T0095429

ALSO BY MALLORY M. O'CONNOR

FICTION

American River: Tributaries, Book One of the American River Trilogy, Archway Publishing, 2017

American River: Currents, Book Two of the American River Trilogy, Archway Publishing, 2018

American River: Confuence, Book Three of the American River Trilogy, Archway Publishing, 2018

NONFICTION

Lost Cities of the Ancient Southeast, University Press of Florida, 1995

"The Art of Hope: Florida's WPA Murals," FORUM Magazine, Florida Humanities Council, Fall, 2005

Florida's American Heritage River: Images from the St. Johns Region, (co-authored with Gary Monroe). University Press of Florida, 2009

"The Art and Soul of Florida." FORUM Magazine, Florida Humanities Council, Fall, 2010 (guest editor)

"Before Bartram: Artist-Naturalist Mark Catesby,"(with Arlene Fradkin), *Fields of Vision: Essays on the Travels of William Bartram,* Tuscaloosa: University of Alabama Press, 2010

Epiphany's Gift

Mallory M. O'Connor

Archway Publishing books may be ordered through booksellers or by contacting:

Archway Publishing
1663 Liberty Drive
Bloomington, IN 47403
www.archwaypublishing.com
1 (888) 242-5904

ISBN: 978-1-4808-7681-1 (sc)
ISBN: 978-1-4808-7680-4 (e)

Library of Congress Control Number: 2019904467

Print information available on the last page.

Archway Publishing rev. date: 4/19/2019

Praise for Mallory M. O'Connor's *Epiphany's Gift*

"Epiphany's Gift, by Mallory O'Connor, takes readers on a journey of the mind as Epiphany learns to rein in her exceptional gift of visions. It isn't often that a book gives me chills, but I have to admit that ... O'Connor makes each of Epiphany's 'encounters' amazingly clear to readers."

—Five-star rating from Literary Titan

"Set against a backdrop of psychic phenomena, corporate corruption and global climate change, *Epiphany's Gift* is a riveting mystery from a writer who is well worth watching. A fast-paced, nail-biting tale of the perennial battle between good and evil."

—Andrew Nichols, Ph.D. *Director, American Institute of Parapsychology*

"Epiphany's Gift, Book One of the Epiphany Mayall series, is a cli-fi paranormal novel that describes the chilling consequences of fracking operations in America. Read it and weep. Better yet, do something about it!"

—Dan Bloom, editor, The Cli-Fi Report

"All the environmental actions and events that O'Connor deals with in *Epiphany's Gift* are grounded in something I, the reader, understand, and want to see exposed and defeated--There is a real-world grounding of the potential apocalypse."

—Steve Surryhne, poet and lecturer in English Literature at San Francisco State University

"Wow, between talking like Blake and digging up some creepy places and references, plus the fracking facts, O'Connor has surely done her homework. [Final thought] … you can't take down the megalith all at once, but perhaps have success by chipping away at it."

—Jessica Eliott, author of *Ghost Lite* and *Tales From Kensington*

Dedication

To my grandfather, N.K., who who knew there was more—if you knew where to look for it.

Acknowledgements

On May 23, 1979, I visited the Spiritualist Camp at Cassadaga, Florida for the first time. I brought along a selection of Native American artifacts. Not much was known about the origin of the small ceramic effigies and potsherds, and I wanted to know more. A friend suggested that I pay a visit to a "psychic archaeologist" who lived and worked in Cassadaga. Skeptical, but curious, I made an appointment and headed for the Camp. Thus began a forty-year friendship with psychic medium Rev. Diane Davis and an investigation of her world. It's been a fascinating journey.

I have many others to thank as well: my husband, John, always supportive, and my son, Chris, editor extraordinaire. Friends Phyllis Saarinen and Steve Surryhne for their edits and suggestions. My mates in the Writers Alliance of Gainesville who helped shepherd along my manuscript, and Beta Readers Diana, Joanna, Ann-Marie, Patty, Anne, Jess, Penny, Daniel and Pat J. Thanks for being there for me.

And special thanks to Dr. Andy Nichols, Director of the American Institute of Parapsychology for his insights into paranormal phenomena, and to Dan Bloom, climate activist and editor of the *Cli-Fi Report* for his encouragement.

Prologue

Kennedy Art Museum, Athens, Ohio
June 2019

"You're sure the alarm's disabled?"

"Absolutely."

The heavyset man wearing a black leather jacket, black jeans and sunglasses paused for a moment, his gloved hands on either side of a drawing encased in its narrow gold frame. The art work depicted a crouching demon carrying a naked man on his back. The demon stood on a ledge of boulders above a dark pool. In the lower right corner, two leering demons looked up in gleeful anticipation. On the left stood two draped figures bearing witness to the scene.

The man with the sunglasses shook his head. Helluva lot of trouble to snatch some crazy cartoon, but fuck it. As long as he got his money what did it matter? Carefully, he lifted the art work up and felt it disconnect from the security hook. His companion handed him a plaid wool blanket that he wrapped around the picture. Tucking the piece under his arm, he nodded. "Okay, let's get outahere."

As the two men walked toward the gallery door, it swung slowly open. The man with sunglasses stopped abruptly.

"What the …?" He glanced at the second man who wore a dark blue security guard uniform. "You see that?"

"Don't sweat it," the guard said with a laugh. "Happens all the time."

"You sure there's nobody else in the building?"

"I swear."

"Then how—"

"Jeez louise, get a grip! It's an old building. Creaky floors. Uneven door frames. Drafty halls. Who knows?" The guard chuckled. "Come on. Let's get your boss's present on the elevator. Don't want to keep Old Silverhair waiting."

The guard closed the door behind them and locked it. As the two men walked down the hall, the one carrying the art work glanced back. For just an instant, he thought he saw a shadow moving along the wall of the corridor.

Or maybe not. *Damned creepy place,* he thought as he hurried toward the elevator.

Part I

Ten years from now, twenty years from now, you will see: oil will bring us ruin ... Oil is the Devil's excrement.

—Pérez Alfonzo, founder of the Organization of Petroleum Exporting Companies (OPEC)

Chapter 1

The Mayall Farm near Mt. Eden, Ohio
June 2019

Epiphany couldn't remember a time when they weren't there—the voices, the visions, the patterns of colored light that flickered around the bodies of her family and friends, the ghostly figures that came and went, appearing and disappearing, there and then gone. But everyone told her she was wrong. That the things she saw and heard were not there. Figments of your imagination, they said. Or worse.

She turned the car off and sat quietly for a moment looking at the house where she had lived for the first eighteen years of her life. It wasn't a large house—just a sturdy wooden structure with a wide front porch and tall windows framed by black shutters. A typical old-time farm house surrounded by gently rolling pastures and a backdrop of maples and hemlock trees common in Southern Ohio.

It had been over forty years since she had left her parents' small farm behind to venture out into another world, a world where she had found friends and lovers, beauty and ugliness, hope and heartbreak. But every time she came back "home," she felt like a little girl again, a little girl with an unwanted talent. It had taken her years to come to terms with the parameters of her "gift."

Even now, she felt a little shudder of anxiety. She was on a mission, but was she doing the right thing? Were her expectations unrealistic? And what about that dream—an unsettling swirl of dark confusion, like being caught in a cloud of heavy smoke. Was it a warning, or just anxiety mixed with fatigue? If only she could see her own future as clearly as she could see those of her clients. "It's hard to be subjective about the things you see coming in your own life," her friend Albert told her. "It's not wise for a psychic to try to read their own future." Albert was right. She should stop trying to see in advance what might come of this little adventure. Still …

Slowly, Epiphany got out of the car. She took her suitcase from the back seat of the nine-year-old Nissan Sentra and walked up the path to the front porch. The door was unlocked, of course. Ed and Susan had always left their doors open. These days it wasn't wise for a ninety-one-year-old widow who lived alone in a rural area to leave her doors unlocked. Epiphany made a mental note to discuss this with her mother. Times had changed.

She stepped into the foyer, set down her suitcase and glanced around. Well, *some* things hadn't changed. The wide-plank wood floors were still a lustrous chocolate brown. The staircase rose before her, making a gentle curve to the left to arrive at the second-floor landing. The cherrywood banister had been cut from the heart of an ancient tree, a single piece of wood that had been carefully soaked and bent to create an elegant arc.

On her right was the living room with its tall windows filled with the original wavy-glass panes. At one end of the room was a huge stone fireplace. The limestone blocks had been quarried from the property when the house was being constructed in the early eighteen-hundreds. When Susan and her husband Ed had bought the house in 1952, it had already been there for well over a century.

And on the far side of the living room was the sky-blue door that led to her mother's bedroom. "Mom?" Epiphany called. "I'm here."

Epiphany heard the clump-clump of Susan's walker. The door opened to reveal a diminutive woman wearing a pink cotton muumuu, white hair piled up on top of her head. She came clomping across the room as fast as the walker permitted. "Fanny," she cried, "oh, my dear. I must have dozed off. I am so glad to see you!" She released the walker to give her daughter an exuberant hug. "How are you? Don't you look splendid? Green always was your best color. Are you tired? Would you like some tea?"

Epiphany laughed as she disengaged from Susan's grasp. "Mom, don't make such a fuss. You'd think I'd been gone for years." How long had it been since anyone had called her "Fanny"?

"Well," said Susan, giving her daughter a reproving glance, "it *has* been almost a year."

"I keep telling you, Mom. You need to move to Florida. Now that Michael and Maddie are with me in Watoolahatchee, you could see us all the time. They'd love to have Grandma Susan join us."

"Hmmm," Susan said,"we'll discuss that later. I'll make some tea." She grabbed her walker and started for the kitchen. Epiphany followed.

The kitchen still had the old white enamel appliances that Epiphany remembered. Susan wasn't the type to worry about having the latest of everything. As long as things worked, she saw no need to replace them. Small pots of herbs sat on the window sill like miniature actors on a stage flanked by blue-and-white gingham curtains. The wavy-glass window over the sink looked out on the back yard—a little clearing of bright green before the dark wall of the woods rose up like a bastion. A row of bright red hollyhocks was lined up like a guard detail in front of the trees.

Susan set aside her walker and used the counter for support as she filled the teakettle and got cups and saucers from the cupboard. Arthritis was making it increasingly difficult for her to get around, but she was determined to remain independent as long as possible.

"Let me help you," Epiphany said, stepping forward to take the china from her mother.

"I'll get it," Susan said. "Consider yourself my guest."

Epiphany sat down at the kitchen table and ran her fingers over the green and white oilcloth cover. Feelings of déjà vu swirled around her—she and her parents eating breakfast at that table, snow falling outside the window, a fire in the hearth. ..

The Mayall Farm
Mt. Eden, Ohio
March 1962

Epiphany heard the hounds baying and stopped to listen. They were some distance away and it was late afternoon, but she felt them tugging at her, imploring her to come to them. She put down the bucket of chicken feed and started toward the pasture behind the barn.

The baying stopped and she paused, her hand on the pasture gate. A puff of wind blew a strand of chestnut-colored hair across her face and she brushed it back impatiently. The air was cold and damp. It had rained earlier and tufts of charcoal clouds still trailed across the sky, moving from north to south like flocks of migrating birds.

The mournful howling resumed. Closer now and more insistent. Epiphany slipped through the gate and followed the packed dirt path across the meadow. Brown grass lay flat and matted on the cold skin of the earth. The path led downward and plunged into a thicket of yew and birch trees. Epiphany could hear the gentle murmur of the creek that rippled past unseen at the bottom of the gorge. A forest of ferns towered over her, and the path was slippery from the recent rain and frost-melt.

She heard the hounds again, their plaintive howls echoing down the gorge. The sound seemed to be coming from somewhere to the north near Old Man's Cave. "Don't you go up there, you hear?" her father had said. "Why, Daddy?" she asked. He shook his head. "It's not safe, daughter. There's wild things up there. Bobcats. Even bears. You stay away from there."

But she couldn't stay away. The hounds were calling her.

Suddenly, the dogs raised their voices in a chorus of howls and yelps. They sounded so close that she jumped and turned around. Two shadows appeared on the ledge behind her. Even as she looked, they seemed to harden into the solid forms of two large hounds.

The dogs ceased their howling and stood looking at her. Her heart pounded with fear. They were huge. Nearly as tall as she was. And their eyes gleamed in the fading light. She was trapped on the ledge with nowhere to run or to hide. And it was growing darker with every shuddering breath.

"Don't you be afraid. They won't hurt you."

She whirled around and saw a man sitting in the entrance to a cave not ten feet away. He was sitting with his legs bent, his elbows resting on his knees. He wore a battered felt hat and his clothes were worn and ragged. A wreath of white hair framed an angular face—a high forehead, prominent nose, hollowed cheeks, thin lips set off by a long white beard. His dark eyes studied her thoughtfully.

"Who are you?" she asked, her voice barely more than a whisper.

A little smile played across his lips. "You know who I am."

Epiphany swallowed and took a deep breath. "The Old Man?"

"Of course," he replied with a little laugh.

"But you're supposed to be dead," the girl said.

He shrugged. "So they say."

The hounds trotted past her and sat down next to the Old Man, one on either side. They panted quietly, pink tongues protruding between their teeth. The man raised his hand and patted the dog on his right. "Come here, lass," he said to Epiphany. "They want to meet you."

She was still shivering with anxiety, but she walked to the man and stopped before him. He looked so real. If he was a ghost, how could he be so solid?

"This here's Rover," he said. "Go ahead, give him a pet."

Epiphany stretched out her hand and gave the burly head a tentative tap. The hound whined a greeting.

"And this one's Bounder." The hound stood up and the girl stepped back. "He won't do you no harm. Just wants to say hello."

She moved closer and brushed her hand across the dog's head. He bumped his brow against her arm and made a little yip.

"They's good dogs, both of 'em," said the man. "Been my friends for a long, long time. Yessir, couldn't have lived out here without 'em." He laughed. "Then or now." He gestured to the space beside him. "Sit ye down, lass and stay a piece. I don't get many visitors these days."

Epiphany sat down and eyed him solemnly. "Everybody says you're dead."

"Maybe I am," he said. "Or not."

The girl frowned. "But don't you have to be ... one way or the other?"

"Hard to say." He looked up at the boulder that jutted out above their heads. "Things is different now. That's true. But this place ..." His arm swept across the landscape. "This place is still the same. Hain't changed a bit since I first come here as a young man. I lived here for years. And now, I still live here."

"Do you remember dying?" she asked.

"I recall goin' down to the crik for water and tryin' to break through the ice with the butt of my gun. I remember hearin' a loud noise and tastin' blood in my mouth. And then I remember some Injuns comin' by and talkin' in soft voices. They was good to me. Wrapped me up in oak bark and leaves. The dogs too."

He paused and frowned. "Don't know why the dogs was there. I thought they was out huntin'. But anyhow," he continued, "they wrapped up the dogs as well and covered us over with grass and twigs so's we wouldn't be cold no longer." He nodded slowly. "They was good people, them Injuns. Kindly."

He looked out at the gorge. The darkness was deepening and a sweet, pungent smell wafted up from the stream. An owl called softly from a hemlock.

The Old Man got to his feet and held out his hand. "Come on then. You'd best be gittin' home while there's still light."

Epiphany scrambled up and took his hand. It was rough and strong. It made her feel ... safe. They walked together along the path above the creek with the hounds following behind. Where the path turned upward toward the pasture, the Old Man stopped. "Reckon you can make it okay from here?"

"Yes, sir," she replied. "I believe I can."

The dogs wagged their tails, then turned and ran back toward the gorge. The Old Man stood and watched her as she started toward the pasture. When she reached the gate, she turned around to wave at him, but he was gone. Puzzled, she looked at the spot where he'd been a moment before. "Don't be a stranger, hear?" said a voice.

At that moment, a little wind came up and the trees made a soft whooshing sound. She slipped through the gate and trotted across the pasture toward home. In the distance, she heard the hounds baying.

"Don't you go sayin' that, daughter. People'll think you're wrong in the head!"

Epiphany knew it was a mistake to tell her father about the Old Man. He always got annoyed when she talked about her *intuitions*—about knowing things before they happened, announcing visitors before their arrival, the invisible "friends" who told her where to find missing objects. She could see his aura—the energy field that surrounded his body—changing from green to grey. Not a good sign.

"But Pa," she objected, "he was *real*. He talked to me. His dogs were with him."

Pa grabbed her arm so roughly that she cowered, shocked at his anger. He was usually so gentle with her. With everyone. "A kindly man," they said of him in the village.

Epiphany's mother, Susan, stood in the kitchen doorway, watching silently, twisting her hands.

"Listen to me," Pa said in a voice she'd never heard before—a grating, furious voice. "Don't you say no more about talkin' with the dead. You got to stop this nonsense."

"But Pa—"

"It's the Devil's business," he hissed, shaking her arm. His clear blue eyes were wild and frightened, like a startled horse. His aura now was shot through with shards of brick-red, like flames erupting around him. "Promise me. No more of this evil talk!"

Epiphany opened her mouth, then closed it and turned away. Pa released her arm. "Promise me," he said more softly.

She glanced up at him. He looked so sorrowful that her heart clenched with guilt. "All right," she said in a small voice. "I promise." She bit her lip, confusion swirling around her. How was she going to keep everything to herself?

He stared at her for a long moment, then nodded. "Good. Go on now and wash up for supper."

Susan let out her breath in a long sigh. "Go ahead, Fanny," she said to her daughter. "Wash your hands." Later that night as Epiphany was getting ready for bed, Susan came to her bedroom to tuck her in. "He's trying to protect you, honey."

"Protect me from *what*?" Epiphany asked.

Susan smiled sadly. "People are afraid of things they don't understand," she said. "You'll find that out soon enough. Let me tell you a story."

Epiphany snuggled down beneath the blue and yellow quilt that Susan had made. "Is it a happy story?"

"Not exactly. But it's a true story and I think you need to hear it."

Then she told Epiphany about her great great grandmother, Susan Travis, who had been well-known for her ability to accurately predict future events. So much so that she was chastised by her minister for "dabbling in the occult," and was subsequently ostracized by the congregation.

"You see, Fanny, this thing runs in our family, but it tends to skip generations. I don't have the gift, but your Grandpa Stephen did. And he paid for it dearly."

"What happened to him?"

"People weren't very … kind to him," Susan said. "They made fun of him and called him names. Eventually, he became very sad. And he … he brought on his own death."

Epiphany's eyes widened. "He killed himself?"

"Shhh," said Susan, her usually light blue aura fading to a muddy blue-grey. "Likely it was an accident, but if he … if they had …" Susan took a deep shuddering breath. She looked down at her daughter, then bent and gave her a tight hug. "Your Pa's just trying to protect you. He's doin' what he thinks is best for you. Please try to understand."

Epiphany thought it over. Was Pa right? Were her impressions really *evil*? Wasn't there *anyone* she could talk to?

From that day on, Epiphany had tried to hide her "gift," tried to ignore the visions, the impressions, the spirits who talked to her, the auras of light that she could see so clearly radiating from the bodies of those around her. She told herself that she was imagining things. Or worse, that there was something *wrong* with her. A brain lesion that caused hallucinations? Some kind of mental illness? She just wanted to be *normal.*

Chapter 2

Epiphany thought that leaving home, going away to college would help her forget about her unwanted talent. But she had no sooner moved into Wilson Residence Hall on the Ohio University campus in Fall 1973, than she began to notice that strange things were going on. At night, it sounded as though someone was rolling marbles across the floor. Doors apeared to open and close on their own.

And then there was the uproar over Room 428. A young man was said to have died in that dorm room, and after his death many students reported hearing footsteps and other unexplained noises.

Next, a female student was also found dead in Room 428. When Epiphany heard about the second incident she was thoroughly disconcerted. One of the students told Epiphany that the young woman was practicing astral projection and trying to contact the dead. She was found in a pool of blood. Some claimed that she had slit her wrists. Others thought she had been attacked by occult forces. The university administrators locked up the room, and no one was ever allowed inside after that terrible night.

Epiphany didn't know what to think. She simply moved out of Wilson Hall as fast as she could and found an apartment a few blocks from the campus. She wanted nothing to do with the ghostly presences who apparently had made the residence hall their home. If anyone brought up the subject, she quickly told them that she "didn't believe in that crap."

She also didn't tell them that the night after the woman's death, she had seen a figure wearing a blood-soaked night gown walking down the hall in front of Room 428.

It was Professor Bernhardt who rescued her from her self-imposed solitude. In the spring semester of her freshman year at OU, Epiphany signed up for his class: An Introduction to the History of Art.

John Bernhardt was in his mid-thirties when Epiphany first met him. Although he was physically small—barely 5'8" and slightly overweight—she soon understood why students clammered to take his classes. From the moment he began to lecture, Epiphany was spellbound.

He radiated energy. He paced. He prowled. He waved his hand at the images on the screen and proclaimed in his dramatic baritone voice, "Civilization is an act of faith." And "Art is the lie that reveals the truth." His clear blue eyes darted here and there, fixing their penetrating gaze on individual students. Yes, he was talking directly to *them*. "History is abstract," he said. "Art is concrete. History looks backward. Art looks ahead."

Under his spell, they watched the history of the world unfold one image at a time from the earliest depictions scratched on the walls of ancient caves to the most recent avant-garde experiments in video installation. "Each and every one of these objects," he told them, "was specifically made by a person, a man or a woman, who was intent on making the invisible visible, who created something using nothing but the power of their imagination and the skill of their hands. This," he gestured at the screen, "is a thought made incarnate." The students looked in awe at the towering image on the screen.

Finally, Epiphany thought, she could use her hidden gift to some advantage. For her term paper, she decided to interview an artist from the past. She chose Phidias, the artist commissioned by the Athenian leader Pericles to oversee the entire sculptural decoration of the Parthenon.

"You have quite an imagination, young lady," Dr. Bernhardt told her when he returned the paper to her with a large "A" in the first page. "Your research is very impressive. You made it sound almost as though you had actually talked to the artist himself."

"Thank you, Dr. Bernhardt," Epiphany murmured. She didn't tell him that she actually *had* talked to Phidias himself. That would have required way too much explaining.

Ohio Route 33 south of Columbus, Ohio
June 2019

The tanker truck lumbered down the highway heading southeast from Columbus. Ray was at the wheel while Beck dozed in the passenger seat. A light rain made the pavement shimmer under the glare of the headlights. On the radio, Chris Janson advised taking a drunk girl home and and leaving her safe in her room.

"That what you'd do Beck?" Ray asked.

Beck muttered something.

Ray leaned toward his companion without taking his eyes from the road. "Say what?"

"How the fuck should I know?" Beck sat up and rubbed his eyes. "Where are we?"

Ray studied the GPS. "Uh, route thirty-three. South. More or less."

Beck sighed. "How much further?"

"Can't be too far. We're out in the middle of nowhere. Keep an eye out for route six-sixty-four." Ray glanced at the older man. "Hey. You hear what I said?"

"Six six four" mumbled Beck.

"You got to lay off the beer when we're on the road," Ray said. "It's cloudin' your mind."

Beck bleated a laugh. "Like you should talk."

Headlights approached and blinked past. "Okay," Ray said. "We're 'bout ten miles from Logan, so our turn's gotta be comin' up."

A few miles farther along, Ray spotted the sign for Route 664 and maneuvered the tanker trunk onto the narrow ribbon of asphalt. The road was even darker and the rain had picked up, blurring the view through the windshield. "Jesus H. Christ," Ray muttered. "Wish we coulda waited 'til it was light to make this drop."

"Yeah, well tell that to mo fos in the front office. We're out here workin' our butts off and they're sittin' in a bar somewhere drinkin' single malt." Beck sniffed and coughed. "Assholes."

"Keep an eye out for Route two-five-one," Ray said. "That's our next turn."

"Like I can see in this fuckin' downpour," Beck replied.

Ray overshot his exit and had to turn the rig around in a 7-11 parking lot. He ducked inside long enough to buy two cups of coffee. Ray said he didn't want any fuckin' coffee, but he took it anyway. Highway 251 was even narrower and the landscape became more rugged—clusters of grey boulders loomed and the forest made a tunnel of the roadway. They hadn't seen another vehicle for at least three or four miles.

Ray slowed the truck and stopped in front of a chain-link gate. "This has gotta be it," he announced.

"Hope the hell we don't get stuck," Beck said, eyeing the dirt road that led into the woods on the far side of the gate.

The tanker crept along the logging road for about a mile until Beck saw a small sign with the Ace Energy logo and an arrow indicating a right turn. The truck shuddered as it bounced along the gravel path. Finally, Ray said, "There it is." He stopped the tanker and he and Beck exited the cab to look at the well-head. A single utility light cast a faint beam on the machinery below.

Standing alongside the cab, Beck helped ease the tanker into position for the discharge operation. Once the tanker was parked in the right position, both men went to work connecting the hose and readying the well to receive the 9,000 gallons of waste-water stored in the tanker's silver hold.

It took about fifteen minutes to set up the various valves and secure the discharge lines. The well itself would complete the process of injecting the contaminated water into the ground.

The Mayall Family Farm
June 2019

"All ready," Susan announced proudly. Then she added, "I guess you can help me put it on the table. I don't want to drop everything in the middle of the floor." They settled themselves at the table and Susan poured them each a cup of tea. "How are Michael and Maddie doing?" Susan asked.

Her eyes shining with pride, Epiphany told her mother about her son Michael's recent promotion to Assistant Professor of Music at the small liberal arts college where he taught. They talked about Epiphany's granddaughter Madison, who would be starting second grade in the fall. And Epiphany filled Susan in on her own work in Watoolahatchee as a psychic counselor—doing readings for clients, conducting workshops on self-realization, giving lectures on the history of Watoolahatchee, the Spiritualist camp that had been her home for almost thirty years.

"Do you ever wonder if it was a mistake, leaving Lloyd and taking Michael with you to Watoolahatchee?" Susan asked gently. "He was what—eight? It couldn't have been an easy decision."

Epiphany sat back and looked out the window at the bright green landscape. When she glanced back at her mother, Susan gave her a wistful smile.

"It wasn't, of course," Epiphany replied. "I knew how Dad felt about my *intuitions*. And Lloyd was just the same. But then I went to Lily Dale and met Albert. When he urged me to move to Watoolahatchee and offered to be my mentor, I knew I had to go. I just couldn't keep on pretending. "

Susan reached across the table and took her daughter's hand. "I think it's worked out well, honey. Michael's a splendid young man. I know it's been hard for him since Shannon died, but he's a wonderful father and Maddie is a joy. Thank goodness they have you there to take care of them."

But who's going to take care of you, Mom? Epiphany thought. *How was she going to help her ever-so-independent mother see the light?* "Well," she said aloud, "I'd better unpack and get settled in." She got to her feet, grabbed her suitcase and headed up the stairs.

Dinner that evening was a simple meal—chicken potpie with carrots and green peas and a wilted-lettuce salad fresh from the garden. Susan brought out a bottle of red wine to celebrate Epiphany's "homecoming."

"How on earth do you get to the store these days?" Epiphany asked. "You aren't still trying to drive, are you?" They had talked about the issue of Susan's driving on Epiphany's last visit.

"Goodness no," Susan exclaimed. "I haven't had a license for nearly a year. Couldn't pass the eye test. But," she added with a smile, "I have a very helpful new neighbor. Her name is Rhoda Miller. She and her husband Sam bought the old Darst place."

"The grey house next to the cemetery?"

"That's the one. They are such nice folks. Rhoda takes me to the store in Logan once a week, and Sam is great about fixing anything that needs it. They moved in just before Christmas. Been a lifesaver for me."

Epiphany held her tongue but she wanted to ask, What happens if they decide to move away? *Patience,* she told herself. *I'll save that lecture for later.*

After supper, mother and daughter made themselves comfortable in the living room and chatted for awhile until Susan began to yawn and said, "I just can't seem to stay up the way I used to. Must be getting old." She chuckled and managed to get to her feet. "Give me a good-night hug, sweetheart."

After Susan went to bed, Epiphany continued to sit in the silent living room. It had been a day of remembrance, and she thought again about what the house, the land, the *place* meant to her parents. And to her.

It was hard to believe that she had been living in Watoolahatchee for over thirty years. She had never intended to embrace her psychic "gifts." Quite the opposite. She had spent the first half of her life denying them, refuting them, disowning them. Strange, the pathways that lead us to ourselves. If she hadn't gone to the museum that day, hadn't met Lloyd Ramsey …

It was summer, 1975. He was vacationing in Maine with his first wife, Dora, and Epiphany was in a museum in Bar Harbor doing research on Colonial women artists. Lloyd and Dora were also visiting the museum and they struck up a conversation with Epiphany. Lloyd invited Epiphany to join Dora and him for dinner, and it was a delightful evening—full of good food, great conversation and intriguing stories.

Lloyd was an attractive man—tall, lean, with collar-length dark hair and beautiful grey-green eyes. Originally from Cardiff, he had attended both the Courtauld Institute and the Edinburgh College of Art before moving to New York. He was a sculptor with a growing reputation on the international art scene. He combined an artist's creativity with a workman's skill, fabricating large abstract metal pieces—a rare combination of brain-hand coordination.

They had talked until midnight. Epiphany remembered, with some chagrin, that poor Dora had hardly gotten a word in during the entire evening. Epiphany was captivated by Lloyd's sophistication, his knowledge of art, and the beautiful flow of his language. (His lyrical Welsh accent hadn't lessened after ten years in the States.) After that night, she couldn't stop thinking about Lloyd Ramsey.

Back in Ohio, she stood before the mirror in the bedroom of her apartment and wondered what he would think if he saw her naked—a thin, almost wispy, young woman with small, delicate breasts, long legs and waist-length auburn hair.

Would he find her attractive? Would he like her cream-colored skin that burned so easily? The little tuft of red-gold pubic hair? She sighed and turned away, and decided she would never know the answers to these questions.

But six months later, Lloyd showed up in Athens, Ohio, and announced that he and Dora had divorced. Three months after that, Epiphany and Lloyd were married. When she moved with him to New York she was already pregnant with Michael. Had she been naïve? Yes. Immature? Of course. But didn't love conquer all? Well, maybe not ...

Chapter 3

New York City
June 1985

"Hurry up, Pip. The cab's waiting." Lloyd Ramsey was not a patient man, and Epiphany could hear the irritation in his voice loud and clear.

"Just a minute, luv," she replied. "I'm trying to find Michael's special pen. He wants to take it along so he can—"

"You should have had that all taken care of in advance," Lloyd exclaimed. "Why do you put everything off until the last minute?"

Maybe if I didn't have to do everything myself, I could be more efficient, Epiphany thought angrily. And immediately felt a twinge of guilt. This was Lloyd's big chance, after all, and the least she could do was to help him as much as she could. She knew how worried he was that something might go wrong.

They were flying to the U.K. so Lloyd could oversee the installation of one of his recent sculptures—a twenty-foot-high tower of stainless steel commissioned by a London bank. It was his first major contract with a European corporation, and he hoped there would be many more to come. So of course he was irritable. And she was a convenient target.

After nine years of marriage, she was still not used to what she referred to as Lloyd's "split personality." He could be perfectly charming when he wanted to—calm, thoughtful, patient. But just as quickly he would become truculant and demanding. She never knew if she would be dealing with Dr. Jekyll or Mr. Hyde.

So, despite the daunting preparations needed to get ready for this trip, she was looking forward to escaping from the confines of the Tribeca loft that was their home where her daily duties of playing secretary, housekeeper, babysitter, confidant and concubine to a proud, stubborn and—face it—arrogant man were becoming a bit exhausting.

"I found it, Mommy!" Eight-year-old Michael held up his favorite felt-tipped pen triumphantly. "We can go now."

Epiphany gave a sigh of relief, tucked the pen into Michael's new Rocky and Bullwinkle backpack, grabbed her suitcase and followed her husband into the hall.

The freight elevator groaned its way down to the first floor. "You're sure you've got everything?" Lloyd growled. "Tickets? Cash? Passports?"

"Yes, yes of course," she muttered. *Bit late now, wasn't it?*

Michael looked up at her furtively, his brown eyes full of concern. Dear, voracious, affectionate Michael who wanted everything and everyone to be perfect. How he hated tension and disharmony. His parent's frequent disagreements caused him enormous discomfort. And allergies.

The cab driver helped them stash their luggage in the trunk and they were off. It was a mild, partly cloudy evening in mid-June. The driver headed east onto FDR Drive and through the Queens Midtown Tunnel toward the Bronx.

Looking out the back window, Epiphany could see the Twin Towers dominating the receding Manhattan skyline. The World Trade Center had opened in 1973, just three years before she arrived in Manhattan as Lloyd's bride, and seeing that symbolic declaration of power built of steel and glass never failed to give her a twinge of pride. She was living her dream of being part of the world of art she had come to cherish. She had a front row seat—married to a successful emerging artist and living in the most important art center in the world. What more could she possibly want? Except …

Never mind.

Everything went smoothly at the airport. She hadn't forgotten *anything* and was delighted that Lloyd's mood had improved by the time they boarded TWA Flight 970. Soon they were 30,000 feet above a gauzy Atlantic, sated with dinner and ready to sleep. Epiphany tucked Michael in and pulled the lightweight blanket up to her chin. The drone of the engines had a calming effect and she soon dozed.

The sky was just beginning to lighten outside the oval window of the Boeing 747 when Epiphany woke with a start and bolted upright. "Oh my God," she cried. "We're going to crash!"

In the seat next to her, Lloyd stirred and mumbled something. She shook his arm. "Lloyd! Wake up! We have to do something. The plane's going to crash!"

Lloyd blinked at her. "What?"

"The plane! It's going to crash!"

"What are you talking about Pip?" he said, sitting up and staring at her.

"There's a bomb on board! It's going to blow up the plane!"

Other passengers began to wake and take notice. "What's she saying?" a man asked.

"Something about a bomb!" said a woman's voice.

Chaos erupted. Frightened passengers sat up. Lights

blinked on. A stewardess came rushing down the aisle and took hold of Epiphany's shoulder. "Ma'am, please calm down. What is it you're upset about?"

"I saw it," Epiphany cried. "I saw the plane blow up. There was a huge fireball and then everything exploded! People, bodies, falling into the ocean. My God, it was awful!" She was sobbing, tears rushing down her cheeks.

"Mommy, what's wrong?" Michael was tugging at her sleeve. "What's the matter?!"

"Just a dream," Lloyd said. He looked up at the stewardess and shrugged helplessly. "She sometimes has nightmares."

Epiphany faced him. "It wasn't a dream!" she said. "I *saw* it, Lloyd!"

"Thanks a lot for scaring us half to death," someone said.

"For Christ's sake," someone else said. "Go back to sleep, will you?"

"Can I get you something?" the stewardess asked. "Water? An aspirin?"

Epiphany recoiled into herself. "I don't need anything," she said. Then added, "Thank you." She took a deep breath and looked down at her hands. They were knotted into claws.

"Jesus, Pip," Lloyd said, his voice low and furious. "What a scene you've made. You embarrassed the shit out of me."

Epiphany didn't answer. She stared straight ahead at the back of the seat in front of her. Michael reached out and patted her arm. "It's okay Mommy," he said. "Don't be scared."

She grabbed him and held him close and began to cry. "It seemed so real," she whispered. "So damned real."

New York City
July 1985

"Lloyd. *Lloyd,* listen to me!" Epiphany waved the front page of the *New York Times* at her husband. "You've got to see this!"

Lloyd looked up with a scowl. He hated being interrupted when he was reading the weekend soccer scores. He grabbed the paper and scanned the front page, then tossed it aside. "So, what's your point?"

"What's my point? Didn't you read it?"

"A plane crashed. So?"

Epiphany grabbed the paper and shook it in his face. "That's *exactly* what I saw in my dream. Listen to what it says: 'Air India Flight 182 en route to London's Heathrow Airport, exploded in mid-air and crashed into the Atlantic Ocean off the coast of Ireland. A total of 329 people were killed.'" She gave him a triumphant look.

"What are you getting at, Pip?"

"My dream! For goodness sake, Lloyd, I—"

"I don't think it's unusual for people on airplanes to dream about crashing. It's a universal fear, after all."

"But Lloyd, it was so—"

"It was a bloody dream," Lloyd shouted, bringing his fist down on the kitchen table. "What the bloody hell else could it be?"

Epiphany stared mutely at her coffee cup. They had been back from London for a week, and she had been unable to forget the frightening vision of the plane exploding in midair. Somewhere in her head, Epiphany felt a dark cavern of guilt. Why hadn't she *told* someone—the airlines, the police, the FBI? But what good would it have done? Would anyone have believed her? Did she believe herself after Lloyd's turning the incident into a comedy routine?

"And then my crazy wife said, 'There's a bomb on board!' You can imagine the reaction."

Red-faced with chagrin, Epiphany tried to make the best of the ridicule. Lloyd's family teased her with good-natured banter. "Maybe the airlines could hire you as a early warning system" and "You know what they say about yelling 'fire' in a crowded theatre, dearie."

After reading about the Air India crash, Epiphany was amazed at the similarity between her vision and the actual event, overwhelmed by a feeling of dread. How could she have foreseen the catastrophe? And what should she do with this unwanted burden? "But it was so *real*," she insisted. "So specific—the explosion, the fireball, the people falling from the sky. And it happened at exactly the same place where I dreamed about it—just off the coast of Ireland."

"Coincidence," scoffed Lloyd. "Nothing more."

But the vision of the plane blowing apart was so immediate, so graphic, so REAL that she had to use all her strength to keep it to herself. To pretend—again-again-again—that it was just the same old problem. Her over-active, delusional, bewildering, scary *imagination*.

This time, she couldn't ignore it. She had *known* that something awful was going to happen. She was *sure* of it. When Lloyd stubbornly refused to talk about it, she turned to her friend Hannah.

Chapter 4

Epiphany had known Dr. Hannah De Groot from the first days of her stay in New York—back when she and Lloyd were newlyweds and the future was full of hope and adventure. The brightly shining city, the talented, good-looking husband, the beautiful new baby. How had it eroded so terriby over the past decade? She blamed herself for being inadequate. And Lloyd for being intractable. And poor little Michael was caught between their two colliding energies.

Hannah, a curator of rare books at the Barnard College Library, had never married. She lived by herself in her Morningside Gardens apartment, one of the first owner-occupied co-ops in New York City. She had moved there in 1976, the year Epiphany and Lloyd Ramsey were wed.

"I should take you to Lily Dale," Hannah said as she and Epiphany sat across the table from each other in a little diner off West 43rd Street.

"What's Lily Dale?" asked Epiphany.

"It's a Spiritualist community near Buffalo. My mother used to take me there. She was interested in the Spiritualists."

"What are Spiritualists?"

"It's a religious movement that began in the middle of the 19th century," Hannah explained, "although it had its roots in Europe with various branches of mysticism and philosophers like Swedenborg. Basically, it's the idea that the living can communicate with the dead. I expect you could trace it all the way back to Shamanism and the calling up of spirits."

Epiphany immediately thought of the Old Man she had encountered as a child. She hadn't told Hannah about her childhood experiences with psychic phenomena. Maybe Hannah would reject her. Like Lloyd had. But now, well she had to talk to *someone* ...

"Pip?" Hannah was looking at Epiphany expectantly, "I said would you like to visit Lily Dale?"

"Sorry," Epiphany replied. "I was thinking about Lloyd and about how alone I've felt since he refused to believe that I'd seen that plane go down."

Hannah reached for her friend's hand and gave it a squeeze. "I can only imagine," she said.

Epiphany studied Hannah's sympathetic face. With her wide, blue eyes and pale complexion and her straight blond hair cut in a simple Dutchboy style, she looked like a schoolgirl. Yet she radiated a gentle depth that was always reassuring. "I don't know what to do," Epiphany said. "I feel like there's this huge gulf between me and Lloyd, and I don't see any way to bridge it. He just ..." She broke off and stared down miserably at her plate of meatloaf, the cooling gravy congealing around the edges of the untouched dinner.

"Why don't we do a road trip. Just the two of us?" Hannah suggested. "I can make a reservation for us at a hotel in Lily Dale and you can take a look around. If nothing else, it will give you some time to think things through."

"What about Michael?" Epiphany said, thinking of her darling boy. Her wonderful son who would be nine in another month, who was growing up at what seemed like the speed of light.

Hannah smiled. "Mikey will be fine as long as he can get to his music lessons. Lloyd can take him, can't he?"

Epiphany had to smile too. Where had her son's love of music come from? Epiphany appreciated music, enjoyed concerts, could distinguish Beethoven from Mozart. But Michael was devoted to it. She honestly believed that he preferred practicing his cello to pretty much anything else in the world. Maybe it was a place where he felt secure. How had he learned to take refuge in Bach?

"I guess Lloyd can do that," she said. Lloyd encouraged Michael's musical ambitions. He was, Epiphany thought, perhaps a better father than he was a husband. She looked at Hannah, who was watching her in silence. Suddenly cold, she shivered.

"Don't be afraid, Pip," Hannah said. "You know what you need to do, don't you?"

Epiphany nodded. Hannah was right. "Take me to Lily Dale," she said.

Lily Dale changed everything. It was there that she met Albert, a psychic who was teaching a workshop on "astral projection." He didn't use a last name. Just Albert. He was short and stout with a black fringe of hair that ringed a bald dome. His thick glasses dominated a face that was almost dainty: a snub nose, rosebud mouth, little pointed ears. She marveled at his diminutive hands and feet. By the time she finished the workshop, she knew what her next step had to be.

And so she walked away from the riches of New York City and the life she had built there—away from the museums and galleries, the concerts and plays, her friends and colleagues in the art world. Left her husband Lloyd and took their nine-year-old son Michael with her, and moved to Watoolahatchee, a small Spiritualist community in Central Florida, to begin her training as a psychic medium.

Watoolahatchee—a village of quaint little houses, many dating from the late 1800s, each with its own patch of yard, where the tallest things around were not the towering glass and steel skyscrapers but the massive Florida live oaks. Where the air smelled of orange blossoms and the dark moldering scent of rotting vegetation, and the quiet of the night was interrupted only by the garbled arias of the mockingbirds and the barking of the tree frogs.

In Watoolahatchee she bought a house, made new friends, became as rooted in the community as the ancient oak trees, as attached as the drifting veils of Spanish moss. She had lived there for well over thirty years.

She had never re-married, though she had enjoyed male companions now and then. Mostly, she concentrated on her work—the clients who came to her for readings and advice, the lectures and workshops she gave, the needs of her family—her son Michael and his late wife, Shannon, and her precocious little granddaughter, Madison.

Had she made the right choice? Had she been fair to her son? She had taken him away from the things he loved—his father, his music lessons at Julliard, his small circle of friends. But he had done well in his new home. Continued his music lessons. Granted, Stetson University wasn't Julliard and Lincoln Center wasn't a few subway stops away, but he had persevered. Finished college, gotten a good job, met and married a wonderful woman, had a beautiful daughter. Did Epiphany ever miss New York? And Lloyd? Of course she did. But the past was what it was. She had made a life for herself, a life that was true to her beliefs and her talents. A life that honored her *gift.*

The Kennedy Art Museum Athens, Ohio
June 2019

The Spirit floated silently along the corridor, following the man in the tweed jacket. He was in a hurry, and when he got to the door of his private office he quickly closed it behind him and slid into the chair in front of his computer screen. Spirit sifted through the closed door and hovered a few feet behind him.

She had seen the activity in the gallery earlier in the evening. Roused from the deep cool pulse of the Afterworld when the man in the blue uniform opened the steel door to the corridor where she spent most of her time, she had followed him up the stairs and into the gallery space. She had witnessed the removal of an art work by a man with sunglasses, and had followed along behind them—at a descreet distance— curious to know what they intended to do with the art.

The two men shivered when they entered the tunnel and complained of the cold. She had to smile, knowing that the drop in temperature was caused not just by the dampness of the underground passageway, but also by the presence of the many spirits who crowded close to see what had brought unexpected visitors to their realm. Most living humans were *so* insensitive.

But after the two men had taken the wrapped art work to the door that opened to the river and had given it to the man who waited there in the darkness next to the boat dock, Spirit had once more followed the men as they retraced their steps and hurried to leave "this damned freezing hole."

She watched as the man with sunglasss left. She saw the guard go back into the gallery and reset the alarm. A few minutes later, the man with the tweed jacket entered the gallery. He spoke briefly with the guard. She was too far away to hear the conversation, but she followed the man in the tweed coat down the hall to his office.

The grey footage from the security cam came up on the computer screen. Spirit wasn't sure what he was doing, but the images on the screen flickered and changed as he went through a series of keyboard maneuvers. Finally satisfied, he sat back with a sigh and shook his head. Then he turned off the computer, got up and left the room, closing the door behind him.

Chapter 5

The Mayall Family Farm
June 2019

Epiphany let the memory of her former life fade until it dissolved. The view out the living room window was like a black canvas—a void, utterly empty. She realized she was exhausted and started to get to her feet, but was suddenly engulfed by a powerful vision.

She was looking at a pond that sat like a dark saucer in the midst of a meadow. As she watched, the water's surface changed from grey to black and the water began to undulate, weak sunlight reflecting iridescent ripples. The water became thicker still—a tar pit with flames licking at the edges of the cauldron. A blue haze rose from the sulfurous mass. Epiphany could smell the sickening sweetness of that lethal cloud. Embers swirled upward in an explosion of smoke. Through the gloom, Epiphany could make out several naked figures being carried toward the pond by a pack of leering demons.

Then the image froze. The color faded and the scene was rendered in black and white like a pen and ink drawing. She stared at the flattened landscape. There was something familiar about it. She had seen this image before—but where? And when? A line of poetry swam into her mind: *Hurled headlong from the ethereal sky, With hideous ruin and combustion down, To bottomless perdition …*

"Oceans of oil," a voice said. "The bedrock of the modern world, flowing in and out of our consciousness one catastrophe at a time ..."

The next morning, Epiphany sat at the kitchen table reading the *Logan Daily News*. She loved community newspapers; they revealed so much about a place and its people—their interests, hopes, priorities, prejudices.

This morning's edition reported that the warden of the local prison had resigned because of allegations of sexual misconduct; that the Meals on Wheels program needed volunteers; that the Chamber of Commerce was hosting a Meet the Candidates night in the run-up to electing a new mayor; and that Ohio was among the worst states in the country with a high unemployment rate and the rising cost of groceries combined with cuts to the food-stamp program. Area events included a cemetery cleanup. And the local girls' soccer team had lost their most recent match nine to two. Epiphany felt encapsulated in a little piece of place and time.

"Now then," Susan said, pushing her walker through the doorway, "what would you like for breakfast?"

"Don't go to any trouble, Mom," Epiphany said.

"How about if I heat up some carrot-orange muffins," Susan said. "Remember how much you loved them when you were little? I couldn't make enough of them."

At that moment, the phone rang. Susan started to struggle toward it, but Epiphany quickly grabbed the phone. "Mayall residence."

There was a pause, then a voice said, "Uh, Susan? Is that you?"

"This is her daughter. Can I help you?"

"Epiphany?"

"Yes?"

"It's John Bernhardt. I—uh—I was just going to ask your mother for your contact information."

"For goodness sakes," Epiphany said. "Professor Bernhardt. How nice to hear your voice."

"Likewise, my dear. So you're visiting the old homestead?"

"I just got here yesterday."

"Well," said Bernhardt, "what a nice coincidence."

Epiphany had to smile. She didn't believe in coincidences. "Why did you want to get in touch with me?" she asked.

"There's been an—uh—incident at the university museum. A drawing by the English artist William Blake was stolen."

"Good heavens," Epiphany exclaimed. "That's awful. Do they know what happened?"

"No. There seems to be some kind of- uh- mystery surrounding the theft. That's why I thought to give you a call. Susan's told me about the work you're doing these days—the *psychic* work—so I thought you might have some ideas about what happened."

"Umm, I'd love to help, but I'm afraid I don't have any experience working on criminal cases," Epiphany said.

"If you'd rather not get involved, I understand," said Professor Bernhardt.

Epiphany thought for a moment. Why not give this type of investigation a shot? It sounded interesting. "Well," she said, "I'd need to get some additional information, but I'd be happy to try to do whatever I can."

"Excellent. Could you come by my office tomorrow around eleven? I'll fill you in."

Epiphany hadn't seen John Bernhardt for at least ten years. After she finished college and moved to New York, they had corresponded now and then, and she had seen him at a dinner party at her mother's during the Christmas holidays a few years ago. He had been in his late-sixties then, and today he didn't look much different. His snowy hair was a little thinner, and when he got up to greet her, his movements were a bit slower. But his handshake was still firm and hearty, and his aura was filled with clear, bright colors, signaling health and energy. And his blue eyes still sparkled as he smiled at her over his spectacles.

"Epiphany," he said, "you look wonderful. Come and sit down. Thanks so much for meeting with me."

"Always a pleasure to see you, Professor."

"Please, call me John."

That would take a little getting used to. She was still in awe of him and of his academic reputation. An authority on the work of Wiliam Blake, he had written a number of books and articles, and had lectured at conferences and museums worldwide. But despite his lofty reputation, he was always ready to help his students better understand the wonders of the history of art.

John launched at once into the mystery of the missing Blake. "It was part of an exhibition I helped organize of the illustrations of Dante's *Inferno*," he explained, "including works by Blake, and also pieces by Doré, Flaxman, Botticelli. I went to London to personally select the pieces for the show from several public and private collections."

"That sounds exciting," said Epiphany.

John smiled broadly. "I had a grand time. The exhibit

opened at the Tate Gallery in London, and then traveled to five other venues before coming here. I was delighted that we could host such a prestigious group of artworks here in the wilds of Appalachia, but my friends at the Tate were most accommodating. As you can imagine, I'm distraught that the piece went missing *here* of all places." He shook his head. "I feel personally responsible."

"It could have happened anywhere," Epiphany said.

He glanced at her. "Yes, but it happened *here* under my watch, and that- uh- distresses me. The exhibition had only been open for a week when the work disappeared."

"Which piece was taken?" Epiphany asked.

"A pen-and-ink drawing with some watercolor added."

"I remember some of those *Inferno* illustrations," Epiphany said. "*Dante and Virgil at the Gate*, the *Simoniac Pope*, the *Whirlwind of Lovers*."

"Good to know you haven't forgotten what I taught you," John said. "The piece in question was never fully completed by Blake. It shows a devil carrying a magistrate to the Boiling Pitch Pool of corrupt officials. Canto 21. The Eighth Circle of Hell reserved for purveyors of fraud and corruption."

Epiphany suddenly realized she had seen the drawing in her vision. She remembered it clearly: the leering demons, the boiling pool of pitch. She inhaled sharply, then said, "So the Blake was the only piece stolen?"

"Correct."

"I wonder why the thief selected that particular piece?"

John pondered the question. "I've wondered about that myself. It certainly isn't the most valuable piece in the show. The Botticellis are each worth far more. It isn't even the most valuable of the six William Blake pieces since it's basically an unfinished drawing, and the others are all completed watercolors." He was silent for a moment, then said, "I have to believe it was the subject matter."

Epiphany raised an eyebrow. "How so?"

"Well, the one stolen represents the torment of the corrupt officials in the Pitch Pool," said John. "The Eighth Circle of Hell is all about liars, hypocrites, seducers, and exploiters. The other images in the show were about other sins—gluttony, suicide, lust, rage. But the one taken is about government officials drowning in the boiling oil of their own corruption. I have to wonder if there isn't some symbolism intended here."

"Who would be especially attracted by an image of political corruption?" wondered Epiphany. She looked at John. "How can I help?"

"I'm hoping you can tell me," John said with a smile. "After all, I've never worked with a *psychic* before. What is it you do?"

Epiphany was surprised to find herself blushing. He was still "the professor," and she had just been handed a tough assignment. "Well," she said, "as I see it, we have two problems. One is to try to locate the missing art and find out how it was taken, and the other is to see if there are deeper implications based on the subject matter of the drawing and why it was the only piece stolen."

"I agree. How do you wish to proceed?"

"Let's pay a visit to the scene of the crime, shall we? That might give me some clues about where to start."

It was a bit of a hike from John Bernhardt's office to the new art museum located across the Hocking River on a site known as The Ridges. Although the museum was new, it was housed in an historic four-story red brick building built just after the Civil War in an elaborate Victorian style. The imposing building was part of a complex that was strategically placed on the top of the hill. Epiphany stopped to take in the scene. "Wait a minute," she said. "I remember this place." She glanced at John and found him giving her an impish grin. "Isn't it the Athens Lunatic Asylum?"

"Right you are," John replied with a little laugh. "But since the turn of the millennium it has become an art museum."

"You're kidding."

"Not at all. The university acquired the property back in the late-nineteen-nineties and began to refurbish it as an educational complex. It's still undergoing renovations, but the museum is housed in the original administration building. There are several galleries, an auditorium, and archive space. Eventually, it will be quite splendid."

Epiphany was gazing at the structure. "When I was going to school here, we were advised to stay away from this place. There were all kinds of stories about it—paranormal sightings, haunted graves. It was said to have an unsavory history."

John nodded. "The treatment of mental illness in the early years was primitive at best," he said. "I'm sure some horrendous events took place here."

"Didn't they do lobotomies using ice picks? That was one of the tales I heard," Epiphany said.

"I've read about that and expect it's true," John said. "However, the asylum started out as a rather noble experiment in rehabilitation for the mentally afflicted. It was thought that a nice quiet place with a pretty view of the river and lovely grounds filled with gardens and orchards would be of great benefit to the mental health of the patients. But it quickly became overcrowded and understaffed, and the treatments changed from therapeutic to outright cruelty. Ice-water baths, electroshocks, and crude lobotomy procedures became the norm." He paused and glanced around at the brooding, shadowy complex. "It became a house of horrors."

Epiphany swallowed hard. The air seemed to be condensing around her, becoming thick and dark like a dank fog. She could hear someone breathing—a rasping, guttural gasp. An art museum filled with beautiful treasures sitting atop a house of horrors? What a peculiar irony. The idea made her cringe.

"Come along," John said. "I'll show you the gallery where the Blake was hanging when it disappeared." He started up the path toward the main building.

Epiphany followed reluctantly. She felt as though she was walking in heavy sand, each step dragging her down. This place has layers, she thought.

She could see images superimposed on top of each other. It seemed as if she was seeing scenes from different periods of time stacked one on top of the next, and there was no way to disconnect them from each other. "The past is too much with us ..." she murmured. What had happened in this place was still very much alive, a persistent resonance of anguish.

"What?" John said, pausing with his hand on the doorknob.

"Nothing."

The temperature dropped perceptibly when they stepped into the vestibule. "Well," John said, "at least we know the air conditioning is working."

Epiphany was silent. She could sense the presence of spirits everywhere. They pressed against her—cold, hungry, frantic. Who were these desperate souls and what did they want? The place was full of negative energy.

The young woman seated behind the reception desk looked up and smiled. "Good morning, Professor Bernhardt."

"Good morning, Gretchen. Is Hugh available?"

"He's out running errands. He said he'd be back after lunch."

"No matter. I wanted him to meet Ms. Mayall, one of my former students. Epiphany, this is Gretchen Turner, one of my *current* students."

Gretchen thrust out her hand. "Welcome to the Kennedy, Ms. Mayall."

"Good to meet the younger generation," said Epiphany.

The oppressive cloud of gloom seemed to lighten in the airy new reception space. Epiphany could feel the spirits moving slowly away, melting into the still air.

She followed John through the double wooden doors leading to a gallery. It was a medium-size room, but the high ceilings and white walls made it seem spacious.

Inside the door was an elaborate arch fabricated to look like Blake's illustration of the gateway to Hell. Above the arch was an inscription: *Abandon hope all ye who enter here*. Epiphany smiled. "Nice touch," she said, pointing to the sign.

"Rather sets the mood, doesn't it? Come on. I'll give you a tour of the exhibit."

"Lead on, Professor."

"The story begins here," John said. "Dante has lost his way and finds he is alone in a dark and dangerous forest."

"Midway in our life's journey, I went astray from the straight road and woke to find myself alone in a dark wood ..." Epiphany read from the label.

"He is pursued by three snarling beasts—a leopard representing worldly pleasures, a lion full of hubris, and a greedy wolf with an insatiable desire for wealth," John continued. "The poet Virgil rescues him and allows him to redeem himself by taking a tour of Hell and witnessing the punishments awaiting the sinners who have strayed from the straight road leading to salvation."

"Lust, pride and greed," Epiphany said. "Three of the most deadly sins."

John looked around the gallery. "They're all represented here. And the sinners Dante described—hypocrites, tyrants, frauds, traitors, and betrayers."

"Where was the missing Blake?" Epiphany asked.

John walked across the gallery and stopped in front of a blank space on the wall. "It was hanging right here last Tuesday," he said, pointing, "but Wednesday morning it was gone."

"So it disappeared overnight on Tuesday?"

"The last person who saw it was the security guard who locked up the gallery around eight p.m. He didn't notice anything unusual, and the alarm system wasn't tripped."

"Could it have been an inside job?" Epiphany asked.

John frowned. "That's hard to believe," he said. "The staff isn't that large—the director, two curators, an education and outreach coordinator. Plus the maintenance and security personnel. They've all been loyal employees for years."

Epiphany put her hand on the empty space and waited. She was familiar with the technique of remote viewing—using her clairvoyant ability to locate and gather information about a person or object in a distant location—so she felt that approach might be appropriate in this case. She closed her eyes, relaxed and let her mind float freely.

After several minutes she feels a door open and she is looking down a dark tunnel. Two male voices are speaking quickly in hushed tones. "Any trouble?" says one.

"Piece of cake," the other responds.

Paper rattles—as if something is being unwrapped. "Good work. Another fine piece for the collection."

She sees a storage rack with dozens of framed art works. A man with silver hair is putting a piece into the rack. The frame is simple, but it glints in the light. Metallic. Golden.

The vision faded and she opened her eyes to find John staring at her. "Are you all right?" he asked.

She nodded, coming up slowly from the trance. "Did the stolen piece have a gold frame?" she asked.

"Yes," John said. "As a matter of fact, it did.

Chapter 6

John stared at Epiphany wide-eyed. "How did you do that?"

"I've learned to project my mind through time and space to see things that aren't apparent using my so-called *normal* senses," she replied. "It's called remote-viewing."

"Does it always work?"

"Not always," Epiphany conceded. "Sometimes my impressions are absolutely clear down to the smallest detail. Other times, I get bits and glimpses, like pieces of a puzzle I have to find a way to put together."

"So what else did you see? Besides the gold frame?"

"There were two men. They were talking about a new piece of art to add to the collection. I'm sure they had the Blake, but it was wrapped up in paper so I couldn't actually see it."

"Any idea who they were?" asked John.

"One was thin," Epiphany said, "and fairly tall. I only saw his back, but he had silver hair that was rather long and carefully combed. And I saw his hands. They were slender with long fingers. A gentleman's hands."

John shook his head. "That just doesn't sound familiar. Is it possible for you to describe the room?"

"It was like a basement. Muted light. Storage racks filled with art. It was cool, but not damp. Air conditioned, I think."

"Any idea where it was located?"

Epiphany pondered for a moment. "There was a tunnel. Very dark. I think I smelled water. Brackish. Standing water. Then I was in a basement or storage room. Wooden racks and shelves. But I can't tell you exactly where it was. I feel it was some distance away. Maybe in another city."

"Hmmm ..."

She glanced at John, who was frowning. "I'm sorry," she said. "I wish I could be more specific."

"Tell you what," John said, "it's nearly noon and I can't think clearly on an empty stomach. Why don't you come home with me for a bite of lunch and we'll talk some more."

"Thank you. That sounds lovely."

John's house was walking distance from the campus— a two-story red brick structure built in the Federalist style with an elegant entry flanked by columns arranged symmetrically. The house had been built around 1820 for one of the early deans of the university.

Inside, the rooms had arched doorways and high ceilings with elaborate crown molding. The furnishings were an eclectic mix of antiques—a Victorian sofa covered in rose dammask, an early American sideboard—and tasteful modern pieces that seemed perfectly at home with their older counterparts.

Trophies from fifty years of traveling abroad hung on the ivory-colored walls—a dark wooden mask from Africa, a Chinese scroll with a lyrical ink-wash landscape, several architectural studies done in pen and ink.

"Francesca," John called, "I've brought a guest home for lunch. Hope that's okay."

John's wife, a small white-haired woman wearing beige slacks and a grey-and-white striped blouse, appeared in the doorway and came toward them. She was, as Epiphany remembered her—immaculately outfitted, every hair in place.

"Darling," the woman cried, hurrying to give Epiphany a hug. "How splendid to see you again. It's been too long."

Epiphany returned the hug. She and Francesca had connected during the two years when Epiphany had been John's assistant while she worked on her art history degree. They had kept in touch now and then through Epiphany's mother, Susan. "Lunch will be ready shortly," Francesca said. "It's such a nice day. Why don't we eat on the terrace?"

"Great idea," said John. He led the way down the hall to the dining room where a set of French doors overlooked a patio and the garden beyond. A wooden table with a green umbrella dominated the terrace. "Make yourself at home," John said to Epiphany. "I'll go give Chessy a hand."

Epiphany settled into a chair under the shade of the umbrella and looked around the garden. Like the interior, there was a mix of styles—from formal boxwood hedges to free-ranging splashes of pink peonies and dark-red gladiolas. A narrow brick path led beneath a rose-covered arch toward a garden shed painted bright blue. It reminded her very much of Monet's beautiful garden at Giverny.

But despite the pleasant scene before her, Epiphany's mind kept wandering back to her remote-viewing experience. Who was the mysterious man with silver hair? Where was this storage room with the racks of art works? She felt it was some distance away. She saw seven roads coming together like spokes of a wheel. But she didn't recognize the place. Nothing looked familiar. If only she could come up with more information for John.

Lunch soon arrived—a quiche Lorraine with thick bacon and sliced potatoes, and a salad of greens brightened by cherry tomatoes and bits of avocado. "It is so lovely out here,"

Epiphany said. "I've always admired the way you two live your lives surrounded by beautiful things."

John and Francesca exchanged a fond look, then Francesca asked, "How is your work going? The way John described it to me sounds intriguing, though I admit I don't know much about psychic phenomena."

"Most of it's pretty mundane," Epiphany said. "People want to know what their future holds and how their decisions will impact outcomes. I try to guide them as best I can—with a little help from my friends on the spirit side."

"John told me he's asked for your help to find out what happened to the missing Blake," Francesca said. "How will you go about locating it?"

Epiphany gave John a weak smile, then said, "This is a new direction for me. I haven't worked on criminal cases before, but I'll do what I can. There are several techniques I can try. Remote-viewing is the most obvious," said Epiphany.

"What's that?" asked Francesca.

"As I told John," Epiphany said, "I've learned how to access and use what's referred to as the biophysical field, a sort of parallel reality that is like a mirror reflection of what we think of as *normal* reality. That gives me an opportunity to see things that are not visible using my ordinary senses."

"I was quite impressed with Epiphany's demonstration at the museum today," John said.

Thank goodness, Epiphany thought.

"Fascinating," said Francesca. "So this *technique* will allow you to see where the Blake piece is now located?"

"It will take some time, but I believe I'll be able to find it."

"We've already made a start," John said. "Epiphany uncovered some clues about where the work is stored, and got some information about the person who is now in possession of the piece."

Francesca's eyes widened. "So now you can tell the police how to find it?"

"Not yet. I need more information. But I can use my remote-viewing skills to learn more. Then we can formulate a plan for the work's recovery." Epiphany looked at John. "But enough of this for now. What else are you up to besides curating exhibits and teaching the latest group of hungry minds?"

"Fracking," said Francesca.

Epiphany looked at John's wife with surprise. "Fracking? Really?"

"It's a big issue around here," John said.

"Why? What's going on?"

"As you may know," John said, "fracking is shorthand for a process called 'hydraulic fracturing.' Basically, it's a drilling process that uses water mixed with chemicals to create fractures in the rock in order to release oil and natural gas. The water is injected under high pressure into wells more than a mile deep. The up-side is that it's a new technology that can capture oil and gas that can't be extracted by ordinary means."

"And the down-side?" Epiphany asked.

"There are several. The chemicals used in the process are toxic and can contaminate the surrounding environment. And, the process uses millions of gallons of water that once used are basically useless for any other purpose and have to be stored, just like the by-products from nuclear reactors."

"So there are oil companies using these extraction techniques right in this area?" said Epiphany.

"No. Not yet anyway," said John. "What has happened, though, is companies that are operating in other parts of the state have been shipping wastewater down here where it's injected into wells."

"Who's doing this?" Epiphany said.

"We know that a company called Ace Energy has been bringing wastewater here," John said. "Over the past few years, this part of Ohio has become a wastewater dump. It's not clear if the water can be contained. If it somehow migrates into another stratum, it could contaminate our drinking water. It also may be the cause of the increasing number of earthquakes this area has seen recently."

Epiphany frowned. "Why aren't there more stringent regulations? Surely it's irresponsible to put the area's water supply at risk."

"It's the same old vicious circle," said John. "People are concerned about their health and about harming the environment, but they're also concerned about economic factors like jobs. The corporations are great at using the jobs issue to circumvent what is usually a more nuanced discussion of environmental hazards."

"The city of Athens has been working to get fracking banned in this area," said Francesca. "But there are so many legal hurdles. And of course, the corporations have unlimited funds to tie up legal questions in the courts." She beamed at her husband. "John has been doing a series of articles for the newspaper that explain the hazards, and why it's important to protect ourselves from the threats that fracking poses, both to nature and to people."

"What about existing environmental laws and regulations?" Epiphany asked. "There must be legal precedents that could be used."

"Many environmental laws, like the Clean Air Act, the Clean Water Act and similar state laws, were put in place over thirty years ago," John said. "And what they do is not to ban environmental harm, but to regulate *how much* pollution and destruction can take place legally. The laws don't *prevent* destruction, they only *codify* it."

"Also," Francesca added, "once certain activities are legalized by federal or state governments, local governments can't ban them even if the local population is in danger."

"Well," said Epiphany, "you certainly have your work cut out for you, John."

"That's the main reason I put the *Inferno* show together," John said. "I very much believe in the power of art to communicate ideas on a deeper and more resonant level than scientific rhetoric. Art can communicate both the science *and* the emotions of living in a polluted environment. I ask the viewer to consider the images of the *Inferno*, of Hell, and compare them to what we are doing to our environment."

John paused to take a bite of quiche. From somewhere in the garden came the rough voice of a crow, like a rebuke.

John continued, "The sins Dante pointed to in his poem are many of the same flaws we still see today—greed, lust, gluttony, resentment, vanity. We still have corrupt officials willing to take a bribe or look the other way, and politicians who will do anything to win. We still suffer from the effects of fraud and tyranny. The parallels are astonishing."

Epiphany nodded. "Always the teacher, Professor Bernhardt."

John laughed. "No new tricks for this old dog."

"Just new interpretations for a new generation," said Epiphany.

She was quiet for a moment, thinking. The polluted pond, the pit of flames. The enormity of the consequenses of such blatant destruction filled her with a sudden terrible dread. *What are we doing*? she thought.

"Epiphany?"

She realized John was speaking to her. "Sorry," she said. "I'm afraid I just caught a glimpse of the future."

Chapter 7

After lunch, Epiphany and John went back to the gallery for another look at the show. "What's the next step?" John asked.

"I'd like to talk to some of the staff and see if they can remember anything unusual about the—"

"John," a hearty voice called. "Hello!"

Epiphany turned to see a heavyset man wearing jeans and a plaid shirt ambling toward them. He crossed the gallery and gave John's hand a shake. "How you doin' partner?" he asked.

"Hello, Chance," John said. He didn't seem overjoyed.

"And who's this pretty lady?" Chance said.

"This is Epiphany Mayall, a former student," John said. "Epiphany, meet Chance Hilliburn."

"Good to meet you, ma'am," Chance said with a grin.

Something about him made Epiphany uncomfortable. It wasn't just because he was large and thick and reminded her very much of a bulldog. His friendly demeanor seemed insincere. She felt a coldness behind the overt show of warmth. And his aura was filled with greys and browns: not a good sign. "How do you do?" she said.

Chance was studying John with his small, mean eyes. "So. I guess your next anti-fracking article will be comin' out in Tuesday's paper?"

"That's right."

"Well, friend, I'm lookin' forward to it."

"I'll bet you are."

"Always good to see you, Professor." Chance winked at Epiphany. "Nice meetin' you, honey."

As he strode out of the gallery, Epiphany glanced at John. He was watching Chance's exit with a look of mild amusement. "Who on earth," Epiphany said, "was that dreadful man?"

John smirked. "He's a field representative for Ace Energy. For some reason, he took a special interest in this exhibition."

"That's odd. He doesn't strike me as an art lover."

"During the installation he kept hanging around asking questions. Who were the artists? When was the work done? Where did it come from? How much was it worth? Drove poor Hugh a bit batty."

"Hugh?"

"Hugh Stillman, the museum's chief curator," said John. "Not that he doesn't enjoy showing off the exhibits, but Mr. Hilliburn was becoming a bit of a pest."

"Hidden agenda?" Epiphany guessed.

"It's possible of course. But why?"

"Maybe he saw the exhibit as threatening. Bad publicity for his company? He didn't seem very positive about the series of articles you're writing for the newspaper," Epiphany said.

"I'm sure he wants to protect the interests of the company he works for," John said. "But I'm surprised that he'd make the connection with the art. He doesn't exactly seem to be an intellectual giant."

Epiphany looked at the gallery door. An image flooded into her mind: Chance, wearing a black leather jacket and sunglasses and carrying a plaid wool blanket, stepping through the door and looking both directions before starting across the gallery. But what happened next? The image faded out, dissolving into a mist. "There's something … not right about him," she told John.

Over dinner that evening, Epiphany told her mother about the meeting with John and the sinister Mr. Hilliburn. "I'm not usually swayed by outward appearances," Epiphany said, "but this Chance Hilliburn just seemed like a bully to me. A pushy, oversized tank of a fellow. And I didn't like his eyes either. Mean little piggy-eyes."

Susan laughed. "Good gracious, Fanny," she said. "You sound like you did when you were ten years old. It was like you could see right through people. We'd be in a crowd of folks at the store, and you'd whisper to me, 'That man is mean. He beats up on his wife.' I always wondered if you were right."

Epiphany smiled ruefully. "Wouldn't be the first time my intuition got me into trouble. Hopefully, I won't have to have any further dealings with Mr. Hilliburn."

But after she told Susan goodnight and went upstairs to her room, Epiphany got out her laptop and searched the net for information on Chance. She found that he'd been arrested twice for minor offenses. There was mention of a bar fight, and he had also been indicted for racketeering five years ago while working for a trucking company in Detroit, but the charges were dropped. Since that time he had been employed by Ace Energy as a field representative. *Definitely a shady character,* Epiphany thought, *but not exactly a serial killer.*

To cheer herself up, she called her son and chatted with him about more pleasant things—Michael's classes at Linden College near Orlando where he taught music history, granddaughter Madison's summer art camp, plans for a holiday gathering at Stargazer Ranch with Ruby and Tom, Maddie's maternal grandparents.

Michael had lost his wife Shannon in an auto accident four years ago, and a few months after the funeral Epiphany had convinced him to move in with her. She offered to help take care of Maddie so he wouldn't have to hire someone. Since then, Michael had been visiting Shannon's parents at their ranch a few miles west of Vero Beach at least once a month to give Maddie a chance to spend time with her mother's family. By the time she told Michael good night and hung up, Epiphany had managed to stop thinking about the nasty Mr. Hilliburn.

She wasn't quite ready for bed, so she went back downstairs and out onto the porch. She sat down in the high-back rocking chair and leaned back, her feet against the rail. The night air was cool and the sky was bright with stars. The scent of grass, perfumed by the sun and now releasing its scent into the cooling evening, filled the air. Fireflies danced in the yard beneath the three old Buckeye trees that were already huge when Epiphany was a child. She could feel the presence of spirits, though none manifested.

She didn't remember falling asleep, but she must have dozed off. Suddenly she is walking across the pasture and down the hill to a creek at the base of a limestone gorge. Birch trees tower above her and giant ferns bend gracefully over the path.

A scraping sound is coming from the gorge, and she starts toward it, walking carefully on the wet and slippery path. Something is moving in the sandy bank next to the creek. It is hard to see in the dim light, but it looks like an animal—too big for a coyote, too small for a bear—digging at the base of the bluff.

Without warning, it stops digging and looks up at her. Epiphany jumps, her heart racing. The creature lets out a low whine, then raises its massive head and bays—a long, mournful howl. *It's a hound,* Epiphany tells herself. *One of the Old Man's hounds.*

Cautiously, she creeps down the path, sliding in the loose dirt. The hound lowers its head and looks at her.

"Are you Rover or Bounder?" Epiphany asks.

The dog tilts its head and studies her with soulful eyes. Then it turns and starts back down the path, pausing to look back. Epiphany takes a deep breath and follows.

At the base of the bluff, the earth is soft and gravelly. The dog stops in front of a small boulder and turns its head to Epiphany, whining. There is a hole in the ground next to the boulder. It must be where the dog has been digging. She kneels down and looks at the hole, then reaches out and touches the loose dirt. When she withdraws her hand, it is covered with black goo.

Startled, Epiphany lets out a cry and shakes her hand, but the tar-like substance sticks to her. She can smell it—a sickly sweet-sour odor that makes her feel dizzy. *What is this stuff*? she hears herself ask. She remembers her vision: the dark pond, the sick-sweet smell, the leering demons. *What is going on*?

Her hand is starting to burn, and she keeps shaking it to try to get rid of the sludge, but to no avail. Then the tar bursts into flame. Panic seizes her and she cries out, "Help! Help me!"

She jumped awake with a shudder. The yard was black, the trees flat silhouettes against the midnight sky. The fire-flies were gone, but she could hear crickets chirping and the faint song of a mockingbird from somewhere in the woods.

Otherwise, it was quiet. She held up her right hand and stared at it. It felt like it was burning.

And something else was wrong. Someone was in danger. She closed her eyes and tried to peer into the gloom of her premonition. Was it her granddaughter Madison? That didn't feel right. She'd just talked to Michael. Everything seemed fine there. She knew this feeling of anxiety was usually followed by something unexpected. Something bad. But she couldn't get an image, a face, a name. Maybe it had something to do with the dream, the burning tar. She rubbed her hand and wondered.

Chapter 8

The next morning over breakfast Epiphany was about to tell her mother about the strange dream she'd had about the hound and the black goo when the china began to vibrate. Then the tea jumped out of Epiphany's cup and sloshed across the table. "Good heavens," she exclaimed. "What the ...?"

The windows were rattling and the kitchen door swung slowly open, its hinges creaking.

"Dang," Susan said. "Not again."

Epiphany could hear a clatter coming from the china cabinet and the tinkling of glassware.

Then everything stopped. It was eerily quiet—no birds singing, no chickens clucking. Nothing.

Epiphany stared at her mother. "Was that an *earthquake*?"

Susan nodded. "We've had a bunch of them lately. A seismic flurry they called it in the paper."

"I don't remember having earthquakes here when I was growing up," Epiphany said.

"There was one just after your dad and I bought this place back in 1952. It was centered in Zanesville, about fifty miles from here, but we felt a pretty good jolt. Then the next year there was one at Crooksville and we felt that one too. Then for a long time"—Susan shrugged—"nothing. But recently, it seems like they've started up again. There was a pretty big one last year just north of Nelsonville."

"I wonder why they would start again," Epiphany said. "Did something trigger them?"

Susan frowned. "There's been talk that it's because of something called 'fracking.'"

"Dr. Bernhardt—uh—John, was telling me about the problems they're having in Athens trying to stop some energy company from moving into the area and using the fracking process," Epiphany said. "He and Francesca think it's a major issue."

Susan shook her head, frowning. "I've been trying to follow the stories in the paper, but sometimes it just seems overwhelming. There's so much bad news these days—pointless wars, crazy politicians, climate change. I try to keep up with it, but I get so tired."

"Mom, you're ninety-one years old. You have every right to be tired," said Epiphany.

"I suppose, but I'm really concerned," Susan said. "I read an article a few weeks back about a family a couple of counties over, down toward the West Virginia border, that had to leave their home because their well got contaminated from the waste-water. It said the whole aquifer in this area could get shot full of chemicals. Then what are we supposed to do?" Susan bit her lip. "It's crazy times, hon. Used to be we worried about how much rain we'd had or whether a late freeze would hurt the apple crop. Now we got people blowin' off mountaintops and deliberately causin' earthquakes. I got to wonder, what's next? We've only got one planet. Where are we supposed to go if we ruin it?"

After breakfast, Epiphany said she was going for a walk and would be back in time for lunch. She headed out across the pasture, stopping to admire the Black-Eyed Susans and Queen Anne's Lace growing along the edges of the field. The path leading to the gorge was barely discernable, a little track of sand between patches of Milkweed and Fleabane. It dropped suddenly into the canyon, a vertical wilderness of cliffs and waterfalls, of giant ferns and towering hemlocks, and the light all but disappeared beneath the thick tree canopy.

She tried to recall her dream about the hound and the hole it dug next to a boulder. It was close to the creek—the sand was soft and wet.

The path flattened out and wound through stands of ferns between the piles of sandstone boulders, following the creek's meandering journey. Little waterfalls splashed their way over the rocks and into deeper pools of undulating water.

Epiphany stopped to look at the creek, examining the sandy bottom, remembering the minnows and little frogs she used to watch as they darted here and there. The water looked clear and clean, but she saw no minnows circling beneath the surface. And no frogs. And no water-bugs skating on the surface. Odd.

Then she noticed a few dark pebbles lying on the bottom of the streambed. Reaching down into the cold water, she grabbed a handful and lifted them to the surface.

The first thing she noticed was the smell. The rocks gave off that same sick-sweet scent she remembered from her dream. And they weren't pebbles. They were slightly soft gobs of what looked like asphalt. "Tar balls," she said aloud. "Good lord."

"They come from farther upstream," said a voice.

She glanced around and saw an elderly man standing on the path about ten feet from her. She recognized her Spirit Guide at once.

A hint of a smile softened his worn features. "It's been a while since you paid me a visit."

"You've visited *me*, but you're right. I haven't been back to this place for a quite some time," Epiphany said.

"That so?" he replied. "Time works different for me than it used to."

"Still have your hounds?" Epiphany said. "Bounder and Rover?"

The Old Man looked around. "They's here somewhere," he said. He looked back at Epiphany and gestured toward the creek. "I reckon it's them goo balls what killed off everything. This used to be a fine little crik. Now it's not good for nothin'."

"When did this happen?"

The Old Man squinted, pondering. "A while back. Not too long. I come out one day and got a whiff of an awful smell, like that stuff they put on fence posts. My dogs was howlin' and carryin' on. I followed the crik upstream ..." He waved his hand ... "and found where the stuff was comin' from. I'll show you if you want."

He set out along the path, and she followed silently.

About half a mile upstream he stopped next to a waterfall that cascaded from between two boulders. "Take a smell," the Old Man said. "You can tell this water's bad."

There was a heavy scent of creosote in the air. "Follow that there side stream and you'll find the source," said the Old Man. Then he faded into a mist and disappeared.

The bluff rose sharply to the top of the canyon. Epiphany guessed it was probably around seventy-five feet above where she stood. There was no path, but the slope was littered with boulders and a few tree roots poked out from the cliff. She might be able to climb up to the top.

It was harder than she thought. The bluff was sandy and strewn with loose gravel. She worked her way slowly up the side, grasping at the rough tree roots and moving from boulder to boulder. Twice she slipped and nearly fell, but managed to regain her footing. Even though it was cool in the gorge, the temperature climbed as she made her way up the side of the bluff, the sun now burning on her back.

She finally made it to the top and pulled herself onto the packed clay. Before her was a meadow filled with dried grass and the stumps of dead trees. It was strangely quiet except for the low gurgling of water off to her right.

Epiphany walked along the bluff until she found a small stream that disappeared between the boulders and catapulted over the edge of the cliff. That pungent, sickly scent rose from the water as she made her way along the stream. She passed through a row of dead willow trees. Their trunks created a natural fence and she had to climb over the bare branches.

A large shallow pond lay before her. There was something strange about it. The water didn't look real—it was glossy, almost iridescent, and moved in slow, murky eddies. The blackened trunks of dead trees rose like grave markers from the cloudy water, and around the edges of the pond lay a wreath of froth encrusted with decayed plants. A stench, thick and sickening, rose from the pond; worse, she thought, than the smell of decomposing flesh. She recognized it at once as the pond she dreamed about just before leaving Florida. "A lake from Hell," she murmured.

A sudden puff of wind made the bare tree branches creak and moan. The back of her neck prickled, and her right hand began to burn.

Chapter 9

"A polluted lake?" Susan set the freshly baked blackberry pie on the kitchen counter and stared at her daughter. "Where is it exactly?"

Epiphany put her coffee cup down on the kitchen table. "About two miles up the gorge on top of the bluff."

"Past the Old Man's Cave?"

"No, not that far. Probably a quarter mile this side of the cave."

Susan frowned and sat down across from Epiphany. "That's odd. I thought that was all state parkland."

"I thought so too."

"Was it fenced?" Susan asked.

"I don't think so. I didn't see any buildings, just the meadow with the stream and then the lake."

"How big was it?" Susan asked. "The lake."

Epiphany thought. "Not big. Maybe a half-acre. But it must have been there a while since all the trees were dead."

"I remember a while back—maybe a couple of years—there was an article in the paper about dead fish found floating in the creek. The authorities said there was pollution in the water and advised folks not to eat any fish they caught in the stream. I don't recall ever hearing any more about it."

"The creek's polluted all right. The water looks clear, but

there's nothing alive in it—not a fish or a frog or a fly. It might as well be turpentine."

"Well, for goodness' sake," Susan said, shaking her head. "That's a pity."

"It's pretty clear that the lake is the source of the pollution. That little stream is carrying it down to the creek," Epiphany said.

A knock on the door interrupted their conversation. "Come on in," Susan called. "It's not locked."

Epiphany bit her lip and glanced at the door.

Sam Miller was a lanky man with light-brown hair and freckled skin that revealed his Scots-Irish roots. He was dressed in well-worn jeans and a green plaid shirt, and wore a Cincinnati Reds baseball cap.

"Howdy, Miss Sue," he said, then spotting Epiphany he grinned and held out his hand. "You must be Fanny," he said. "I'm Sam Miller."

"Good to meet you," Epiphany said. "Mom tells me you've been helping her out. I really appreciate you folks keeping an eye on her."

"What are neighbors for?" He turned to Susan. "I reckon you felt that little shake this mornin'? Everything okay?"

"No damage," Susan said.

"That's good. By the way, I'm headed into Logan to get some feed for the horses. Can I bring you anything from the store?"

"I could use some milk. But won't you sit with us a minute, Sam? I just took a blackberry pie from the oven. I'll bet you and Rhoda might like some for dessert."

"Thanks kindly, Miss Sue. That does sound awful good."

"I'll wrap it up for you."

Sam sat down and smiled at Epiphany. "Miss Sue tells me you're livin' in Florida."

"That's right. I keep telling her she should come on down. We've got flocks of retired folks from Ohio."

"Reckon the winters are a lot warmer than here."

Susan brought Sam a coke and settled down at the table. "Sam," she said, "Epiphany has come across a mystery—a very sorry mystery."

"That so?"

"I was hiking in the gorge and noticed there weren't any fish in the creek," Epiphany said. "I was able to trace the cause to a polluted lake a couple of miles upstream."

Sam gave her a troubled glance. "I've heard tell about that, but I haven't actually seen it. So it's true?"

Epiphany nodded.

"Damn."

"What's going on?" Epiphany said. "Do you have any ideas?"

"Yes, ma'am, I'm afraid I do. A couple of years ago up in Youngstown this company started doin' what's called hydraulic fracturing."

"Fanny was talking about that this morning. But what exactly is it?" Susan asked.

"Basically, you find a deposit of shale, and pump in a liquid with enough pressure to crack open the reservoir rock and release the oil that's trapped in the shale field."

"Why don't they just drill an oil well?" Epiphany asked.

Sam shook his head. "It's a different process. If you drill a well in a regular oil field, oil and gas flow up through the reservoir rock, often sandstone, usin' geologic pressure. But shale-field rock isn't that porous. Just drillin' a hole isn't enough to release the oil. So the producers have developed a way to crack open the rock and release the oil."

"How do you know all this, Sam?" Susan asked.

Sam grinned. "Used to work for an oil company up in the

Cleveland area. That was before I met Rhoda and decided to get back to nature, so to speak. She wanted to bring up our kids on a farm, and I figured that would be a pretty good life."

"That's quite a switch," Epiphany said.

"Yes, ma'am, it is. But since I left the oil business, I've found out about a lot of problems I didn't think were so important at the time. I don't know ..." He hesitated. "When you're working for a company, it's easy to sort of overlook problems. Hell, you want to get paid, so you do what's expected. But now that I'm away from it, I can see it's a pretty dirty operation."

"But what I saw was a lake of polluted water," Epiphany said.

"A lagoon, as they say in the business," said Sam. "That, of course, is even worse than a well because the pollution can contaminate groundwater and run off into the surrounding creeks and rivers."

"And that's legal?"

"There are regulations, of course, but they're not always followed." He sucked in his breath. "Plenty of ways to get around the rules."

"Isn't anything being done to stop this mess?" asked Susan.

"Folks are workin' on it. But it's slow goin'," Sam replied. "Take the university, for instance." He frowned. "Back in 2007 OU signed off on what they called a Climate Commitment. A bunch of colleges and universities put together a sort of pledge sayin' they was gonna shift away from usin' fossil fuels because of the pollution problems."

"Sounds like a great idea," Epiphany said.

"Yeah, but here it is twelve years later and not much has been done." He paused for a moment before continuing. "Well, they did put in a gas pipeline across the campus 'cause natural gas is supposed to be 'greener' than coal. Trouble is, gas that's got from frackin' has its own pollution problems. The process contaminates the water supply, and it also generates methane gas."

"And methane gas is bad?" said Susan.

"Yep. Puts out lots of CO2, which is the stuff that's causin' global warmin'." Sam shook his head. "We gotta accept the fact that there's no free lunch when it comes to energy. The key is to reduce consumption."

"How would we do that?" Susan glanced around. "Should I give up my refrigerator and my AC?"

Sam laughed. "No, ma'am. You don't have to go that far. But how about gettin' energy from renewable sources like solar or wind? Ohio State University just up the road apiece is already getting' a big chunk of their energy from wind farms. Savin' money on their electric bills too."

"But I heard that wind farms and solar panels can cause problems too," Epiphany said.

"Sure. Like I said, no free lunch. But they's both renewable and they don't produce CO2. That would sure help."

"I hope that pond up on the hill isn't going to get bad stuff into my well," Susan said.

"I've been monitorin' my well water," Sam said. "I can keep an eye on yours too. Just need to take a sample to the county office once a month."

"That would be wonderful. Thanks, Sam," Susan said.

Chapter 10

That night, Epiphany had trouble falling asleep. She couldn't stop thinking about the unexpected problems she'd found in her old neighborhood. She'd always considered her childhood to be generally pleasant—a happy memory marred only by her unusual *impressions* and the confusion and embarassment they caused her.

But aside from that, she had lived in a wonderful world of natural beauty—pristine streams, old-growth forests, sparkling waterfalls, meadows filled with flowers and birds. A true Eden. What a dreadful idea that what she had taken for granted would be lost, destroyed by the pursuit of profits. What a miserable trade-off.

She looked out the bedroom window. The night sky was a black ocean speckled with stars. It reminded her of the southern sky—huge and open, an arc that spanned the Florida peninsula from the Atlantic Ocean to the Gulf of Mexico.

Over the years, she had come to love Florida in the same way she had loved the Southern Appalachians. It was a place of great natural beauty with amazing hidden treasures—springs and lakes, caverns, underground rivers, forests filled with magnificent trees and flowering shrubs.

And the wildlife! Waterbirds everywhere. Deer and bears, turtles and alligators. She had even managed to accept the snakes, though she was no fan of the poisonous ones. She shivered a little, wondering if the entire natural world would soon be ravaged by profit-seeking predators. When they finished their assault, would there be anything left? Eventually, she fell into a troubled sleep.

John and Epiphany are walking along the creek toward Old Man's Cave. Epiphany wants to show John the polluted lagoon so he can write an article about it for the paper. He follows her along the path between the ferns and hemlocks, and she urges him to be careful because the rocks are slippery and he might fall. He ignores her warning and keeps interrupting her to ask questions about the health of the creek, the types of pollutants she has seen, the size of the lagoon. "I'll show you," she tells him, "but you have to be careful." Why won't he listen to her? She twists her hands together and wishes she hadn't invited him to view the lagoon.

Then they see the Old Man. He is standing on the path in front of them with one of his hounds. He holds out his palm to them. "That's far enough," he says. "Don't you go no further. It ain't safe."

John starts talking to the Old Man, trying to get him to take him to the lagoon. When he refuses, John starts to go around him, but the hound growls and blocks the path. John looks at Epiphany in frustration. "For God's sake, can't you reason with him?" he asks. "I need this for the article."

"He's just up ahead," the Old Man says to Epiphany.

"Who?" she asks. "Who's up ahead?"

"The bulldog with the pig eyes," he replies. "I seen him

this mornin'. He has the right tools to do the job. And he's got helpers too."

"You mean Mr. Hilliburn?" says Epiphany.

"Aye. That's the one. He's up to no good. Watch out for him, hear me?"

John takes the opportunity to continue along the path. "Wait," Epiphany calls to him. "It's not safe. John? You have to be careful. John!"

She starts after him, but he disappears.

"Dang," says the Old Man. "Too late. He's already gone."

Epiphany woke filled with frustrated concern. *I need to tell John to be careful,* she thought. *Hilliburn is definitely up to something.* As she slowly fell back to sleep, she thought she could hear a hound baying in the distance.

At breakfast the next morning, Epiphany read Susan the article John had written for the newspaper. It was the second in a series that he'd authored on the topic of oil and gas-extraction in the Athens area.

He began by inviting the readers to visit the Kennedy Museum and look at the exhibition of illustrations of Dante's *Inferno,* noting that the exhibit was intended to serve as a starting point for examining the consequences of human folly.

"By linking past and present, environment and human action, infirmity and healing, the show provides a template for engaging one another in a dialogue about the impact of our present actions on the future of our community. The fact that one of the art works in the show has mysteriously disappeared gives additional urgency to our quest for information—and answers."

The article continued by giving a basic overview of the process of hydraulic fracturing. Citing numerous examples, he showed that the process posed a threat to water, air, land, and the health of people living in the area—dangerous levels of toxic air pollution near fracking sites, smog in rural areas at levels worse than downtown Los Angeles. Oil and gas production had also been linked to increased risk of cancer and birth defects in neighboring areas, as well as to a risk of increased seismic activity.

The rest of the article provided statistics on the benefits of using cleaner, renewable sources such as wind and solar to meet energy needs, including job creation, reducing health care costs, and preventing emissions that contribute to global warming.

"We deserve better," John stated in the last paragraph. "And we have the technology to realize the dream of a future free from fossil fuels. The only question remains: do we have the will?"

"He's so courageous," Susan said. "Look how he spells everything out and makes it so clear."

"He always did that in class," said Epiphany, remembering. "He was such a good teacher." *Was? Still is, right?* She shook her head.

"What do you think we should do?" Susan asked. "I mean, there must be something we can do to help. Write letters or protest? Something."

"A letter of support would be a good idea," Epiphany said.

The phone rang and Susan answered. "Francesca," she said. "Good morning. Epiphany and I were just reading … What? What's wrong, dear? Yes. She's right here. Of course."

Susan handed the phone to Epiphany. "She wants to talk to you, Fanny. She seems upset."

"Hello, Francesca. What is it? What's wrong?" Epiphany slumped in her chair and her hand flew to her face. "Oh, my God. How did … When? Where are you, dear? Yes, of course. I'll be right there."

As Epiphany hung up the phone, Susan said, "What's wrong, Fanny? What's the matter?"

"It's John," Epiphany answered. "He's dead.

Chapter 11

Two police cars and an ambulance sat in front of Siegfred Hall, their lights flashing. Epiphany parked close by and ran across North Green to the Fine Arts Complex. At the top of the steps, a uniformed officer blocked her way. "I'm sorry, ma'am. You can't go in there. There's been an incident."

"Yes," Epiphany said between breaths, "I know. Francesca, John Bernhardt's wife, called me. She asked me to come right away." When the officer hesitated, Epiphany looked past him through the door and spotted Zoe Hernandez, John's long-time assistant, standing with a group of people near the elevator. "Zoe!" Epiphany called, waving.

Zoe glanced up and hurried to the door. "Ms. Mayall! Mrs. Bernhardt said you were on your way. God, isn't this just awful?"

Epiphany looked at the officer. He nodded and motioned her inside. She and Zoe hugged. "What happened?" Epiphany asked as they moved toward the elevator.

"I must have been the last one to see him alive," Zoe said, her voice trembling. "He was fine. He was having his morning coffee and getting ready for a class. He asked me to make a copy of some notes for him and when I came back he ... he had slumped over on his desk and he ..." She began to cry.

Epiphany patted her shoulder. "I'm so sorry, Zoe. I know how close you were to him."

"All those years ..." Zoe murmured. "So many years ..."

When she got off the elevator, Epiphany saw Francesca talking to two paramedics and a policeman in front of John's office door. The door was open, and Epiphany could see two more medics lifting John's body onto a gurney. She embraced Francesca. "Zoe told me what happened," she said.

"He was fine this morning. Everything was normal. How could this have happened?" Francesca searched Epiphany's face. "How?"

"I don't know. But I intend to find out."

An investigator was methodically examining the office. Epiphany watched for a moment. There were no visible signs of a struggle or anything unusual in the office, but she felt a sinister presence. Something hidden. Someone running. Breathless words in a language she didn't recognize. A gun or weapon of some kind. But that didn't make sense, did it? She tried to focus on the present and pulled her attention back to the scene before her.

After Francesca left with the medics to accompany her husband's body to the morgue, Epiphany went back downstairs and found Zoe. "Let's go find a place to sit down, okay?"

They went out a side door and sat down on a bench overlooking a patch of lawn. The morning sun was bright. Small white clouds paraded past the shingled rooftops and hid behind the maple trees.

"Can you tell me anything else about what happened?" Epiphany asked.

Zoe shook her head. "I don't think so. Like I told the officer, I came in to work about seven-thirty. John came in a few minutes later and I brought him a cup of coffee and asked if he needed anything. He was getting ready for a lecture on

Byzantine architecture and he asked me if I'd make copies of some floor plans he wanted to hand out to his class, so I took the drawings down to the office and made the copies."

"How long did that take?"

Zoe paused, thinking. "I don't know—maybe ten or fifteen minutes? Then I took the copies back to his office, and he was slumped over with his head on the desk. I asked him if he was okay but he didn't answer. I went to him and shook his shoulder. Then I saw his face." Zoe stopped and took a shuddering breath. Tears rolled down her face.

Epiphany put her arm around Zoe's shoulders. "It must have been a terrible shock."

"I couldn't believe it," she whispered. "It was so sudden."

Epiphany could see the image in Zoe's mind—the bulging eyes, the gaping mouth. Like a fish suffocating on a dock. She studied the image calmly as she held the trembling woman in her arms. Was there anything unusual in the picture? Something that didn't belong? Anything at all?

She scanned the face and then moved down to the neck. She noticed that John's tie was loose—perhaps he'd clawed at it, trying to get his breath? Just above the shirt collar on the left side of his neck was a small red spot. Perhaps an insect bite? Or maybe he'd nicked himself while shaving? Something about the little spot bothered her. But no additional images came up on her mind-screen. Then she heard a little "zing" and immediately lifted her hand to the left side of her neck. What the heck was *that*?

"I'm sorry." Zoe was trying to straighten up and stop crying. "He was so good to me, and I'll miss him so much."

"I know. He was good to all of us."

The two women got to their feet and walked back into the building. "Do you want me to give you a ride home or get you anything?" Epiphany asked.

Zoe gave a blurry smile. "Thanks, but I think I'll stay in the office. I have work to do. Maybe it'll distract me, you know?"

"Of course. I think I'll see if I can find Francesca and make sure she's all right." She started to leave, but stopped and turned back to Zoe. "Are you sure you didn't see anything or anyone unusual around this morning?"

Zoe thought for a minute. "Not really. The only thing I can think of is there were a couple of students sitting on the steps when I came into the office. I didn't recognize them, but that's not unusual. But they ..." She frowned.

"What?"

"I don't know. They looked different. *Foreign*. Of course, we have quite a large number of foreign students here at OU, but they seemed sort of furtive. They stopped talking and watched me until I went inside." Zoe shrugged. "Probably nothing, but it did seem a little out of the ordinary."

"Thanks," Epiphany said. Again she heard voices speaking some foreign language she couldn't understand. Who *were* these people?

Epiphany caught up with Francesca at the coroner's office. She had just finished giving a statement to the medical examiner, and was relieved that the death had been ruled due to "natural causes" and that an autopsy would not be necessary.

"There is no evidence of any crime," Francesca told Epiphany. "Since John was seventy-eight and had high blood pressure, they have concluded that the cause was myocardial infarction—a heart attack—and closed the investigation."

"What about the little red spot on his neck?"

Francesca looked puzzled. "Red spot?"

"Yes. There was a small red dot on his neck on the left side just above his collar."

"I … I don't know. No one said anything about a red spot." She gave Epiphany a quizzical look. "I didn't think you'd seen his body."

Epiphany didn't know what to say. She realized she had seen the red spot in a vision based on what Zoe had seen when she discovered John's body. How could she explain that to Francesca? "Don't worry about it. It's probably nothing. Do you need a ride home?"

Francesca shook her head. "Our son is flying in from Dallas. He's going to pick me up here so we can go to the funeral home and talk to them about arrangements for transporting the … his body." Her face crumpled. "Oh, Epiphany. What a terrible day this is!"

Epiphany hugged Francesca and told her to call if there was anything she could do. She drove home slowly, trying to process what had happened.

When she got home, she told her mother the details of the tragic events. They sat on the porch and talked for over an hour—about John and his work and his influence on Epiphany. And what a fine teacher he had been and how sorry they were to lose him.

Susan decided to distract herself by listening to an audio-book and went inside. Epiphany sat on the porch and stared at the garden. The row of red hollyhocks parading along the back edge of the lawn caught her attention—the collection of bright red dots seemed to scream at her.

She sat looking at them for several minutes. Then she went inside and called the medical examiner's office. She *had* to talk to him. The receptionist made an appointment for her for later that afternoon.

"I determined that based on the evidence there was no need for an autopsy," said the medical examiner. He was a pleasant-looking middle-aged man with a shock of grey hair and a neatly trimmed moustache. He peered at Epiphany through thick-rimmed glasses. "I know that Mrs. Bernhardt was happy to avoid any prolonged investigation. She's already been through enough."

"But you *did* notice that little red spot?" asked Epiphany.

The examiner looked down at the papers on his desk. "The investigator noted it but didn't see that it had any bearing on the case. It appeared to be a very small puncture wound—likely an insect bite that was slightly irritated. There was no swelling and no sign of infection or trauma or bruising. His blood work didn't show anything unusual." He sat back and gave Epiphany a patient look. "We just don't have anything to go on here. I can't authorize further investigation without any evidence or reason. I know you'd like to be sure no extenuating circumstances were connected to Dr. Bernhardt's death, but we need more than a hunch."

Epiphany got to her feet. "All right. Thank you for your time." At the door, she paused and turned. "But, if I find additional evidence, will you agree to reconsider?"

"Yes, of course. We want to be sure this case is fully resolved."

⟡

Once again, Epiphany had trouble falling asleep that night. She tossed this way and that. Put on an extra blanket. Took it off. A full moon hung above the trees, sending a searchlight in through the window. It was after midnight when she finally dozed off.

When she woke, the moon was gone and the room was dark. She sat up to look at the clock and gave a little cry. John Bernhardt was sitting in the wing chair next to the bed, looking directly at her.

"Don't be alarmed," he said. "I just need to talk to you."

"I know." She quieted her breathing and felt a sense of calm descend around her.

"Don't bother Chessy with an autopsy," he said. "It would distress her and they wouldn't find anything."

"It wasn't a natural death, was it, John?"

"I was poisoned."

"Poisoned?" Epiphany was surprised. "How?"

"I believe it was one of the young men Zoe saw outside the Fine Arts building," John said. "The fellow had on a grey jacket and a dark slacks, and he was talking to another young man, but when I started up the steps they both stopped and looked at me. One of them came toward me. I thought for a moment he was going to run into me, but he stepped aside at the last minute. I suddenly felt a strange little sting on my neck and I glanced back at him. He met my look for an instant and then turned away. I didn't think anything of it at the time. It felt like a biting fly or some other bug. Not even as much as a bee sting. So I went on inside and up to my office. Zoe brought me some coffee, and I set to work on my lecture.

"But after a few minutes, I started feeling strange. I

couldn't breathe and I felt like I was floating out of my body. The next thing I knew, I was looking down at myself. I felt a sense of detachment. That poor fellow was obviously dying, and I felt sad for him, but I knew that I was not him, nor was he me. Then I was moving into a sea of magnificent shades of blue light. But a voice was telling me to go back. That I had more work to do. So, here I am."

"Do you have any idea who attacked you?"

"No. I'd never seen him before. But I want you to talk to a man named Blake King. Francesca can tell you how to reach him. I think he'll be able to help us."

And with that, John disappeared.

Part II

There's a crisis of epic proportion occurring on our planet 24/7, 365: the war against nature has become a prolonged looting spree.

—Dr. Reese Halter, Conservation Biologist

Chapter 12

"Blake King?" Francesca's brown eyes widened. "I don't know him very well. He and John had a close relationship, but I found Blake rather, how should I say, daunting?"

"How so?"

"He's really quite, umm, eccentric. Actually, that would be an understatement." Francesca seemed perplexed. "He's, umm, an artist, but I've known a number of artists over the years and he's, well, *unusual*. In every way."

Epiphany waited. She was aware of Francesca's distress and her struggle to find words to describe Blake King. Her aura was swirling with greys and reds, confusion. Even fear. They were sitting on the Bernhardt's brick terrace at the same table where they shared a lunch two days before.

Everything was the same—the garden with its rush of pink and red flowers, the roses twining around the arbor, the little blue garden shed at the end of the path—yet everything had changed dramatically as though the light had somehow shifted and taken on an overlay of grey. The spirit of the place had changed.

Francesca set down her teacup and took a breath. "All right. I'll just tell you what I feel. I honestly think the man is mentally unstable. I find him hard to be around."

"What did John think of him?"

"John found him amusing. No, more than that. He found him *intriguing*. Maybe because John was a scholar of William Blake and Blake King is a devotee."

"Blake is a follower of Blake?"

"Oh, that's not his real name. He took the name Blake King after he left his wife and family and moved out to that cabin in the woods. Before that, his name was Scott Golden. He was on the OU faculty for a while, but he retired when he moved out to Carbondale and bought some land. That was back before you were in school here—late sixties, I think. He became a sort of recluse, though he had his followers. They said he was a New Age prophet. In my opinion, they had all taken too many drugs and couldn't see straight. But that was the culture of the day." Francesca shook her head and took a sip of tea.

"Anyway, John kept in touch with him because of their common interest in William Blake. He felt that Scott, or Blake, provided a unique interpretation of the poet's work through a kind of spiritual identification, almost like a case of possession in which Scott became the spiritual embodiment of William Blake so he could carry on his work. I was never certain how exactly that differed from a delusional disorder, but John loved to have long conversations with the man. To me he made almost no sense."

"Do you know how I could get in touch with him?" Epiphany asked.

"Why would you want to?"

"I thought since he's interested in William Blake he might know something about the theft of the work from the museum. The, uh, investigation doesn't seem to be progressing very quickly, so I thought I'd see what I could dig up. After all," she added, "John did ask me to help him find the missing work."

"Yes. That's true." Francesca thought for a moment, then

said, "I'll be happy to give you his phone number. I know John had it here somewhere. But I've heard that Scott, er, Blake, is difficult to reach. He values his privacy."

"I understand," said Epiphany, "but I'd like very much to talk to him."

Epiphany tried the number several times without getting an answer. She decided to try to find out where Blake lived. Perhaps she could contact him personally since he apparently didn't answer his phone.

R.R. #7, Carbondale, Ohio, was the address Francesca had given her. She drove west from Athens on Route 56, the same road she took to get to her family farm in Mt. Eden. After passing through the little community of New Marshfield, she was soon surrounded by the towering white pines and other oldgrowth trees of Zaleski State Forest. The village of Carbondale was nothing more than a collection of weathered wooden houses and a tiny post office. She turned off the main road and followed her GPS directions to the address.

The narrow road wound through patches of woods and briefly followed a stream before plunging into a steep gorge. After navigating a series of hairpin curves and crossing a fast-flowing creek, Epiphany wound upward, emerging from the thick woods at the top of a ridge. A dirt drive led from the main road to a small farmhouse. The number seven was painted in bright-green letters on the mailbox.

She approached the house slowly. In the front lawn was a large oak tree. A derelict-looking tractor sat in the drive between the house and a small shed, and an old hand-mower had been abandoned in the middle of the yard.

Epiphany got out of the car and looked around. There was no sign of life—no dogs or other animals. It was so quiet she could hear her own breath. Her scalp tingled. She felt eyes watching her, but she walked calmly to the front door and raised her hand to knock.

The door swung open, and she found herself face to face with a man of medium height wearing jeans and a blue sweatshirt. Shoulder-length iron-grey hair framed a tan face with prominent cheekbones and large, heavy lidded eyes. "Good afternoon," she said, "I'm Epiph—"

"Behold, the Phoenix rising, its wings ablaze with fire," the man said loudly. His voice was melodious, like a singer or a preacher. "I search out the remnant that it may be called into readiness. Every step is covered on a calloused knee. We must make haste. And carry a big stick. God in his heaven will not intervene on our behalf."

Epiphany stared at him. "I'm a friend of John Bernhardt's," she said. "Of Professor Ber—"

"Beleaguered, I admit to nothing," the man said. "And you, more bidden than the sea from sheets of basalt risen, isn't it time, just short of the direct downfall of seismic fissures, to tread on Ancient Soil again?" He stood aside and motioned her into the house.

"Have you heard about what's happened?" Epiphany said. "The missing art work and about John's—"

"John is gone. Long live John."

Epiphany had no idea what to say, so she remained standing in the middle of the semi-dark room and glanced around.

There was a large stone fireplace at one end of the cabin. Next to it was a wooden table and several metal pots—perhaps a makeshift kitchen? At the other end was a cot covered with a ragged quilt. A shelf of books hung above the bed. In a corner next to the only window was a rocking chair.

"Sit ye down, daughter. Rest ye," said Blake, pointing to the chair.

Epiphany complied and sat watching her host as he watched her. "Some drink, I think," he said. He went to the "kitchen" and brought back a glass of water and gave it to her. "A toast," he said, raising an invisible glass. "To what is lost and what is found and what is flowing all around."

"Okaaay. I'll drink to that, I suppose," said Epiphany. The water was cool and sweet, unusually refreshing. She set the glass aside and studied him. "Do you know why I'm here?"

He stood next to her and looked out the window. "The Daughters of Albion send sighs toward America," he said. "They long in vain for the country's soft soul, the vast and unspoiled garden of Arcadia. But the wheels turn one against the other. The quenching oil makes smooth the machinations of the chariot, but a series of slippered footfalls snaps the bough of rotten pearls and lets loose a cacophony of colonial prosperity. Unleash the slaves! Turn loose the hounds!" He glanced at Epiphany. "I wish," he said, "there was a right and proper solution. They have built a Kingdom of the Dead beside the burning lake. The scaffolding is crumbling beneath their feet, and yet they do not heed the cries of helpless infants waiting to be born."

"The search for oil has brought about environmental degradation and the future is in peril?"

Blake's mouth twitched in a little smile. "More prophet he than me."

"John?"

Blake nodded. "The thunder of our present-day knowledge is but the piping of a bird. The Sons of Albion sail across the Erythraean Sea, and the shaking ground is put to rest in the great temple of Postponement. The sea is red with the blood of martyrs. Generations come and go and still we finance further bleeding upon the slipping plane of this tilting earth. Do they not see the Tyger burning in the night? Can they not read the warning in its eyes? No arrow exists that wasn't thrown down by the stars. What hand dare seize the fire?"

"Do you think someone killed him?"

Blake looked away. "Two bleeding contraries cover their hurried footfalls. The blood of the lamb is on their hands. Yet they bear witness to the Serpent and the Serpent to the Dragon. The evil day can be put off no longer. The Tyger laps up fire. Knot by knot, the web was knit while the moral fiber weakened. Cops and Robbers play at the same game. The still man wins no victory with his silence."

Suddenly, Blake froze and looked up at the ceiling. "He's here," he said in a low voice.

"Who's here?"

"Why John, of course."

Chapter 13

Epiphany could feel John's presence, but he didn't fully manifest to her. It seemed that he wanted a private word with Blake, so she sat quietly while Blake wandered here and there and spoke in a low voice. She couldn't make out the conversation, but after about ten minutes he stopped his wandering and stood still before her. "The Man has yet to leave," he said.

"Why does he stay?"

"We are to provide proof of the folly. The still man sits upon the bridge without a course of action. We must penetrate the darkness wherein the invisible god lives. Behold! Up from the depths he comes! We have long been betrayed by wishful thinking."

"Who is the still man?" Epiphany asked.

"I can only hint at my theory," said Blake. "Should he wish to assert himself he must find his better foot. He writhes in agony, no longer able to ignore the plea of numbered stars. He thought to save himself from ever wanting to know. There is an agenda to all this." Blake turned and once more gazed out the window. "He is there, even now. He walks in Tyger circles and mutters to himself. The gloom is a bruising rod. People-destroying sulphur is having an effect upon the weather. Bits of rock from space were visited from long ago upon the earth. If you require a sign, look for Hunger!"

Suddenly agitated, Blake collapsed on the bed and buried his head in his arms. "Hark! Can you not hear her screams? She fulfilled her mortal task of hungering once and for all by laying out her corpse at the feet of the medical professionals. They mistook her for a rat, small creature that she was. The walls still hold her shadow and the floor as well. The still man has heard her footsteps in the darkness of the halls. Starving, she weeps. A thing apart, a separate animal alone in her cave. He hurries past without a look."

Epiphany stared at Blake. "You're talking about Margaret Schilling, aren't you?" Epiphany said. "The inmate at the asylum who starved to death when she wandered off and got locked in a cleaning closet. And her spirit must be there. So the still man works at the museum?"

"He eats guilt for his dinner and feels decay with every breath. But fear stays his hand. He seeks justification for his inaction. These empty spreading sounds do not work for him alone. I say again, there is an agenda here." Blake sat up and rubbed his face with his hands. "Come," he said, getting to his feet. "I will show you the Tyger."

Epiphany followed Blake across the yard and down a dirt road that wound through a meadow. Bluebells and pink phlox bloomed in the ditch alongside the drive. The road stopped at the edge of a steep embankment and a narrow path led downward to a creek.

"What's wrong with the water?" Epiphany asked, stopping to take in the slow moving brownish-orange stream. An acrid, metallic scent filled the air.

Blake looked back at her from the water's edge. "Our souls tremble at the sight of such a loss—metallic streams perplexed by iron rust. Acid reigns supreme in these far valleys. This state of possession is laid out on the grid of an abandoned pit where thieves applied their ambitious assault upon the mother and conceived of monsters yet to be born." He shook his head and began walking along the edge of the stream.

Epiphany had seen acid mine drainage before. The pollution from mining operations—even years after the activities have ceased—lowers the pH of waterways, making the water acidic and harmful to most organisms. Drainage from long-closed mines can seep from abandoned sites for centuries. Chemical reactions can also cause a condition called "yellow boy," bright-orange water indicating high levels of iron hydroxide. As well as contaminating local streams, the poisonous brew can find its way into wells and pollute drinking water for thousands of people.

About a quarter mile up-stream, Blake stopped in front of a large opening in the side of the bank. A metal gate covered the opening. He undid the padlock. "Behold, the Gates of Hell." He motioned Epiphany to enter.

"What is this place?" she asked.

"This mine is mine, I own this mine," Blake said. "This mine's my home, the home I own. I am the guide, so come inside." He threw open the gate. "I know them well, these bowels of hell," he confided with a wink.

She followed him through the gate and found herself in a long narrow shaft that tunneled into the hillside. Beneath her feet, the ground was soft and slippery.

Blake flipped a switch and the tunnel brightened to a dull glow. At the far end of the shaft, she could see a macabre light that matched the unnatural orange of the polluted stream.

They walked through the tunnel and into a large

underground room about the size of a basketball court. A domed ceiling rose high above their heads. The place smelled strongly of rubber and enamel.

In the center of the room stood a huge sculpture made of what appeared to be scrap metal and an assortment of cables, wires and parts taken from machines—electric panels, metal rods, circuit boards, spark plugs—all welded together to create a monstrous creature.

The top half of the sculpture was painted bright orange, while the bottom half, which was a mirror reflection of the top, was black. The effect was of a monstrous mechanical creature looking down at its own reflection in an invisible lake. The eyes of the creature were painted with a luminescent material that made them glow with menace. Epiphany stared in amazement at the sculpture.

"Behold how he burns with fearful symmetry in the eternal night of the underworld," said Blake, looking up at his creation. "Upon what anvil were his innards twisted to life? What chain can hold him? His brain is a furnace that spews forth a rain of frogs. Six thousand years of homo sapiens revived in imitation of the Beast." He glanced at Epiphany and said in a low voice, "East is east and west is where the gates are locked."

"Who has seen this Tyger?" asked Epiphany.

Blake turned back to the sculpture. "He waits in the forest for the eternal eye to envision him. He waits for darkness and sorrow to cover all flesh, for that time which was and is and is to come when the piping bird will fly above the City of Ashes to announce the descent of the Divine Child. Misunderstood, abused, he comes, finally, to burn himself out in the current of life called Memory." He gave Epiphany a sorrowful glance. "If only we could remember to forget."

He fell silent for several minutes, then said, "There is a

burning lake that stands in the midst of a meadow. Tentacles of death reach out from its shores. I have seen this in a dream."

Epiphany thought at once of the lagoon with its toxic font of poison. "I know this lake. I've seen it too."

He looked at her sharply. "By fire shall the filth be consumed. Woe to the serpents, that brood of vipers. We have overslept upon the moon of indulgences. Mammon has come home to roost. Even now his emissary stalks the halls of Malebranche. He of the silver hair and the violet eyes. His velvet words obscure vile thoughts while all the time he magnates to himself the treasures of the world—rare volumes, priceless works of art, gemstones, comely maidens. But make no mistake," Blake paused dramatically, "Make no mistake, inside he is rotten. When he makes a trumpet of his ass you realize how foul he smells."

"Do you know his name?"

"Look no farther than the rape of Oothoon," Blake replied. Then he turned abruptly and started toward the tunnel entrance. "Come. The fumes are strong. We must leave this place at once."

Back at her mother's house that evening, Epiphany sat for a long time on the front porch watching the fireflies wink, and hover and listening to the rasping chant of the katydids. Now and then, an owl hooted from among the branches of the elms.

She tried to piece together the events of the past four days. The dream about the hound and the black goo. The next morning's earthquake and her discovery of the polluted lake. Meeting Sam Miller and hearing about the oil company activities in the area.

Then, the next day, meeting John Bernhardt and the tour of the gallery with its exhibit of art works based on Dante's *Inferno*. The missing work by William Blake. Her dream that John was in danger and then the next morning, news of his death.

And then today the strange meeting with the artist Blake King, seeing his Tyger sculpture, hearing about his vision of the burning lake. What should she make of this unusual man? His ravings were ambiguous, but she had found that she could follow his ideas once she grew accustomed to his bizarre use of language. She had no doubt that he could be helpful.

A mockingbird began a complicated soliloquy. The moon was making an appearance from behind the trees, throwing beams of silver across the lawn. The katydids buzzed more loudly, boring into her brain, overwhelming her thoughts. She closed her eyes and put her hands over her ears and tried to think beneath the din of nature's symphony.

What did she *know*? What did she *need* to know? A work of art had gone missing from an exhibition that was deemed controversial only because the art works focused on certain sins and the punishment of the sinners. The sins had to do with greed, fraud and corruption. The sinners were depicted being thrown into a pool of burning pitch. Blake's burning lake?

Her friend and former teacher, John Bernhardt, had been critical of the activities of oil companies in the area, and had spoken out by writing a series of articles explaining why the practices used by the company were a threat to the health of the community. The day his latest article appeared in the paper, he was found dead, apparently of natural causes. And yet he had appeared to her and told her he was poisoned. But there was no medical evidence of any toxin and so no autopsy.

Who were the suspects? Both John and his assistant Zoe had seen two suspicious men on the steps of the building where John's body was found, but how could they have poisoned him? It had to be someone who was in the building around the time of his death. Zoe was the last person to see him alive, and she hadn't seen anyone go near his office. But what about those two students? John thought they had something to do with his death, but how? Were theirs the voices she heard speaking in a foreign tongue?

And who stole the painting by William Blake? Epiphany suspected Chance Hilliburn, the field representative for the oil company. She had "seen" him entering the gallery with a wool blanket, but where was the evidence? Could he have just walked into the gallery, removed the art work, put it under the blanket and walked out? And what would he want with the painting anyway? He hardly seemed the sort of person who would care about stealing a work of art.

Maybe he was working for someone. What had Blake King said about an "emissary of Mammon" who surrounded himself with beautiful things? Blake had said "look no farther than the rape of Oothoon," but what did that mean? Who was Oothoon?

Epiphany got up and went inside. Susan had gone to bed and the downstairs was dark. Epiphany locked the front door and made her way upstairs to her room. She opened her laptop and typed in "Oothoon."

"The central narrative in William Blake's poem, *Visions of the Daughters of Albion*, is of the female character Oothoon, called by Blake the 'soft soul of America,' and of her sexual experience," Epiphany read. "Scholars have suggested that Blake had been influenced by Mary Wollstonecraft's *A Vindication of the Rights of Woman*, which was published in 1792, a year before Blake's book appeared. In the narrative, Oothoon is in love with Theotormon, who represents the chaste man, filled with a false sense of righteousness. Oothoon desires Theotormon but is suddenly, violently raped by Bromion. After Oothoon is raped, neither Bromion nor Theotormon will have anything to do with her."

"So," Epiphany said aloud, "the man who raped Oothoon was named Bromion. If Blake King was right, then the person who stole the drawing—or had it stolen—is named 'Bromion.'"

Before she went to bed, Epiphany began a list that she hoped would lead her to the answers to several pressing questions. First, she needed to find out who stole the William Blake drawing. Next, she needed to discover the identity of the elusive collector "Bromion." And third, she needed to follow up on that peculiar red dot on John Bernhardt's neck. She decided to tackle the question of the theft first.

Chapter 14

The next morning was hot and steamy. Sam and Rhoda picked Susan up to take her on a shopping trip to Logan to look for a new fan for her bedroom. They invited Epiphany to join them, but she said she wanted to have another look at the art exhibit at the museum. "I'll be back in time for dinner," she told them as they climbed into Sam's antique "woody" station wagon.

Epiphany drove through the countryside past fields of wildflowers and groves of elm and maple trees. The sky was hazy with moisture, the sun a dun-colored disk moving between wisps of clouds.

She turned onto Route 682 and followed the course of the Hocking River until a cluster of red-brick buildings to her right announced the entrance to The Ridges. At the end of the drive, she stopped and parked across from the imposing facade of the Kennedy Museum of Art.

Still chilled by the history of the complex, she spent a few minutes looking at the buildings. The identical towers of the Kennedy Museum loomed upward into a colorless sky. Three white balconies connected the towers, the lowest one serving as the roof for the porte cochere extending outward from the façade.

There were more than thirty buildings in the Ridges complex. The grounds had once been an idyllic park with gardens, ponds, and fountains meant to calm the most distressed minds. The facilities included a livestock barn, greenhouses, a dairy and a carriage shop. Inmates, as they were called, could work in the gardens or learn a trade.

Epiphany recalled that in the eighteen-hundreds, any kind of unusual behavior was considered to be a "mental illness," including moral lapses such as alcoholism and unwanted pregnancy or hormonal problems like menopause and puberty. Mental retardation was also a condition that allowed for commitment to an asylum. Records indicated that by 1918, nearly four thousand people had died at the "hospital," succumbing to everything from tuberculosis to botched lobotomies.

She got out of her car and gazed around at the foreboding structures, thinking about the thousands of souls who had perished here. She could feel a restlessness in the heavy air. It was hard to breathe. The alleyways between the walls seemed full of sighs and muttering. She shivered despite the heat and remembered Blake King's mention of one of the patients at the asylum, Margaret Schilling.

They mistook her for a rat, small creature that she was. The walls still hold her shadow and the floor as well … Starving, she weeps. A thing apart, a separate animal alone in her cave.

Margaret was fifty-three years old when she hid herself in one of the asylum's rooms and then discovered she couldn't get out. The doors were self-locking. Unable to escape, she starved to death. Her body was found several weeks later by a maintenance worker. The corpse left a stain—the perfect outline of her head, arms, legs and buttocks. Despite repeated attempts to remove it from the concrete floor, the stain remained. Epiphany wondered which of the buildings still bore witness to Margaret's lonely demise.

Epiphany wandered past the auditorium and stopped to look at the Biotech Research Lab, then walked back past the

Child Development Center and through a complex of offices before reaching the museum. She was once again aware of of dozens of spirits following her, moaning pitifully. It was, she thought, definitely the most haunted place she had ever experienced. Indeed, according to the British Society for Psychical Research, Athens, Ohio was the thirteenth most haunted place on earth. The town was also built in a location where several magnetic fields called "leylines" met. These lines of energy are thought by some to be associated with paranormal activities.

And, as if that weren't enough, Wilson Hall was also at the epicenter of a pentagram formed by five cemeteries that surrounded the city. No wonder, Epiphany thought, as she headed for the museum's front entrance, that she could feel the presense of multiple spirits

"Hi, Ms. Mayall." Gretchen jumped to her feet as Epiphany approached and came around her desk to give her a hug. "I just can't believe it. Dr. Bernhardt was the best teacher I ever had. God, I'm going to miss him!"

"So will I," Epiphany said. She and Gretchen embraced silently for a moment, then Epiphany stepped back and said, "I came by to take another look at the exhibit. I hope that's all right. I want to remember the good times—the classes I took with him, all the things I learned."

Gretchen nodded. "Sure. Go on in." Then she added, "Oh, you might be interested to know that a private investigator was here this morning to look into the theft. I think the insurance company sent him. I guess the local police just aren't equipped to handle something of this significance."

"I'm not surprised," said Epiphany. "It's not everyday a million-dollar work of art goes missing."

Still, she thought, how would the locals feel about an unknown player descending on their little bailiwick? Would they welcome the assistance? Or would they resent an outsider's interference?

For just an instant, she got a strong impression of a young man. He looked *different* somehow, exotic. His hair was very dark and thick, and his eyes had a coldness that was not sinister but more *remote*. Guarded. She felt that he needed her help, but she didn't know why. Puzzled, she wondered who he could be.

The gallery was dim after the white light of the summer day. The lights were deliberately lowered in order to protect the two-hundred-year-old drawings and prints. Epiphany sat down on a bench in front of the empty space where the Blake piece had hung. She relaxed and half-closed her eyes and let her thoughts sink into a meditative state. Breathe in. And out. And in ...

The image of a stone house rippled in her mind. There was a large expanse of lawn and then several birch trees. She could see the black-and-white patterns of the peeling birch-bark. A large picture window overlooked the lawn. The house had an unusual roofline that included a raised central section with a row of clerestory windows beneath the eaves. The door was also strange—it appeared to be made of metal. Bronze perhaps? A car was parked parked in the driveway—a sleek, late-model silver Bentley.

Epiphany moved back away from the house, trying to get an idea of the neighborhood. From the street, she saw that the house was surrounded with a wrought iron fence that had elaborate gates with a geometric pattern. The brass plate next to the gate said: *Malebranche*. Bad branch? Blake said that the silver-haired man was at Malebranche. Was it the name of the owner or the name of the property?

"Hello there," came a male voice.

Epiphany came up fast and turned to see a stout,

dark-haired man wearing old-fashioned horn-rimmed glasses and a tweed jacket coming toward her. "You must be Epiphany, John's protégée," he said heartily. He held out his hand. "I'm Hugh Stillman, senior curator here at the Kennedy."

Ah, Epiphany thought, *the still man.* "Nice to meet you," she said.

"We're in shock around here," he continued. "First the Blake goes missing and now … It's really quite distressing."

"Yes, my quiet little vacation has turned into a nightmare," Epiphany conceded.

"Would you like a cup of coffee?" Hugh asked. "We can go to my office and chat."

"I'd like that."

She followed him past the reception area and down a hallway. His office was small, but well organized—a tidy desk, a computer with a pleasant, mountain scene screen-saver, several bookshelves filled with volumes. An arched window overlooked the parking lot and the river beyond. In the distance she could see the sports arena and university campus.

Hugh brought them each a cup of coffee and sat down behind his desk. "This is the first time we've had to deal with the theft of a work on display here at the museum. We had just finished doing a complete study of the security protocols and thought we were quite safe."

"I know art theft is a huge problem," Epiphany said.

"Indeed it is," Hugh agreed. "It seems hard to imagine, but art crime is the number three most-lucrative criminal trade after guns and drugs. Most people underestimate the enormity of the problem. And the profits."

"Millions of dollars, I'm sure."

"It's the highest-grossing unregulated business on the planet," said Hugh. "And there's hardly any paper trail to follow. Only a few big cities even have an art crimes unit as part of their police force. The U.S. has one art crime officer for every twenty-one million people—that's about sixteen total for the whole country."

"So when the Blake was stolen, what did you do?" asked Epiphany.

Hugh shrugged. "Followed the regular protocals: called the police. Called the museum director. Notified our insurance company. That's about all we *could* do."

"So the police treated it like any other theft of, say, a television set or a computer?"

"That's right," Hugh said. "They did the usual stuff—dusted for fingerprints, checked for DNA, looked at the security-cam video. They put a high-rez image of the work on the website. Like somebody's going to call in and say, 'Oh, I just saw that picture hanging over my cousin's sofa.' Not likely."

"What about the insurance company?" Epiphany asked. "They can't be happy about paying out a huge settlement."

"They usually send a report to the Art Loss Register, a private database of lost and stolen art," Hugh said. "They can assist with search-and-recovery services. But until the thief—or thieves—try to sell the piece, there's really no way to locate it. It could be anywhere."

"Gretchen told me that a private investigator has been called in," Epiphany said.

Hugh looked a bit startled, then collected himself and said, "Yes. That's right."

"How will that help?"

"Our insurance company recommended it. He … uh … the PI has an art recovery service. His company can obviously cover a larger area than local law enforcement can. Since the work might have been taken out of the country, he can connect with the FBI and Interpol. Watch to see if the piece turns up at auction."

"Hugh," Epiphany asked, "do you think there's any connection between the theft of the art and John Bernhardt's death?"

Hugh visibly flinched. "Uh, why do you ask?"

"It seems strange, don't you think?

"Well, it's an odd coincidence, of course. But after all, he was almost eighty. The shock of a piece of art disappearing from a show he'd helped to organize might have been too much for him." He nodded. "Yes, I suppose it could have been a contributing factor."

"What if the death wasn't due to natural causes?"

"There's nothing to suggest it wasn't," Hugh said quickly. "Nothing at all." His aura had just gone from yellow to the dull ochre of secrets and dishonest intensions. He was clearly hiding something.

"I believe that may not be accurate," Epiphany said.

"On what grounds?" Hugh was suddenly stiff in his chair.

"The morning John died, were you here at the museum?"

"I didn't come in until about ten," Hugh said, his voice rising. "Professor Bernhardt had been dead for two hours, and the police and the paramedics were here . It was chaotic."

Epiphany set her coffee mug down on the desk. "I know. I was here too."

"Well, then you know how it was," he said lamely.

"Did you see anything out of the ordinary? Anything suspicious?"

"No. Nothing."

"You're sure?"

"Absolutely." Hugh got to his feet. "Uh, I'm very pleased to have met you, Epiphany, but I really need to get back to work." Black and brown energy swirled around him, a flurry of confusion and fear.

"Of course," Epiphany said. She got up and held out her hand. "Nice meeting you, Mr. Stillman."

"I think," he said, "it's best to leave everything to the professionals. I'm sure they know what they're doing."

"Yes, of course. Good day." As she left the office, she could feel him staring at her. *He's afraid of something,* she thought. *I wonder what—or who—has scared him*?

An image unfolded in her mind—a man dressed in a blue uniform. He was medium-height and looked as though he might be in his fifties. He didn't *look* exactly intimidating, but something furtive about him made her uncomfortable.

What should she do? She felt she had important insights about the case, but who could she talk to? The police would likely refuse to take her seriously. One reason she'd never gotten involved in "pyschic sleuthing." She wasn't eager to incite ridicule. But was she really equipped to find out who had murdered John and stolen the Blake? This was way out of her comfort zone! Maybe Hugh was right—leave it to the professionals. But John had asked her to help! Conflicted and frustrated, she started down the stairs.

When she got to the foyer, Epiphany saw Gretchen heading for the front door. "Off to lunch?" she called.

Gretchen looked back. "Oh, Ms. Mayall. Yes, I was just going to Cutler's to get a bite."

"Mind if I join you?"

"Gosh, no. That would be great!"

Outside, the humidity had gotten worse. Clouds were beginning to pile up behind the hills to the west, and the sunlight had weakened to a sullen brassy glow. "Looks like we're in for a shower," Epiphany said as they walked down the drive toward the conference center.

Gretchen stopped and consulted her cell phone. "Sixty percent chance. Should have brought my umbrella."

The restaurant wasn't busy. The student population diminished during the summer, and there were no events on campus to attract a crowd. After they ordered minestrone soup and ham sandwiches, Epiphany asked Gretchen how the investigation was going.

"I don't know," she said. "At first there was a lot of excitement. People coming and going—police, insurance people. Then yesterday, that guy from the PI firm was there when I got to work. He met with Hugh for about half an hour and then left. I don't know what they talked about, but when he went out he seemed kind of pissed."

"Interesting. I talked to Hugh about the theft, and he seemed hesitant to discuss it," said Epiphany. "I suppose that's understandable. I wouldn't be so insistent, but I did promise John I'd try to help locate the missing piece, so I feel obligated to look for leads. Do you have any ideas about who took it or why?"

Gretchen put her spoon down and spent a moment staring at the soup bowl before she looked up at Epiphany. She started to speak, then stopped and glanced around the dining room. Only a few people were in the room and they were not close by. "I think," Gretchen said in a low voice, "there's something really strange about the whole thing."

"Really? Like what?"

"John expected some kind of protest or action from the energy company," Gretchen said. "His arguments with them about the fracking business had been escalating even before the show opened. The newspaper used the exhibit as an opportunity to write an editorial opposing the plan to open the state forest to oil and gas drilling, and the guys from the energy company were royally pissed. They came back with letters in support of the operations—the usual stuff about jobs and economic development—but they were clearly on the defensive.

"Then Professor Bernhardt went to work writing that series of articles for the paper outlining why fracking is a bad idea, and pointing out the damage already done. The first one came out a couple of days after the exhibit went on display. Of course that just upped the ante. Things were getting pretty nasty."

"Is that when the art disappeared?" Epiphany asked.

"Yes," Gretchen said. "It was the day after Dr. Bernhardt's first article appeared in the paper. The next morning, the Blake was gone."

"What day was that?"

"Let's see," Gretchen thought for a moment. "His article came out on Tuesday, so the drawing must have been stolen Tuesday night or early Wednesday."

"He called me the next Sunday and asked me to help him with the investigation," Epiphany said. "Two days later he was dead. What's wrong with this picture?"

"Too many coincidences?"

Epiphany nodded. "Any ideas?"

"I wish I could tell you 'yes,' but I really don't have a clue. Except that it seems … fishy. I tried to bring it up when I talked to the police, but they didn't seem interested."

"The problem is that there's no evidence to connect the theft with John's death," Epiphany said.

They finished lunch and walked back to the museum. The rain was still holding off, building momentum as the clouds thickened and the heat became more oppressive. Epiphany decided to head for her mother's house before the storm broke, so she told Gretchen goodbye at the museum door and started toward the parking lot.

Something stopped her. Almost as though a hand had grabbed her by the shoulder and turned her around. She found herself looking at one of the windows on the second floor of the building. Very clearly in the center of the arched window she could see a face looking down at her—the face of a woman with unkempt white hair.

Even as Epiphany looked up at the woman in the window, the image faded from view. Despite the heat, she felt a sudden chill. Had she seen the ghost of Margaret Schilling, or that of some other unfortunate inmate of the Athens Lunatic Asylum? She needed to talk to that spirit.

Chapter 15

Epiphany was distracted by a black sedan roaring up the drive and pulled into the parking lot, spraying gravel as it came to a halt. She recognized the man who got out: it was Chance Hilliburn, dressed today in khaki slacks and a red tee shirt with an Ace Energy logo. His short-cropped, slate-grey hair made his face look round and fleshy, while the heavy jowls added to his bulldoggish appearance. When he saw Epiphany, he stopped and waved. She gave an inward groan and went to meet him.

"Howdy there, young lady," he said in his blustery voice. "How you doin'?"

"Fine, thanks. What brings you back to the crime scene?"

His little eyes narrowed slightly, then he grinned and said, "Just checkin' on the progress of the investigation. Any new leads on mister what-his-name's painting?"

"His name is William Blake, and it's a drawing, not a painting," said Epiphany. "And no, no new leads that I know of."

He gave her a disdainful look. "Well, that's too bad. Hope they catch the perp real soon and get it back." He nodded to her. "See you around, honey."

She watched him head toward the door. *I'd like to honey you up and sit you on an anthill,* she thought. The image made her smile as she walked to her car.

She was driving across the river when the storm finally broke. Huge clouds drifted in, low and fast—a tsunami of moisture spilling over the horizon. Lightning flickered, and sheets of rain poured down. Epiphany decided not to try to drive home through the deluge, so she headed for the center of campus to visit the library. It was a short walk from the parking lot to the building that housed the library, but despite the umbrella, her legs and feet were soaked by the time she got to the door.

Epiphany left her umbrella next to the entrance and took the elevator to the third floor, where the Fine Arts Library was located. She found the digital archive and began looking through collections of works by William Blake until she located the illustrations for Dante's *Inferno.*

Blake's drawings and watercolors illustrating Dante's *Divine Comedy: Inferno, Purgatorio* and *Paradiso,* were among his last works. Indeed, Blake never finished the illustrations commissioned by his friend and mentor John Linnell, although he worked on them literally until the day he died.

The subjects of the illustrations—sin, guilt, punishment, and salvation—were similar to the subjects that had captured Blake's imagination in his own illustrated books. Despite the five centuries separating their lives, Blake shared Dante's disdain for materialism and its corrupting influence as well as his appreciation of the "womanly virtues" of graciousness, empathy, and natural beauty as expressed in Dante's love for Beatrice.

Epiphany had always been intrigued by Blake's connection with the spirit world—his vision of the soul of his dead brother Robert ascending to heaven, his fascination with ghosts, and the stories of Blake's psychic experiences, including precognition and telepathy.

She was also touched by the fact that one of his last drawings was a portrait of his wife, Catherine. Blake's biographer Peter Ackroyd wrote, "His only thought now was completing his work on Dante and one of the very last shillings [he] spent was in sending out for a pencil. On the day of his death, he stopped work [on the Dante illustrations] and turned to Catherine who was in tears. 'Stay, Kate,' he said. 'Keep just as you are—I will draw your portrait—for you have ever been an angel to me.'"

After reading through the information on Blake's illustrations for Dante's masterpiece, Epiphany focused on the missing work of art: *The Devil Carrying the Lucchese Magistrates to the Boiling-Pitch Pool of Corrupt Officials*. Who were these "magistrates" and what corruption had they indulged in?

She found that the Lucchese family was originally from Sicily, but by Dante's time they had immigrated to several places in Italy, including Dante's hometown of Florence. They were a prosperous family and had a great deal of political influence. The family was especially powerful in the city of Lucca in Tuscany which rivaled Florence during the early thirteen-hundreds.

She learned that Dante was a magistrate, or civil officer, charged with administering the law in Florence during a time of bitter political rivalry between factions known as the White Guelphs and the Black Guelphs. The Blacks were supporters of the Pope's claim to become sole leader of all Italy, while the Whites supported secular leaders. The black-and-white spotted leopard came to represent Florence since it was divided by loyalties to these two factions.

Dante, as chief magistrate in Florence, made enemies among both the Blacks and the Whites, especially after he banished several of the feuding Guelphs. Two years later, the Black Guelphs seized control of Florence and forced Dante into exile. *Okay,* Epiphany thought. *That explained a lot about the motivation for writing the Inferno.*

Embittered by his political experiences, Dante saved a special place in Hell for his enemies. He blamed the corrupt officials for allowing greed and arrogance to distort their views, opening the doors for bribery, fraud and other crimes. "Newcomers to you, O Florence, and sudden profits, have led to pride and excess that you already mourn!" he wrote in his *Inferno*.

Epiphany wondered why the name "Lucchese" sounded so familiar until she Googled it and was reminded that one of the most powerful crime families in US history was the Lucchese family, one of the "Five Families" that had a seat on the "Commission," the ruling body of the American Mafia. Interesting, she thought, that six hundred years after the creation of Dante's *Inferno,* the same family was still associated with corruption. The ancient sins of greed, lust, hatred, and pride were still very much alive on the sidewalks of New York.

A sudden flash of lightning illuminated the reading room, followed by a resounding crash of thunder that made the building shake. Several people nearby gasped in alarm. There was a buzz of conversation and a few nervous laughs. Then the lights went out.

Epiphany sat very still. The lightning strike had initiated a sudden intense vision unfolding in her mind almost like a flickering black-and-white movie. Naked figures were struggling with several reptilean-looking demons. Even as she watched, the spike-tailed demons grabbed the nude men and lifted them to their shoulders, carrying them to the top of a rocky cliff. At the base of the cliff was a bubbling pool of black pitch.

She remembered seeing all this before—the demons, the writhing nudes, the burning vat of darkness. It was the subject of the missing Blake drawing. Suddenly, it all made sense—her vision, the trip to Ohio, meeting with John a few days before his death. All part of the plan. But what should she do next?

She felt as though the floor was tilting. The black pool became a fountain gushing upward. Flailing helplessly, several figures disappeared into the darkness. Their companions struggled to get away, but they too were swept into the tide.

Epiphany could feel the floor trembling beneath her feet, but she couldn't move. More fissures were opening up all around her and the black sludge was rising up, creating a web of linest crisscrossing the sand.

Abruptly, she found herself in a white room with dark hardwood floors. Track lights bathed the walls with light. It appeared to be some sort of gallery, for the walls were lined with works of art of various sizes. She moved in for a closer look.

And there it was! The missing Blake drawing, still in its gold frame, hanging next to a large photograph showing a rusted pipe spewing froth into a pool of green slime. The trunks of dead trees stood like sentinels amid the lime-colored slush.

There were other art works on the wall—a lushly painted aerial view of the Gulf of Mexico oil-spill with flames spiraling up from a black whirlpool; a photo of a clear-cut landscape of eroded mountains and the stumps of dead trees; a sculpture of a melting polar bear; a group of wailing children covered with oil.

"Aren't they beautiful?" a soft voice said. "Now *that's* what I call progress."

Chapter 16

"Hannah?" Epiphany was sitting up in bed in the upstairs room at her mother's house in Mt. Eden holding her cell phone to her ear. She had left the library shortly after the lights came back on and drove straight home. It was still raining lightly, but the major impact of the storm had passed.

"Hi, Pip. What's up?" Epiphany's good friend Hannah De Groot was her usual cheerful self.

"I'm working on a project," Epiphany told Hannah, "and I'm beginning to feel like I'm running in circles. I thought I might come to New York for a short visit so we could do a bit of brainstorming."

"Can you wait a couple of weeks? I'm off to Cleveland tomorrow to do some work at the museum there."

"Oh," exclaimed Epiphany, "then you'll be right up the road from me."

"Where are you?"

"I'm visiting my mom in Ohio," Epiphany said. "Just south of Columbus. Cleveland's only about a three-hour drive from here."

Hannah paused and then said, "I'd planned to have a look around Cleveland over the weekend and then see my cousin for a day or two. I'm not due at the museum until Wednesday morning. Why don't I drive down and visit with you for a few days? I've always been curious about where you grew up."

"You're sure that wouldn't be too much trouble? I know you're a busy lady."

"Sounds like an adventure. I've never been to Appalachia," Hannah replied.

"All right. I'll email you directions."

"I'll see you Saturday around four."

Epiphany spent Saturday morning doing some more research on the fracking issue. She found several websites with information on earthquakes in Oklahoma where intensive fracking had been going on for over a decade, and where numerous waste-water injection wells had been drilled. As a result, the occurrence and intensity of earthquakes in the area had increased dramatically to six hundred times the historical average.

Epiphany was reminded of the impact the prophetic writings of Edgar Cayce had on her when she was beginning her studies on psychic phenomena. She had been delighted to discover that there were other people who could see the spirits of the dead, who could "know" about things before they happened. She wasn't alone after all!

Now, she recalled Cayce's predictions about the awakening of the New Madrid earthquake fault and the resurgence of seismic activity along the Mississippi River—"The waters of the Great Lakes will empty into the Gulf of Mexico," Cayce had said. How, she wondered, might this prophecy be related to the recent unprecedented earthquake activity in Oklahoma? And in Ohio?

She had also read a recent paper written by researchers from the U.S. Geological Survey confirming that the cause of the Oklahoma quakes was the result of "300-million-year-old subsurface faults that had not been active" suddenly coming to life following the 2010 oil spill in the Gulf of Mexico.

A retired geophysicist who had studied the Gulf of Mexico's geological make-up for over forty years, hypothesized that the "oil volcano" unleashed by the BP oil spill had sparked renewed seismic activity in the region. He wrote that there was substantial evidence that the New Madrid fault zone was directly related to the "deeply buried tectonics" in the Gulf.

The report did not look at whether the reactivation of the faults was related to the energy extraction process known as "fracking," and energy companies continued to deny any link between fracking and major seismic activity. To Epiphany, the connection seemed obvious. She also wondered if the ley-lines that crisscrossed Ohio had any connection to the recent earthquakes? She would have to do some more reseach.

Late that afternoon, Epiphany saw a blue Toyota sedan coming up the driveway. She briefly tried to straighten the pile of books and papers that were strewn across the bed, but gave up and was almost to the stairs when she heard Susan calling, "Fanny, sweetheart. Your friend Hannah's here."

Over an early dinner of Susan's delicious chicken and

dumplings, the friends caught up on recent activities. "Why are you going to Cleveland?" Epiphany asked.

"We're building a new library at Barnard," Hannah said. "I've been overseeing the relocation of a lot of the collections into storage while the construction is taking place, but I wanted to continue my research on Chinese scrolls. So I decided to spend some time with a friend at the Cleveland Museum. They have a fantastic Asian collection. I've taken a bit of vacation time during the summer slow season. You know, of course, my dear, that *nobody* stays in the city during the summer season."

They both laughed at her pretended snobbery. Hannah was probably one of the most down-to-earth people on the planet. She was, in a word, plain. Her round face was devoid of makeup. She had worn her light-blond hair in a Dutch-boy bob forever. She was of medium height and neither fat nor thin. And her clothes were a kind of uniform—tailored slacks, white blouse, no jewelry—that she rarely accessorized. She described herself as a "secular nun," dedicated to her work and to the "church of the holy aesthetic."

That evening after dinner, Hannah and Epiphany helped Susan with the dishes. After Susan went to bed, the two friends went out to sit on the porch and watch the evening display of fireflies.

"Hot sex out there," Hannah remarked.

"Excuse me?" Epiphany said, her eyes widening.

"During mating season," Hannah said, "fireflies use bioluminescence for sexual selection, synchronizing their flashing pale green lights to attract females. The males cruise around, flashing their lights to let the ladies know they're ready for love. When the girls see a pattern they like, they flash the same signal back at the male as an invitation to get together."

"Since when are you a firefly expert?" asked Epiphany.

"Hey," Hannah said, "we have fireflies in New York too. I like to follow the action."

"Well," said Epiphany, "I'm having some issues with signals. That's why I invited you to visit—that and your eternally good company."

"Let me guess. Some hot guy is sending you flashes, and you're trying to decode the message?"

"It's a bit more sinister than that, I'm afraid," Epiphany said. She went on to describe the chain of events that had intruded on her vacation visit to her mother. "What I have so far," she concluded, "is a bunch of seemingly unrelated events I *know* are tied together, but I can't figure out *how*. And my usual techniques—remote-viewing, meditation, spirit guides, lucid dreams—aren't working very well."

"Okay," Hannah said. "You've got a missing masterpiece, a dead professor, a polluted lake, an unusual series of earthquakes, and a rogue energy company. What's the connection?"

"Exactly."

"What have you got so far?"

Epiphany filled Hannah in on the list of people and events over the past week: the disappearance of the Blake drawing, the call from John Bernhardt requesting Epiphany's help, her discovery of the polluted lake, the vision of the silver-haired man, the shady Mr. Hilliburn, John's unexpected death on the same day his article against fracking appeared in the paper, the strange meeting with the artist Blake King, and the slow progress of the investigation into both the stolen art and John's "coincidental" death.

"I'm certain there's a pattern here," said Epiphany, "but I feel like I'm missing something. I just can't get my mind around the gestalt of it—I've got parts, but not the whole picture."

"It's a convoluted puzzle. We have to figure out how to

assemble the pieces if we're going to get an accurate image." Hannah glanced at Epiphany. "There are a lot of players, but who can help us?"

"Not Chance Hilliburn," said Epiphany. "He's a closed book. And I feel the same way about Hugh Stillman, the museum curator. He's not very forthcoming. I haven't tried to confront the local police. In fact, I hear they don't believe that anything sinister has happened and have ruled out murder. But there's Sam Miller, Mom's neighbor. He's been helpful." She thought a minute. "Also, there's an artist friend of John's, Blake King. He's full of information, but his delivery is so esoteric that it's like trying to make sense of someone speaking a dialect of an extinct language."

"How so?" Hannah asked.

"It's like he's speaking in ... parables. Like some Old Testament prophet."

"That sounds interesting. I've spent lots of time unscrambling parables." Hannah grinned at Epiphany. "Why don't we pay him a visit?

Chapter 17

The next day was Sunday. Sam Miller and his wife came by to pick Susan up for church. They were members of the Episcopal Church in the village of McArthur, a ten-mile-drive south of Mt. Eden. Epiphany and Hannah headed east toward Carbondale.

When they arrived at Blake King's property, Epiphany was surprised to see a small group of people gathered in front of the cabin. They were nicely dressed in what appeared to be their "Sunday" clothes—most of the women wore dresses and the men slacks. The children were also tidy even though they were scampering around the yard, laughing and shouting.

"I thought you said he was a recluse?" Hannah said.

"I thought he *was*," said Epiphany. She spied Blake standing next to the door of his house talking with an elderly gentleman. The man wore a dark suit and a black hat and looked as if he had just stepped out of a nineteenth-century daguerreotype.

Epiphany parked the car, and they got out and approached the group. Blake caught sight of them and waved. "Two by two. Drops of Dew," he cried. "Put on the full armour! Get into the cleansing songs!"

Hannah gave Epiphany a WTF glance.

"I told you," Epiphany said. "Just a bit eccentric."

"A *bit*?" Hannah said.

The group was dispersing. Mothers called to their children. The men were shaking hands and nodding to each other. The old gentleman said to Blake, "I see ye have some company, so I'll be leaving." He tipped his hat to Hannah and Epiphany. "Good day, ladies."

They murmured a reply and looked at Blake.

"Truly fed, they go," he said, his face glowing with benevolence. "Heaving anchor from a dead start, abounding with health. Is that what God looks like raising waves? Punt, pass, and play!" He smiled broadly and raised his hand in blessing to the departing flock.

He looked back to Epiphany and Hannah and gestured toward the door of his cabin. "The places of Albion provide entrance to those on the highway. Kiss the pillar of salt and don't look back."

Hannah followed Epiphany through the door.

"It smarts to see you again," Blake said, sitting down in the chair next to the window and gesturing toward the cot. "My visual acuity is neither challenged nor impaired. It is thee that I see before me."

"Yes," said Epiphany. "And this is my friend, Hannah De Groot. I've asked her to try to help me resolve some of the problems we're facing."

Blake nodded. "The manger is empty. The animals run about helter-skelter searching for sustenance. The path leads downward into darkness. It is there the priceless object lay, wrapped in well-striped wool."

Epiphany straightened up. "A plaid wool blanket?"

"The lines are forming between the verdant pastures," Blake said. "Expose the paucity of his excuses!"

"Is the still man involved?"

Blake hesitated. Then he said, "Delicate men in the harvest

are cut up for their parts. He says what he says and then again utters it. He takes refuge in the basket case of good intentions. But his hands are dripping excrement."

"Should I talk to the police?"

"Do not look to them, but rather to another who has yet to appear."

"How will I know him?"

Blake jumped to his feet and began pacing back and forth in front of the window. "There is a man," he muttered, "who came across the burning bush of desire. And out of this came a leprous body. The dog pushed him 'til he fell. And greased the skids to hasten his descent. It wasn't long before he qualified for the mob. The serpent worked its electric charm on him and he succumbed." He stopped and stared at Epiphany. "A magistrate, bald as a newborn babe, stands before the door. It is too late for him to flee the pools of burning pitch. He puts the treasure of tax-payers' blood on the line. There is a cheaper way to heat our houses." Blake shook his head sadly and began once more to pace back and forth. Then he stopped and turned his eyes on Epiphany. "Read the script," he said.

On the way back to Mt. Eden, Hannah and Epiphany tried to piece together Blake's message.

"So the first message," Hannah said, looking at her notes, "was 'kiss the pillar of salt and don't look back.'"

"Obvious reference to Lot's wife who was turned into a pillar of salt when she looked back to Sodom. So a warning not to look back at worldly corruption?"

"But why "kiss the pillar of salt'?" Hannah asked.

"Hmmm. What's the next message?"

"'The manger is empty and the animals run helter-skelter,'" Hannah read.

"There's something missing, presumably the drawing, and people are running around in a panic trying to find it?"

Hannah nodded. "I guess that makes sense. Then the next clue is 'The path leads down into darkness and that's where the package lay wrapped in a blanket with green and white lines.' Getting anything from that?"

"Actually, yes. At least in part. I did see a green and white plaid blanket in one of my visions," Epiphany said.

"Really?"

"Yes. I saw Chance Hilliburn, the Ace Energy field rep, standing in the gallery door holding a plaid blanket."

"What about the path that leads down into darkness?" Hannah asked.

Epiphany shook her head. "Doesn't ring a bell."

"But if the package lay on the dark path wrapped in the blanket, then maybe it means there was a place where the art was hidden?" Hannah said.

"I wonder if the museum has a cellar or a basement? Something underground?"

"Well, he goes on to say that 'the still man' is trying to cover up something, but his hands are dirty." She looked at Epiphany. "Who's 'the still man'?"

"I think that's a reference to the museum curator, Hugh Stillman."

"Okay, now we're getting somewhere," said Hannah. "The curator must have had a hand in the theft, but he's trying to cover up his involvement."

"Right," said Epiphany. "When I tried to talk to him about

the investigation, he was guarded. Didn't want to say much." She glanced at Hannah. "What's next?"

Hannah looked at her notes. "Um, okay, avoid the police but find someone else who can help you." She glanced up. "Any ideas?"

"I don't know. Sam maybe?"

"Then Blake mentioned a bald magistrate standing before the door. The dog pushed him until he fell. What exactly is a magistrate?"

"A public official," Epiphany replied.

"So we have a bald public official who is pushed by a dog?"

Epiphany frowned. "What comes after that? Wasn't there something about a pool of pitch?"

"Yeah. 'It's too late for him to avoid the burning pool of pitch.'" Hannah thought for a moment, then said, "That's a clear reference to Dante. The corrupt official being thrown into the boiling pitch pool."

Epiphany threw Hannah a triumphant glance. "And that, my dear, is the title of the missing Blake drawing: *The Devil Carrying the Lucchese Magistrate to the Boiling-Pitch Pool of Corrupt Officials*."

"And the last clue is *Read the text*."

"So, if we want to follow the trail, it's a pretty clear map," said Epiphany. "People are running around looking for the missing drawing, but it was wrapped in a blanket and hidden in a dark place underground. Hugh Stillman was involved, but the real culprit is a corrupt public official."

"With a bald head," Hannah added.

"And then," said Epiphany, "I had a vision of someone else—a man with silver hair—who was also involved. It appears he is now in possession of the drawing, but I don't know who or where he is. However, I did see a name plate on the gate of his house that read 'Malebranche.'"

"Another reference to *The Inferno,*" said Hannah. "The fourteenth-century followers of the corrupt mayor of Florence, Manno Brancea, were called 'Malebranchee,' the bad branches."

"We're getting closer," Epiphany said.

Chapter 18

Epiphany tried to go to sleep, but the messages embedded in Blake King's ramblings seemed to twist this way and that, and she kept trying to make sense of them. Every time she thought she had a clear picture, the images clouded over as though they were submerged in murky water.

When she finally did get to sleep, she kept dreaming hundreds of miserable people were milling around, whimpering and moaning. They were trying to tell her something, but she couldn't understand them. She kept saying, "Speak up, please!" and "Don't you speak English?" but they only muttered and sighed.

She woke up totally frustrated. But as the last dream image dissolved into mist, she heard a voice say, "Come and visit me, and I will show you something."

"Wait!" she cried. "Who are you?" But the vision evaporated. All she got was a momentary glimpse of an old woman with disheveled white hair.

Epiphany took a quick shower and got dressed. Hannah was already downstairs chatting with Susan. They were seated at the kitchen table, and the sun was shining through the window. The room was so bright Epiphany wanted to cover her eyes. What was wrong with her this morning?

"Good morning, sweetie," Susan said. "Coffee or tea?"

"Coffee. Extra strong."

"Didn't you sleep well?" Susan asked.

"So-so." She sat down thinking that Hannah looked way too chipper. But the coffee helped, and by the time they were finishing up their scrambled eggs and sausage and blueberry muffins, she felt better.

Susan declared that Monday was laundry day and told Epiphany and Hannah to gather up anything that needed washing and she would take care of it for them. They both told her they would be happy to do their own laundry, but she stopped them with a stern "That's what mothers are for."

After rounding up a basket of clothes and delivering it to Susan, they decided to drive into town and take another look at the museum. "It's closed to the public on Monday," Epiphany said. "Might be a good time to have a look around."

"Maybe we'll find that path that leads down into darkness," Hannah said.

They were in the driveway and Epiphany had her hand on the car door when she felt a shudder beneath her feet. She looked up and saw the trees swaying and jumping. There was a sound like some huge machine roaring, and the landscape began to jitter like an antiquated movie. When she looked toward the house it seemed that the chimney was swaying. "Mom!" she cried and tried to run up the drive, but the ground was heaving beneath her.

"Pip!" she heard Hannah shout. "What's going on?!"

"Earthquake," Epiphany managed to say.

Then it stopped. Everything calmed into silence. Only the wind chimes continued to tinkle softly.

"Mom!" Epiphany bolted through the front door. "Where are you?"

"Down here," came Susan's voice. Epiphany ran down the stairs to the basement. Susan was sitting on the concrete floor in front of the washing machine. Her walker lay on its side next to her.

"My God," Epiphany said, kneeling down beside her. "Are you okay?"

"Help me up, would you, Fanny?"

"Are you hurt? Don't try to get up," Epiphany said.

"I'm fine, dear. Just give me a hand please."

Epiphany gently helped her mother get to her feet. "Dang," Susan said, "That floor is hard!"

This is exactly why I hate having you live alone, Epiphany thought grimly. From upstairs she heard Hannah calling, "Where are you, Pip? Is everything all right?"

"We're down here," Epiphany answered. "We're fine."

Hannah came running down the stairs. "Good God, that was frightening. I've never been in an earthquake before. Do you have many of them around here?"

"They do now," Susan returned wryly.

"We think it's the wastewater wells from the fracking operations I told you about," Epiphany said. "The injection wells destabilize the ground structure and activate faults, even those that have been inactive for years."

"Scary."

"Couldn't agree more."

The phone rang, and Epiphany hurried upstairs to answer it. Sam Miller's voice was agitated. "Everybody all right over there?"

"Fine," said Epiphany. "How about you folks?"

"We're both in one piece. But Rhoda's grandmother's clock is all over the living room floor. It fell off the mantel and hit the hearth. She's pretty upset about it."

"That's so sad. I'm sure it meant a lot to her."

"Yeah. Well, glad you folks are okay. Tell your mom if she needs any help cleanin' up, I'm available."

"Thanks, Sam."

Epiphany went back downstairs. Susan was tossing clothes into the washer. "Just hope this thing is still workin'."

Epiphany and Hannah exchanged looks. "Guess maybe we should stay here," said Epiphany.

Hannah nodded.

"Don't be silly. Things are fine here. You girls go ahead. You can't let a little earthquake get in your way," Susan said with a laugh.

After checking the house to make sure there was no significant damage, Epiphany and Hannah decided to follow their plan to go into town and visit the museum.

They were only a few miles from Athens when Epiphany's cell phone chirped. "Epiphany, hello," said the caller. "It's Francesca. I have a … well, a message I'm supposed to deliver to you."

"Who from?"

"It's from that strange Mr. King. You know, John's artist friend?"

"Blake King?" Odd. She had decided that he was totally against using the telephone and so hadn't bothered to give him her number. "He called you?"

"Yes. Just a few minutes ago. Right after that little earthquake. He insisted I contact you at once. Said it was very important."

"What was the message?" Epiphany asked.

Francesca paused. "He told me he just had a vision. About the silver-haired man. He said he is a disciple of Mammon, whatever that is, and you would find him at Malebranche. Does that … make any sense to you?"

"More or less. Blake mentioned this man before. I think his name is Bromion, but I haven't been able to find anyone with that name. Or any place called 'Malebranche.' So I'm stuck."

"He told me to tell you to look to the skies for an answer and it would become clear to you where to go."

"Was that all? Just … look to the skies?"

"That's what he said."

Epiphany thought for a moment. "All right then. Thanks, Francesca, for delivering the message."

"Oh, and one other thing. He said that the bald man's uniform is blue. Dark blue."

Chapter 19

The museum was closed on Monday, but Epiphany had called Gretchen and asked if they could visit so her friend from New York could see the exhibit John had organized. Gretchen greeted them at the door and opened the gallery for them. "I'll be in Professor Bernhardt's office if you need me," she said. "Zoe and I are going through his books and trying to pack things up for Francesca."

Hannah and Epiphany studied the paintings and drawings in the exhibit and talked about the message Francesca had relayed from Blake. "He'd talked before about a silver-haired man with violet eyes," Epiphany told her friend. "And I know about the Malebranche connection, though I have no idea where it is."

"So the only new clue is 'look to the skies'?"

Epiphany nodded. "Sunrise? Sunset? Weather event? I have no idea what to look for."

"So what else should we do here?" asked Hannah.

"Maybe," said Epiphany, "we should check out the 'dark passage'?"

They found Zoe and Gretchen in John's office going through a large pile of books and papers. They were cataloguing the contents of the desk and the bookcases, making notes on the boxes and listing titles on the computer.

"Is Hugh in the office today?" Epiphany asked.

Gretchen looked up from her laptop. "No, he's taken a couple of days vacation. Said he'd be back next week."

Epiphany was vaguely irritated. She had several key questions for the elusive Mr. Stillman. But maybe Zoe or Gretchen could help. "Is there any sort of basement or cellar in this building?"

The two women exchanged looks. Then Gretchen said, "Sure. There's a basement. It's used mainly for storage and now and then for prep space. Why?"

"I'm trying to figure out how the Blake drawing was removed from the building without anyone noticing," Epiphany said.

"Mr. King said something about a dark passageway," Hannah added. "Maybe a tunnel or hallway?"

"I don't know of any tunnels," said Gretchen, "but there are plenty of hallways down there."

"Could we take a look?" Epiphany asked.

Gretchen and Zoe exchanged another apprehensive glance.

"What?" Epiphany said, looking at the two.

"It's just kind of … spooky," Gretchen said.

"Spooky?" said Hannah.

Zoe gave a little laugh. "People have heard noises."

"What kind of noises?" Epiphany asked.

"Weird sounds. Doors slamming. Things rattling around."

"We, I mean the staff, don't like going down there if we can help it," said Zoe.

"Well," said Hannah, "there'll be four of us. That sounds pretty safe."

Gretchen nodded slowly. "I suppose."

They took the freight elevator to the basement level and got out into a cavernous room.

The light was dim, but Epiphany could see rows of wooden crates and shelves lined with boxes and some uncrated items—Native American ceramic pots, small wooden statues, African masks. "This is huge," she exclaimed.

"About eight-thousand square feet in this section," Zoe said. "And two more rooms as big, though they've been divided into smaller sections for prep space and shipping operations."

Epiphany could feel the presence of spirits all around. She could hear their sighs.

"Come on," said Gretchen. "We'll give you the grand tour."

Half an hour later, the four women had made their way through the maze of storage units, offices, and work rooms. Epiphany hadn't seen anything that looked like a dark passage unless it was some of the hallways that connected parts of the complex.

Then, on the way back toward the elevator, she noticed a heavy steel door at the end of a hall. "Where's that go?" she asked.

Gretchen glanced at the door. "I think that's the furnace room. Some kind of maintenance space."

"Could we take a look?"

Zoe shrugged. "Sure. Why not?"

However, the door was locked. Zoe tried her master key, but couldn't get it to work. "Want me to try to find a maintenance worker?"

Epiphany considered, then said, "No. We've taken up enough of your time and we ought to head for home. I'll drop by next week and try to catch up with Hugh. Maybe he'll know something more about the layout."

Zoe, Gretchen, and Hannah started off toward the elevator. Hannah was asking them questions about the Native American collection. Epiphany lagged behind, still eyeing the mysterious door. She had a feeling the door was hiding something. It seemed to be whispering to her. She took a step closer and listened intently. There was a rustling sound coming from beyond the door and then a tapping. She stood gazing at the door, trying to decipher the sound.

She saw a misty form taking shape in front of her. "Who are you?" she said quietly. "Talk to me."

The form solidified into the body of a haggard-looking woman with long white hair. The woman wore a shapeless hospital gown and was barefoot. Her hair was matted to her forehead and hung around her shoulders in ragged curls. The woman's eyes were wide and wild. "I saw him take it," she said in a raspy, low voice, barely more than a whisper.

Epiphany strained to hear her. "Saw who? What did he take?"

"The man that looks like a dog. He took the picture and wrapped it in a blanket."

Excitement grabbed Epiphany in a quick embrace. "You saw him take the drawing off the wall and put it into a blanket?"

The old woman nodded.

"Then what happened?"

The woman pointed to the door. "He came down here. Then he went into the passage."

"There's a passage behind this door?"

Again the wraith nodded.

"Where does it go?"

The woman raised a thin arm and pointed again to the door. "To the river. Come," said the spirit. "I'll show you."

Epiphany closed her eyes and held out her hand. Immediately, she found herelf inside a dark hallway. The air was damp and musty, and she could feel the silent brush of spirits passing next to her. The atmosphere was heavy with dread. She picked her way along the passage, careful not to trip over the cobblestones slippery with moisture.

She saw a faint light ahead and moved toward it. The tunnel made a sharp turn to the right and widened into a small room about the size of a garage. In the middle of the room, Epiphany saw a group of figures huddled around a bed. Three of the figures were men. They wore white uniforms and round white caps. They were attended by four women dressed in long skirts and white aprons.

Moving closer, Epiphany could see a figure lying on a table in the midst of the group. It appeared to be a man. He was covered up to his chin with a white sheet, and his head had been shaved. A cloth band stretched across his eyes and was secured on either side of his head. A restraint of some kind.

As she watched in horrified fascination, one of the men—a doctor?—held up what appeared to be an ice pick, a long steel spike with a wooden handle. He inserted the spike into the man's left nostril. He then was handed a small metal hammer and proceeded to tap the pick's handle, driving the spike into the "patient's" head.

Epiphany wanted to scream, but she realized she was experiencing a vision of the past and that there was no way she could alter the events taking place. What was done, was done. She turned away, gasping for breath.

The spirit was standing beside her, watching. "Yes," she said. "This is what they did to us." She moved past Epiphany, then turned and beckoned to her. "Come."

Still shuddering with horror, Epiphany followed. When she glanced back at the "operating room," the figures had disappeared.

The tunnel continued. The floor sloped down, and once again Epiphany saw faint light ahead. Beneath her feet, the ground was even wetter, with little puddles of water standing between the stones.

The passage widened and then she was outside. It was dark. In front of her, the river was a black flow of slow-moving water. A primitive wooden boat dock hugged the shore, a few weathered planks beside a single upright post. She looked back and could see the tunnel's entrance.

So that's how he did it, Epiphany said to herself.

Suddenly, she was back in the museum's basement outside the metal door. The spirit was looking at her with a vacant, emotionless stare. "The other one had the keys," said the ghost.

Epiphany caught her breath and managed to ask, "Who is the other one?"

"The man with no hair."

"Did he have on a blue uniform?"

The apparition began to vibrate softly.

"Wait," said Epiphany. "Don't go yet. You're Margaret, aren't you? Margaret Schilling?"

The ghost continued to dissolve, but as it faded into mist, Epiphany heard a voice say, "I'm so very hungry."

"Yes," said Epiphany. "I know." She started to turn away, then looked back and said, "Thank you, Margaret."

There was no reply.

Chapter 20

Over breakfast the next morning, Hannah and Epiphany filled Susan in on the latest developments—the message from Blake King, the spooky basement with its dark hallways and locked door. Epiphany didn't mention seeing the ghost of Margaret Schilling. Or the lobotomy operation.

As they were finishing their scrambled eggs and cinnamon toast, Epiphany said to Hannah, "I guess you'll be leaving tomorrow to head for Cleveland."

Hannah looked thoughtful. "You know, Pip, I've been having such a great time playing art detective I think I'll just stay here a while longer. My sabbatical doesn't actually start until September, so I have a few weeks of free time." She looked at Susan. "Providing I'm not too much trouble."

"Stay as long as you like," Susan replied heartily. "It's wonderful having both you and Fanny here."

"Thanks," Hannah said. "I do appreciate your hospitality." She turned to Epiphany. "So what's next?"

"I think we need to find out more about who we're up against. Let's do some research on Ace Energy," Epiphany suggested.

They decided to use the resources of the OU library because of the access to information, but also to put a layer of protection between themselves and the subjects of their research. "Something tells me," said Epiphany, "we're not dealing with Mary Poppins here."

"More like the Wicked Witch," Hannah agreed.

The weather was mild and bright as they drove past pastures and forests on their way into town. The low ridge of hills was a flat powder blue in the morning light. They crossed over a fast-running stream and wound their way between small farms and the little villages of Orland, Starr and New Mansfield.

The library was quiet. Only a few students sat at the study tables or wandered through the stacks. Hannah and Epiphany set up a base of operations next to a large window overlooking the lawn. They had written up a checklist of topics and began with an investigation of Ace Energy.

They soon discovered that the company had a long history in the Buckeye State. A copy of the corporation's annual report began with an introduction praising the merits of the shale oil industry. The author pointed out that the extraction operations originally began in the mid-1600s when three Englishmen came up with a way to essentially squeeze oil from a certain kind of rock.

An ebullient essay followed showing the amazing economic benefits Ohio had enjoyed as a result of the shale oil industry. "Because of the economic opportunities afforded Ohioans by fracking and its support industries," the essay stated, "residents of the Buckeye State have access to good jobs. And businesses in small towns throughout the state are getting a boost from energy production." The author credited the fracking industry with creating 200,000 jobs that added $12.7 billion dollars to the state's labor income.

There was a special article that purported to address safety concerns. It pointed out that hydraulic fracturing had been successfully used in Ohio since the 1950s, and that as the steel industry had wound down, it was the fracking industry that had risen to provide communities with jobs, resources and a better standard of living.

The author acknowledged that, "development does bring some challenges," but assured the reader that Ace Energy was committed to developing resources in a "safe and responsible way" and would work with concerned citizens, regulators and policy makers to meet their expectations.

There was no mention of the threats posed by the extraction process including the use of huge amounts of water not legally reusable because of serious contamination by chemicals. Instead, the essay pointed out that the average fracking job used "only" four million gallons of water per well. Except in some areas—such as California—where the average was 116,000 million gallons. But that was less than half of what was used to irrigate the average golf course. Nothing was said about air pollution, methane emissions, or carcinogenic toxins.

It was apparent, however, that Ace Energy was careful to comply with state and local regulations, at least publicly. They were able to find only a few legal actions against the company. Ace Energy covered its tracks effectively and avoided controversial situations whenever possible.

There was only one negative newspaper article about Ace in which members of a largely minority community argued that they were being used as "lab rats" to see what percentage of local citizens became ill as a result of the company's activities. Despite soaring rates of newly diagnosed cases of cancer and respiratory ailments, the company steadfastly maintained that it had followed all permitting procedures and safety precautions. To show their good faith, the company cut a deal with local politicians to provide the city with substantial new tax revenues through job growth and property taxes.

"Such concern," Hannah said, as she finished the report and put it down on the table.

"Wonderful neighbors," Epiphany agreed.

Next, Hannah and Epiphany dove into the articles and other information *not* authored by Ace Energy. They found a very different story.

In several articles by investigative journalists, the company was accused of playing fast and loose with the permitting process to the point that one legislator from a Dayton suburb, a first term Congresswoman named Beatrice Falco, suggested that the company was "paying off local officials to look the other way." The company refuted the charges, stating there was no credible evidence to support the idea.

"Of course there isn't," said Hannah.

"I'm shocked—*shocked*," said Epiphany "to hear that bribery has been going on in here!"

"But think of all the poor devils who can't meet Ace's price."

"No exit visas for them," said Epiphany.

"So who got paid off in our little case?" Hannah asked.

"Let's consider the usual suspects. There is Hugh Stillman, the quiet curator," Epiphany said. "And Chance Hilliburn, the nasty watchdog."

"And the two guys on the steps who disappeared just before John's body was found," Hannah added.

"John didn't believe it was an inside job," Epiphany said, "but I think *someone* had to be in on it who knew where the security cameras were and how the alarm system operated."

"So who are the staff members?" asked Hannah.

"Besides Hugh there is the director, Marshall Monroe, but he was out of town that week at a conference in London," said Epiphany. "There's John's assistant, Zoe Hernandez, but she's been with John and the university for years. I can't believe she'd betray him. And there's Gretchen, the intern, but she's been eager to help and was very open."

"Aren't there two curators?" Hannah asked.

"Yes. Besides Hugh Stillman there's a young woman who works with the Native American collection, but she was out of town on vacation at the time of the theft. And there's the education curator, a little old lady who's been around forever. Her name is Judy, I think. Or maybe Trudy? Nice lady."

"Ah, but it's always the nice ones you have to look out for," Hannah said.

"Okay, fair enough. But who else would have had access and opportunity?"

"Maintenance and security," said Hannah. "The janitor did it."

They looked up the staff names on the museum website and found one security officer, a retired city councilman named Ray Lucas who had also served in the Army. The two maintenance workers were Arnie Wilson and Jack Vance who had both been with the museum since it opened.

"Slim pickins as suspects," said Epiphany. "But our lead is a bald guy in a blue uniform. We need to find out more about the security officer."

"Let's dig a bit," Hannah suggested. "Maybe something will pop out."

After another frustrating hour, the two women decided to take a break and get some lunch. Traffic was light in the conference center café. Over bowls of chicken chili, they went over what they had discovered during the morning session.

Ace Energy, an old and powerful corporation, had been very successful in doing its business even when it took short cuts and found ways around regulations. Company officials obviously had plenty of resources to keep them looking clean, no matter what they did behind the scenes. No one on the museum staff looked suspicious, even though Hugh Stillman seemed reluctant to talk much and apparently was acquainted with the Ace Energy field rep, Chance Hilliburn.

"What about the security guy?" Hannah asked. "Ray something?"

"Ray Lucas. He seems like a good guy—ex-city councilman, ex-Army ranger. Retired. Looks like anyone's grandpa," Epiphany said.

"But he does wear a blue uniform," Hannah pointed out. "Didn't Blake King say something about a guy in a blue uniform?"

"That's right," Epiphany agreed. "I'd forgotten about that. A bald man in a blue uniform." Suddenly her vision of a middle-aged man in a blue uniform came back to her. He must have some connection to the theft.

Back at the library, they searched through photographs and newspaper articles until they finally found a photo of Ray Lucas without his hat. He was bald.

"Bingo," said Epiphany. "That's something to follow up on."

"Let's do one more thing before we call it a day."

"What?" said Hannah.

"Let's see if we can find any of the Ace Energy executives with long silver hair."

"And violet eyes?"

They went through lists, annual reports, news articles—everything they could think of and were ready to give up when Hannah found a piece in "Town and Country Magazine" about a museum charity event in Cincinnati sponsored by Ace that honored one of their top executives, a man named Derrick Rarian, who had donated a piece to the museum from his "extensive collection."

"Is there a photo of him?" Epiphany asked.

Hannah thumbed through the article, then stopped and said, "Look here. The guy shaking hands with the museum director. What do you see?"

Epiphany looked hard. "I see silver hair," she said. "Is there a name in the caption?"

"It says, 'Director Michael Willard is seen thanking art collector Derrick Rarian for his gift to the museum.'"

Epiphany shook her head. "I'm looking for someone named 'Bromion.'"

Hannah looked up. "Bromion?"

"It's from a William Blake poem about the Daughters of Albion. Blake King told me that I should look for the man who raped Oothon if I wanted to find out who stole the art. And in the poem, his name is Bromion. He said it means 'loud roarer.'"

"But look," Hannah said pointing. "His name is Rarian."

"So?"

Hannah grinned. "In Old English, Rarian means *loud roarer*."

Epiphany looked again at the photograph. "My god, Hannah," she said. "We have our Bromion!"

"Yeah," said Hannah, "But where is he? How do we find him? And if we do, what do we do then?"

Part III

Three hundred men, all of whom know one another, direct the economic destiny of continents and choose their successors from among themselves.

—Walther Rathenau, Foreign Minister of the Weimar Republic, Germany

Chapter 21

"You should talk to Sam," Susan said. Hannah and Epiphany were sitting at the kitchen table. It was the day after their trip to the OU library and their discovery of the identity of the silver-haired man, Derrick Rarian. Sunlight streamed in through the wavy panes of glass. Outside, the day looked bright and bold.

Susan brought a plate of bacon from the stove and sat it on the table. "Dig in," she said. "It's no good if it's cold."

"Why should we talk to Sam?" Epiphany asked as she speared a piece of bacon.

"Well, you know he worked for that company, Ace Energy. I just thought he might be able to tell you something about your silver-haired mystery man. Also," she continued, spreading butter on her toast, "he told me the other day that you two oughta be careful when you're diggin' around. Said it might be dangerous. You'd do well to listen to him."

"Blake King said there was 'an agenda.' Maybe all of this is tied together somehow," Epiphany said.

"Meaning?" Hannah asked as she poured maple syrup on her pancakes.

"Let's follow the timeline," Epiphany said. "Ace Energy comes to town and begins dumping their contaminated water into injection wells. Local officials haven't done much about the issue. Nor has the university. The citizens get upset, including some of the faculty like John Bernhardt. They start asking questions and stirring up public opinion. John organizes an exhibit that questions the integrity of the public watchdogs. He also starts writing articles about the shady practices of the company. Then, one of the art works from the exhibition is stolen."

"Then John mysteriously dies," Hannah chimed in, "and it's officially determined to be from 'natural causes,' but there seem to be a lot of unanswered questions."

"And no one wants to talk about it," Epiphany finished. "The university officials are mum. The chief curator is still. The police don't seem very interested. And it looks like the art work may have ended up in the private collection of an Ace Energy executive." Epiphany looked at her mother. "Do you think Sam will level with us and tell us what he knows?"

Susan nodded. "He's worried about you."

That afternoon, Epiphany, Hannah and Sam Miller, Susan's neighbor, sat on the front porch drinking iced tea and watching the squirrels chase each other among the branches of the hickory trees. The sky was a hazy blue with small puffs of clouds perched on the horizon.

Susan had gone inside to take a nap. Epiphany waited for Sam to finish a story about how his dog had once gotten tangled up in a hammock and had to be rescued on Christmas Eve. "Thank God at least it wasn't snowin'," he exclaimed. "We'd have all froze to death." They all laughed.

After a moment, Epiphany said, "Mom tells me you have

some concerns about the research that Hannah and I are doing on the missing art work."

Sam glanced at them, then gazed out at the garden. "I can understand why you all want to help out with tryin' to figure what happened. 'Specially with your friend the professor dying like he did." He looked back at Hannah and Epiphany. "I just want to make sure you know what you're up against."

"We know Ace Energy is a multinational corporation with a ton of money and endless legal resources," Epiphany said.

"And we know that one of their executives is behind the theft of the art from the university museum," said Hannah. "We just don't have the details."

"Yet," said Epiphany. "And," she added, "I'm pretty sure John Bernhardt's death was not from 'natural causes.'"

Sam let out his breath and was silent. Then he raised his head and gave Epiphany a level look. "Okay. I reckon you've got no mind to stop, so I'll tell you what I know."

They waited while he struggled for a moment. Then he said, "I've known them guys quite some time. Started workin' for Ace back in the mid-eighties. About that same time, they started to be more earthquakes than normal. In nineteen-eighty-six there was one just east of Cleveland around where I was workin' at the time. They was aftershocks for two months. Scared the bejesus outta me. Course, I didn't tie it to Ace at the time. Nobody did. But after a few more years, I began to see a lot of things that worried me."

"Like what?" Epiphany asked.

"Like usin' up water at such a fast pace. Frackin' uses a ton of water, and it seemed to me that you couldn't just go on usin' it day after day and not run out. And the water they used ended up bein' so polluted it wasn't worth nothin'. Had to be put back into them injection wells which is sorta like puttin' sewage into septic tanks except with no linin'. When you think about it, that's a darn stupid idea. 'Cause water got a mind of its own. It's gonna run and go where it wants, and if it's not contained somehow there's not much you can do to stop it. Pretty soon, folks was complainin' about bad water. They denied it, but Ace was the cause. Just nobody could prove it."

Sam continued to talk about the bad practices that Ace had used—the dubious decisions, the cover-ups large and small, the illegal dumping of wastewater into streams and rivers, the legal machinations that kept the company from being prosecuted for its offenses against regulations and what Sam called "common sense."

"When I saw the figures that in twenty-eleven the oil and gas companies had injected five-hundred-eleven billion gallons of wastewater into Ohio wells, I finally decided I'd had enough," Sam said. "The money was good, but money's not everything. I needed to get away. I didn't want my kids to grow up livin' next to toxic waste dumps." He shook his head. "Trouble is, it's hard to get away from it, you know? Now they got wells down here and that damned lagoon up on the bluff. Seems like there's no way to escape."

"Do you know the name 'Derrick Rarian'?" Epiphany asked.

Sam looked up sharply. "You mean the Shadow?"

"The Shadow?"

"Yeah, that's what we called him. Spooky kind of guy. A big shot with the company, but he seemed real slippery to me. Had a way of smilin' that made me get a chill down my spine."

"We think he might be involved in the theft of the art work from the museum here," Epiphany said.

"If that's true, then you really better watch your back," said Sam.

"Why is that?"

"He's one of the top guys. See, Ace Energy isn't some local

company. They's like an octopus. Got their tentacles wrapped around an international cartel of corporate heads, politicians, lawyers, banks. You name it and they got a finger in it." He shook his head. "No way to stop an enemy that's everywhere and nowhere."

"So you have no idea where this Derrick Rarian might live?" asked Epiphany.

"The corp HQ was in Cleveland back when I worked for them, but then they split the company up into smaller units. It's like a hydra. Chop off one piece and it grows a new head. Makes it harder to track what's goin' on. It's like there's no one place to look. It's a dice game." He gave them a hard look. "These guys don't play nice. You best be careful."

"Can you think of anyone who could help us?' asked Hannah.

Sam thought for a moment, then said, "There's that PI fella that's made a couple of visits. He knew I'd worked for Ace and wanted to ask me some questions, but I played dumb and he left it at that."

"Do you know his name?" said Epiphany.

"Yeah. Kinda a strange sort of name. Maro somethin'. Maro Gaido, that was it. Looked kinda foreign. Asian maybe. You might could look him up."

"I think Gretchen might know how to reach him," Epiphany said. "She told me an investigator had been to see Hugh Stillman. I'll give her a call."

They both thanked Sam for his help. As he started down the steps, he turned and said, "Remember now what I said. You be careful. These folks is big. Real big. They're not scared of nobody, but everybody's scared of them. Know what I mean?"

"I hear you," said Epiphany.

After Sam left, Hannah and Epiphany sat silently on the

porch, both lost in thought. Sam's warning was ominous. How should they proceed?

Epiphany gazed at the tranquil landscape. If only she could process the dizzying amount of information tied to this strange sequence of events. How could she sort it all out?

Two invisible planes had drawn a gigantic X across the southern quadrant of the sky. Epiphany studied the contrail lines with vague interest. Suddenly, her mind was fixated on the image. X. What was the meaning of X? Look to the skies, Blake King had said. She felt a sensation of sinking or falling, and then envisioned a dark pool. A pool that reflected no stars.

Slowly, the surface of the water began to ripple and undulate. From somewhere in the depths of the darkness, illuminated letters began to rise to the surface and arrange themselves. A. E. N. I. X. Then they reformed: X. N. I. E. A.

Epiphany struggled to read the message. X. I. N. No, X. E. N. I. A. Xenia. "Xenia!" she cried.

"What?" Hannah looked at her in surprise.

Epiphany turned to her friend with a huge grin. "I know where the Blake drawing is."

Chapter 22

"Thanks for coming all the way out here to talk to us," Epiphany said.

"No problem," said the man who sat across from her at Susan's kitchen table. Hannah sat next to Epiphany. The scene suddenly struck Epiphany as incongruous—she and her friend Hannah sitting at the family breakfast table chatting with a total stranger—a lean, dark-haired man with intensely black, almond-shaped eyes that suggested a Japanese ancestry.

From her phone conversation with him, she learned that before retiring five years ago he had worked as an art theft agent with the FBI, one of only a handful of investigators who specialized in art crimes. After retiring, he had set up his own private investigation company, ArtTracker, Inc. She had imagined he would look like the typical G-man or private detective from the movies—dark suit, white shirt, maybe a hat. But instead he was dressed in a blue polo shirt and khaki slacks. He seemed relaxed, yet formal. Distant. Wary. Something about him seemed familiar to Epiphany, but she couldn't quite put her finger on it.

"You said you have some information about the missing art?" he said. His voice was very level. Just like his gaze.

"I think so. I've had some ... impressions about what happened," Epiphany said.

Maro Gaido waited politely for a moment, but when Epiphany continued to hesitate he sat back and gave her a tight smile. "Look, Ms. Mayall," he said, "I know what you do for a living. I've done a background check. I haven't personally worked with psychics before, but some of my colleagues at the Bureau did. I'm open to any leads you have that might be helpful in this investigation. This is a complex, difficult case. So," he inclined his head slightly, "let's hear what you've got."

Epiphany was surprised, but she recovered quickly and said, "I think it's all connected." She launched into the timeline she and Hannah had constructed—Ace Energy's wastewater dumping, the lack of interest or action by local officials, the growth of citizen concern and John Bernhardt's effort to raise awareness through the art exhibit.

Then came the theft of the Blake drawing and John's sudden and rather mysterious death. "And now we find out the Blake is in the private collection of one of the Ace executives. I just wish I could connect the dots."

Maro stared at Epiphany with his unnerving dark eyes. "Do you have an idea who took the art?"

"I don't have proof, but my sense is that it was Chance Hilliburn, the Ace field rep."

"Any idea how he did it?"

"I'm sure he had inside help," said Epiphany.

"Ninety percent of museum thefts are inside jobs," Maro said. "A custodian, a docent, an academic, a curator, even a wealthy patron. They all have access. And opportunity."

"But the museum employees refuse to believe any of them would do such a thing," Hannah said.

"Most museum staff are blind to the possibility. They want to believe they're all family," said Maro. "When they make a new hire, they rarely even run a background check. It's as though if you're interested in working at a museum, you're automatically a really good person. But the fact is, the biggest art crimes are usually the result of an insider working either alone or with someone on the outside. Often the artwork is already pre-sold to a collector or a dealer. It's a huge racket."

"Here's what I think happened." Epiphany glanced at the agent. "I expect you know the name Derrick Rarian?"

Maro straightened up. "He's head of exploration and production for Ace. And," he added, "an avid art collector."

"He has the Blake," said Epiphany.

Maro's eyes narrowed. "How do you know that?"

"I've ... seen it."

"You've ... seen it?"

"Yes."

"Go on."

"I think Derrick had Chance steal the Blake," said Epiphany. "Chance had help, likely the museum security officer, a man named Ray Lucas. The curator, Hugh Stillman, had some role in the theft, but I don't know exactly how he fits in."

"Interesting," said Maro. "Any thoughts on how they pulled it off?"

"Do you know about the tunnel that leads from the museum basement to the river?" asked Epiphany.

"There's a tunnel?"

"Yes. There's a steel door at the north end of the basement. Museum staff told me it was a furnace room, but they couldn't get the door open."

"Then how do you know there's a tunnel?" Maro asked.

"Trust me. It's there," said Epiphany.

Maro raised an eyebrow but didn't object.

"I believe that Ray knew about the tunnel and worked

with Chance to find a convenient time to grab the art and get it out of the building through the tunnel," Epiphany continued. "The tunnel exits a short distance from the river. Someone could have been waiting there with a boat to receive the art and take it away. Ray and Chance go back upstairs. He lets Chance out, locks up and sets the alarm. It's as though nothing happened."

"What about the security camera tape?" Hannah asked. "Wouldn't have they spotted something?"

"That might be where Hugh comes in," said Epiphany. "He could have edited the tape and changed the time on it so it looked as though nothing was missing."

"I remember something similar happened at another museum," Maro said. "A custodian heisted two Civil War presentation swords from a display case in full view of the cams, but his son was a techie who was able to disable the tapes for just a few seconds, time enough to lift the lid, grab the swords and rearrange the other objects so it didn't look as though anything was gone. The theft wasn't even discovered until a month after it happened." He gave Epiphany a hard look. "So, you think Rarian has the Blake?"

"I do," said Epiphany.

"Do you know where? I mean the location?"

"I think he lives in Xenia in a sort of mansion. There's a brass plate next to the gate that says 'Malebranche.'"

"His river house," Maro said

Epiphany looked confused. "How many houses does he have?"

Maro shrugged. "Three or four that I know of. His main headquarters is in Cleveland, but he has a weekend place in Xenia. Then there's the apartment in Manhattan. And a condo in St. Moritz."

"So you've dealt with him before?"

"His name has come up in several investigations. Collectors like Rarian are good at flying under the radar. They have lots of contacts with art dealers around the world. The business is basically unregulated, so a dealer can pick up a stolen work, provide false documents for it and sell it to the highest bidder. Goes on all the time."

"Provenance is hard to prove," said Hannah.

Maro gave her a questioning glance.

"I'm a rare book curator," she told him. "Barnard College Library."

"Then you know what I mean." He looked back at Epiphany. "Too bad we don't have hard evidence that Rarian has the Blake."

"Can't you get a search warrant or something?"

Maro shook his head. "On the basis of a ... vision? I don't think that would fly. We need reasonable cause to get a warrant."

Epiphany bit her lip but said nothing.

"On another note," Maro said, "What about John Bernhardt's death? What do you make of it?"

"Too coincidental," Epiphany said. "He organizes an exhibit to protest Ace's fracking operations, starts alerting the public by writing articles for the newspaper and then has a heart attack and dies. Way too convenient."

"So you believe that he might have been ... murdered?"

Epiphany sucked in her breath. "Uh, well, uh," she said.

"What?"

"Uh, that's what he told me."

"He?"

"John."

Maro stared at her for a moment. "All right. John told you this. When?"

"The day after he died."

Maro sat back in his chair and looked up at the ceiling. After a minute he looked back at Epiphany and said, "Okay. You talk to dead people. I'm going to go with that."

Epiphany gave him a weak smile. "It's one thing I do."

"Could you tell me what he … said."

"He told me that when he came into work that day, he saw two young men on the steps outside his office. He looked at them for a moment and made eye contact, then he started to go inside. He felt a little sting on his neck, but didn't think any more about it. But when he got to his office he felt strange and very quickly he died. He believed he was poisoned and that the young men he saw were somehow responsible."

Maro didn't say anything. Just stared at Epiphany.

"That's all he said," she told him.

"Damn!" Maro's voice was hard. "That's not good news."

"Excuse me?" said Epiphany.

Maro got to his feet. "I … uh … need to get back to town." He took a quick breath and forced a smile. "Thank you, ladies," he said holding out his hand to Epiphany. "It's been a … valuable conversation."

After Maro left, Hannah and Epiphany continued the discussion. "I wonder what he knew about the murder that he wasn't sharing?" Hannah said.

Epiphany nodded. "That was one quick exit. Clearly we hit a nerve."

"Let's see what we can find out about that little red spot on John's neck. That seemed to catch our PI's interest," Hannah said.

After an hour on the net, they made an exciting discovery.

"It's called a HAG," Hannah announced.

"Meaning?"

"Heart attack gun. Listen to this. *In the early sixties, the CIA developed a secret weapon Code name HAG for heart attack gun. It shoots a tiny dart that can pierce through clothing and leaves no trace. The dart is laced with poison. It disintegrates after piercing the skin. A few minutes later, the person suffers a massive heart attack."*

"Good Lord," Epiphany exclaimed. "The perfect murder weapon. But they did a blood test on John. Wouldn't the poison show up in the victim's blood?"

"It says here that it leaves no trace," Hannah said. "Even an autopsy wouldn't catch it unless they checked for that particular poison. They'd have to know what they were looking for. Once the damage is done, the poison denatures quickly. The only evidence of the attack is a tiny red puncture wound at the entry point."

"Like the one that John Bernhardt had on his neck," said Epiphany.

"Exactly," said Hannah.

Chapter 23

The Campus Inn
Athens, Ohio

Maro Gaido sat down on the end of the bed and took a few moments to reflect on the past five years. It wasn't something he did often—what was the point? The past was gone. Retained only by memory, and memory was something he was very good at forgetting.

He had spent ten years, beginning in 2001, as a Special Agent with the FBI working as a translator—he was fluent in seven languages including Arabic and Farsi—and as an art crimes investigator. But when his father passed away in 2010, Maro received a small inheritance. He used some of the money to help his younger half-brother, Colin, finish law school. With the remaining resources he set up his own investigation service.

It hadn't been an easy decision. He enjoyed his work with the Bureau and still kept in touch with a network of colleagues he could turn to for assistance, but the tangle of bureaucracy and regulation annoyed him. He kind of missed the title. After all, PI Gaido didn't have quite the impact that Special Agent Gaido had. But he liked being in charge. Having control. Maybe that meant more than a charismatic title.

He got up and went to the window. It was getting dark—shadows gathering beneath the trees across the street, a rust-colored afterglow from the departed sun. The lights above the parking lot made the asphalt look like black metal. The same color as Chrome Molybdenum steel, the metal used to make the barrels of guns.

How had "the bad guys" gotten hold of the HAG? Sure, the prototype had been around for almost half a century, but the plans were highly classified. Had someone leaked the information or had the other side come up with the idea on their own? Didn't matter. If the Mayall woman—the *psychic*—was right, then it was likely John Bernhardt had been murdered by someone using a heart attack gun. If true, it was a dangerous development. An assassins' dream come true.

But how did she *know*? That was the real question. Did she know more than she let on? Could *she* somehow be connected with the professor's death? Maybe her description of the HAG was some kind of red herring meant to throw him off track. But he had done a thorough check. Nothing in her background indicated that she might be mixed up in anything like international espionage. She seemed innocuous. Except for these peculiar ... powers she was said to have. Not that he believed in any of that ... crap.

Angrily, he turned away from the window. The hell with it. He was too tired to think this through just now. And he was hungry. He grabbed his duffel bag from the closet and set it on the bed. Rummaged through it until he came up with an energy bar. Raspberry-walnut crunch. Whatever. He opened the plastic water bottle, switched on the TV and settled down on the bed to have his "dinner." Tomorrow, he would make some calls. Check things out. Tonight he'd just zone out and watch something mindless until he could sleep.

"Undercover?" Hannah stared at Epiphany as if she'd just proposed flying to Mars. "You mean like a spy?"

"Look," Epiphany replied, "the PI said he needed evidence that Rarian has the Blake, and that he's a very slippery guy. As I see it, Rarian has one weak point—his art collection—and I think I'm the perfect person to exploit his weakness."

"Gee," Hannah said. "I don't know ...".

Epiphany looked out the window. The sky was a blurry grey-white, as tentative as her thoughts. *What am I doing,* she asked herself. *I never signed on for spies and monsters and international art thieves. I was just an ordinary psychic living quietly in Watoolahatchee, Florida. Then I paid a visit to my mother ...*

She glanced back at Hannah. "I've done a little research on the subject. I found this really interesting blog by an ex-FBI art crimes investigator and he talked about lots of ways to undertake an investigation."

"So ... what would you do?"

"Undercover work seems to be a lot like chess," said Epiphany. "You need to rely on your own intuition. As a psychic, I shouldn't find that too difficult."

What did she do for a living? She "read" for people. Sat down with them and envisioned their lives, their hopes, their problems. Saw inside them. "The main mantra is simple: befriend and betray."

"Befriend and betray?"

"Yes. Here's how you do that." She filled Hannah in on the basics: First, assess your target and get to know his game. Know the vocabuary. In this case, she had a perfect background for the subject: art and art history and the market for fine art, both legitimate and shady. She'd also recently had the chance to do some research on Ace Energy and their operations in the area.

Next, how to approach the target. Epiphany had a plan. She had a former client who now lived in Dayton. The client had married a wealthy businessman who was an art collector. Epiphany had kept in touch with Stella Martin-Lubworth. She could find out if Stella knew Derrick Rarian. If so, Epiphany planned to pose as a South Florida art dealer. Maybe Stella could arrange for Rarian to meet her "special guest."

Then, it would be up to Epiphany to build rapport with Rarian, draw him out about his collection, flatter him into giving her an invitation to view it at his estate in Xenia. Once inside his home, she could verify that he indeed had possession of the stolen Blake, and maybe even convince him to sell the drawing to an interested collector who would "pay anything" to get it. If Rarian could be trapped into selling the Blake, he could be charged with dealing in stolen property. And maybe with other crimes as well. "In any event," she said, "I could alert the PI about what I found and he could use the information to build his case against Rarian. Maybe even get that search warrant."

"Isn't it dangerous?" Hannah wanted to know.

"I suppose it could be. I mean, if Rarian found out I was working with a PI, I can't imagine he'd be exactly thrilled."

"What if he doesn't invite you to see his collection?" asked Hannah.

"Nothing ventured, nothing gained I guess. It's worth trying."

Later that evening, she and Hannah were still discussing the undercover idea. The kitchen table was a little globe of light in the darkness of the house. Thick clouds had obliterated a feeble sunset and pulled a black cover over the hills. Epiphany could hear thunder grumbling in the distance.

"When would you be, uh, pulling this caper?" Hannah asked with a grin.

"Hey," Epiphany countered, "I'm the good guy here." She studiously dissected the iceburg wedge glistening in a puddle of dressing. "Anyway, I'd have to do some *backstopping*."

"What's that?" asked Susan.

"Creating a false identity. I need to invent a persona Rarian would find believable. I'm thinking I should be an art dealer from Miami, so I'm going to call myself Rebecca Cohen. There are hundreds of Cohens in Miami, so I could hide in the herd if Rarian checked on my name.

"Then, I'd need to create a paper trail—ID cards, email account, anything a person might have to back up their identity." Epiphany paused, her fork in the air. "Maybe I'd need a Twitter account."

"And glasses," Hannah said. "You should definitely have glasses."

"Tortoise shell or leopard?" Epiphany asked.

"I'd go with the tortoise," said Hannah.

"For goodness sake," exclaimed Susan. "I think you should be more serious. You could get into trouble, Fanny!"

"What else is new, Mom?" Epiphany asked.

It took over a week to set up Rebecca Cohen's identity. Besides a Florida driver's licence, she carried credit cards for Neiman Marcus and Saks Fifth Avenue, a Platinum American Express card, a Delta frequent-flyer card, an international museum card, and a membership card for an exclusive spa and fitness center. Epiphany called her son and told him that she had decided to stay in Ohio for another couple of weeks to help her mother put some of her papers in order. Michael told her to take her time.

Next, she and Hannah visited the Saks store in Cincinnati and picked out a wardrobe from the Caribbean Collection—tailored white slacks, two flowing gossamer tops in turquoise and mint green. They added a cashmere sweater, an elegant black-and-white cocktail dress, stiletto heels, an oversized Gucci bag.

"That's enough shopping," Epiphany groaned. "My feet hurt."

"Oh, no," Hannah said. "We're not finished with you yet."

Epiphany looked alarmed. "We're not?"

"Hair," said Hannah emphatically.

The young lady at "Marie's Coiffeurs Elegantes" told Epiphany she had "lively" hair and went to work. When Epiphany emerged, Hannah tossed her copy of *Elle* aside and raised her eyebrows. "God, Pip," she murmured. "You look amazing!"

Epiphany glanced in the floor-to-ceiling mirror. There stood a tall, elegant lady with a sweeping curve of softly sculpted platinum hair highlighted by a copper streak that ran from forehead to temple. She stared at the image. "Meet Rebecca Cohen," she whispered.

Chapter 24

It was less than a two hour drive from Susan's farm to Dayton. Epiphany got into her rented Lexus, took Route 56 to Laurelville, then turned south and picked up Route 35, a straight, fast piece of road that by-passed the Hopewell Indian Mounds and the small towns of Jasper Mills and Wilberforce before heading for Dayton.

As she drove past Xenia, Epiphany thought about trying to find Malebranche, Derrick Rarian's "week-end house," but decided to go straight to the address she had for Hunter's Glen Manor, Stella Martin-Lubworth's palatial estate. Her GPS directions led her past the University of Dayton and southward through the fashionable communities of Oakwood and Kettering to a winding private road that ran along the edge of a forest.

A uniformed guard met her at the black wrought-iron gate and gravely inspected her invitation. "Thank you, Miss Cohen,' he said, touching the brim of his cap. "Please take the first drive on the right. The valet will see to your car. Have a lovely evening."

The house was a huge brick and British half-timber affair with an ocean of green lawn surrounding it, interrupted by islands of fir trees and maples. The large, bright-red John Henry sculpture with its modernist steel angles seemed out of place in the pastoral lawn, like a spaceship sitting in a meadow of wildflowers.

Epiphany joined the line of cars creeping up the slope toward the house, discharging their occupants beneath the massive porte-cochere. She got out and handed the valet her key fob. She had dressed her part, wearing the clinging black and white cocktail dress, and the black stiletto heels. She hoped she wouldn't have to move very quickly.

Once inside the marble foyer, she was greeted by a formally-dressed gentleman with a white beard who asked her name. "I'm Rebecca Cohen," she told him. "An old friend of Stella's."

His face lit up. "Of course, Ms. Cohen," he said. "How delightful to see you again. Madame is waiting for you in the library." He gestured toward an open door halfway down the hall.

Stella Martin-Lubworth was a stout, grey-haired lady with a round face and chubby arms. She looked to have been poured into the tan silk dress that hung almost to her thick ankles. But when she spotted "Rebecca" she beamed and raised her hand in greeting.

"Becky, darling," she called in a high-pitched voice. "How wonderful of you to come for a visit, knowing how busy you are. Come here, dearest, there's someone I want you to meet."

The man standing next to Stella turned to assess the new arrival. Epiphany had to catch her breath—it was Derrick Rarian. Trying to calm her pounding heart, Epiphany moved toward them hoping that she looked more confident than she felt.

Stella gave Epiphany a quick hug and took hold of her hand. "Becky, this is my dear friend Derrick Rarian. He has the most fab collection. Very exclusive and unusual. I know you'd love to see it!"

Stella turned to Derrick. "As I told you earlier, Rebecca is an old friend of mine from Miami," she said. "I've known her forever. We used to get into all sorts of trouble together!" Stella placed a plump hand over her mouth. "Oh my, I shouldn't start telling stories, should I? It would take all night. Let me go find a waiter. I'm sure the two of you could use some champagne." She bustled away as Derrick and "Rebecca" stood appraising each other.

Derrick spoke first. "Stella tells me you're in the art business," he said. His voice was silky. It had a smoothness that made Epiphany uneasy, like a polished marble floor that felt slippery underfoot. He tilted his head slightly and watched her with narrowed eyes. His eyes, she noted, were an odd color. Somewhere between grey and blue. He had a mane of silver hair that caught the light when he moved his head. His face was tanned, as though he'd just returned from an island vacation—or spent lots of time in a tanning bed.

Epiphany met his eyes with a look of mild amusement. "Art is one of my interests."

Derrick raised an eyebrow. "In what way, Ms. Cohen?"

"A bit of this and that, actually," Epiphany said. "I do appraisals, consulting. I had a gallery at one time—An Eye for Art—but I found it too confining. I like to travel, and running the gallery was a problem." She sighed. "I tried having someone manage it for me, but it's so difficult to get reliable help."

"I agree. Some things are too important to be left to amateurs." A hint of a smile played over his mouth.

She wondered if he was aiming the remark at her, but she gave him a conspiratorial smile and said, "What I really enjoy is going to auctions. I crave the adrenaline rush, the competition. I'm sure you know what I mean."

A waiter, smartly dressed in black, offered them each a glass of sparkling wine and retreated with a deferential bow.

Derrick raised his glass and offered a genuine smile along with a toast: "To art."

"And all the other finer things," said Epiphany.

She didn't see Derrick again for a while. There were swarms of guests and Stella made a great scene of introducing Rebecca, her best friend from Miami, to everyone.

Epiphany had reviewed her profile of Stella—her education (University of Miami), marriages (currently working on number three), children (two boys and a girl, all married and living in New York, Los Angeles and Vancouver respectively), and affiliations (Garden Club, museum benefactor, ballet company board member, etc.). Husband number three owned a container company. He made boxes. They sold very well. Epiphany knew where Stella had grown up (Coral Gables), where she went to high school (Coral Gables Senior High), and even who her first boyfriend was (Howard Strauss).

It wasn't until after the sumptuous dinner (roast leg of lamb, potatoes gratin, grilled asparagus, arugula and pomegranate salad, glasses of Romanée-Conti), that Epiphany found herself standing next to Derrick in the upstairs hallway admiring a Degas painting of three lounging ballerinas.

"Ethereal, aren't they?" Derrick said.

Epiphany leaned in for a closer look. "A bit *too* ethereal."

Derrick glanced at her, then looked back at the art. Cradled in an elaborate gilded frame, it was a small work, 12 by 15 inches, depicting three ballerinas dressed in diaphanous pink and yellow costumes. The young women were apparently taking a break from rehearsal or class—one sat with her feet apart, another was adjusting her slipper.

"They're too pretty," Epiphany said. "Too elegant."

"They do seem a little … refined."

"And look here," Epiphany said, pointing. "It's dated 1884. By that time Degas was losing his eyesight, and his work had gotten much more gestural, less precise. These brushstrokes are tentative, careful. Degas's late works were vibrant and expressive, and the color was richer."

"I see what you mean." He looked at Epiphany with that strange little half smile. "So what are you saying, Ms. Cohen? Do you think it's a forgery?"

"If I were Stella, I'd definitely have it checked out. I wonder where she got it?" she added thoughtfully. "I know she used to visit a gallery in Pompano Beach. I can't remember the dealer's name, Charles something I think. I later heard the gallery had been closed after the authorities found a number of forgeries among the works for sale."

"You're thinking of the C.B. Charles Galleries," Derrick said. "The Art Dealer's Association tipped off the Feds that the gallery was going to auction off a group of works that were suspect, and the sale never took place."

"That's right. There was quite a commotion about the sale of a fake Matisse from the same gallery." She looked back at the painting. "I hope I'm wrong, but I think I should tell Stella this may not be a real Degas."

"You have a good eye, Ms. Cohen."

"Please, call me Rebecca," said Epiphany, giving him a warm smile.

"Very well, Rebecca."

That silky voice bothered her. For an instant, she saw a dark shadow surrounding him, a smokey aura like a burned log left to smolder. She could even smell the bitter scent of ashes. There was something violent in his past, an incident that had scorched him like a burst of flame. She felt an undercurrent of rage and humiliation that had left him empty, a burnt-out husk.

The dream came back to her—the swirling smoke, the suffocating haze. Momentarily shaken, she looked back at the fake Degas. Then she glanced at Derrick and said, "Stella told me you have a wonderful art collection yourself. I'd love to see it sometime." She couldn't believe she was being so bold. Was she moving too fast?

But Derrick looked pleased and replied, "I'd love to show it to you. How long are you going to be in town?"

"At least another week. Then I'm off to London for a meeting with some corporate clients."

"What about next Thursday? Cocktails at six and an early dinner?"

Epiphany swallowed hard. It couldn't be this easy. Straight into the dragon's lair? Alone? When she hesitated he added, "I don't think Stella will mind if I invite you to come take a look. I may need some … consultation in the future."

"In that case," she replied, "it would be rude of me to decline your generous offer."

Chapter 25

Later that night, Epiphany put through a call to Hannah. "He's invited me to see the collection," she told her.

"That was quick," she said. "When's the meeting?"

"Day after tomorrow," she said. "Here's the plan. The goal is to talk Rarian into selling the Blake, but first we need verification that he has the art. Once I'm sure it's in his house, the authorities can set up a sting operation."

"What if you don't see it on the wall?" said Hannah.

"I'll try to get him to talk about it. Maybe mention that I have an interested buyer with similar tastes who would love to own an original William Blake—something like that. If he takes the bait, I think the PI or the police can set up a meeting between Rarian and the supposed buyer. Once he consummates the sale, they'll have him on dealing in stolen property."

"That sounds sort of … tricky," said Hannah. "Why don't they just send in a SWAT team and arrest him?"

"They don't have probable cause," said Epiphany. "So they can't get a search warrant. They need to know first that he has the art, and second that he's willing to sell it. Then they have him."

"Well," Hannah said uncertainly. "Stay safe."

⟡

The house looked just as she had envisioned it—a sprawling Mid-Century Modern with an unusual roofline, a raised central section, and a row of clerestory windows beneath the eaves. It was separated from the street by a wide expanse of lawn and a small grove of birch trees, their trunks marked with black and white patterns that were almost geometric—just like she'd seen in her remote vision.

She stopped in front of an elaborate metal gate with a Frank Lloyd Wright design. And there, next to the gate, was a brass plate with the name "Malebranche." "Evil Claws," according to Dante, Epiphany thought. The demons from the Eighth Circle of Hell led by Malacoda who tells Dante and his companion Virgil about the earthquake that destroyed the bridges leading from ditch to ditch within the Circle. The job of the Malebranche was to torment those who have committed fraud—the liars and flatterers, the seducers and hypocrites, who use their abusive power to corrupt and pervert.

She reminded herself that one of those bad guys lived here, and that it was her job to help bring him down. Even if he was sleek and slick and disturbingly attractive. And smart. And rich. He was a BAD GUY. "Right," she said. "*Bad.*"

The gate opened mysteriously. When she drove through, it closed behind her. She noticed a silver Bentley parked in the driveway.

She expected to be met by a butler or a maid, but Mr. Silverhair himself answered the door and graciously ushered her into the foyer. He looked relaxed and much less formal, wearing a pale blue linen shirt, open at the neck, and tan Chinos. She was glad that she too had "dressed down" for the meeting, choosing the white slacks and a blue-green top she and Hannah had purchased.

Inside, she found herself in a two-story entryway made of polished gray marble. At the end of the foyer was a half-circle alcove dominated by a dramatic spiral staircase whose cantilevered wooden steps seemed to float in thin air.

To her right was a vaulted living room with wooden beams and a wooden-plank ceiling that soared high above her head. One side of the room was floor-to-ceiling glass overlooking an austerely beautiful Japanese garden with raked gravel simulating waves between carefully positioned rock "islands." A dense grove of evergreens provided a backdrop for the garden's abstract simplicity.

The room was sparsely furnished with two elegant black leather sofas facing each other across a low glass coffee table. Track lights bathed the white walls with illumination, while the polished concrete floors gleamed softly. At the end of the room was a huge stone fireplace rising like a pillar from the dark floor to the distant ceiling.

And everywhere she looked there was art—paintings, drawings, prints, sculptures, a framed video screen that gleamed and moved, colors fading and brightening as she watched.

Derrick smiled and took her arm. "Let's have a drink before we get to work, shall we?"

She nodded mutely, dazzled by the surroundings. He steered her across the room and through glass doors onto a flagstone terrace overlooking another Japanese style garden, this one featuring a pond flanked by carefully shaped junipers set atop moss-covered banks. Two of Eero Saarinen's Tulip chairs sat beside a graceful Noguchi table.

A servant magically appeared with an ice bucket and a tray that contained two wine glasses and several small bowls of nuts and olives. He opened a bottle of white wine, poured two drinks, set the bottle back in the ice, then disappeared as silently as he had arrived.

"Your home is stunning," Epiphany said. She raised her glass. "To excellent taste."

Derrick responded with a smile. "Welcome to Malebranche," he said, and took a sip of wine.

"Why would you name your house 'Malebranche' when it's so amazingly lovely?"

Derrick chuckled softly. "Because it's Number Eight, Shadow Drive. I found the incongruity amusing."

"I wouldn't exactly describe it as Hell,"

"It's where I come to relax," he said.

"It is quite tranquil."

She was captivated by his hands—the long slender fingers, the graceful way he gestured. But even as she watched, his hands seemed to become transparent, as though they were made of ice. Or glass. Something cold and empty. She shuddered, then composed herself and smiled brightly. "Have you lived here long?"

"I had this place built about ten years ago," he said. "I realized I was spending all my time in cities—Cleveland, Chicago, New York. I missed the color green, so I bought ten acres here and had the house designed by an architect friend in the MCM style."

"Did you grow up surrounded by green?"

"I grew up surrounded by filth," he said curtly. "But I won't bore you with the details." He sipped his wine.

Epiphany backed off quickly. "So, how did you become an art collector?" Stick to business, she told herself.

"It wasn't intentional. The idea never occurred to me until about ten years ago. I suddenly realized that art is actually ahead of science in describing the reality of our existence. Art is the prototype, the template, and the artist brings an idea into existence for all to see." His voice had risen with excitement and his expression became animated. "Culture," he said, "has always been more powerful than politics."

"You make it sound like a religion," Epiphany said.

"Indeed, it's the only religion I have." For a moment he seemed lost in thought. Then he smiled at her and said, "Let's save that discussion for later, shall we? Tell me about Rebecca Cohen. Who is she and what does she believe in?"

Remember your lines, Epiphany reminded herself. "Because I am a dealer—not a collector—I have to be careful not to get too attached to my children. I'm good at finding things other people want. I sense their tastes, their ... needs." She leaned forward slightly. "I like to get close to my clients."

She felt a door slam shut. He was suddenly opaque, unreadable. She sat back and studied him. She was once again aware of a coldness at the core, but also of the charred interior. The words of T. S. Eliot's poem came to her: "Shape without form, shade without color ... There are no eyes here in this valley of dying stars, in this hollow valley ...". She shivered involuntarily.

Derrick got to his feet. "It's getting chilly out here," he said. "Let's go in, shall we?"

She followed him into the house. He gestured toward one of the leather sofas. "Make yourself comfortable. I'll ask Jackson to bring the wine in here."

Epiphany settled herself on the sofa and resisted the urge to kick off her shoes. She wasn't going to get *that* comfortable. She was still in the dragon's lair, and he was a perplexing opponent. She wished again that he was less difficult to read.

"Now then," he said, striding in and dropping onto the sofa across the table from her. "You were telling me about your ... self."

"I buy and sell art. I travel a great deal. When I'm not traveling I live in Coral Gables."

"That's it? No family?"

"I once had a cat," Epiphany said. "But it died."

"I'm sorry for your loss."

"Don't be. She was old and sick and better off leaving when she did. But," she continued brightly, "what about you? Family? Children? Cats?"

"No cats. No dogs. No kids."

"Married to your work?"

"I'm very good at what I do," he said quietly.

"And what is it exactly that you do, Mr. Rarian?"

"I destroy things."

Chapter 26

When she thought about it afterward, Epiphany was surprised she had stayed. But at the time, she felt like a spectator at an accident—horrified but unable to look away even as the metal crumpled and the glass shattered and the screams rent the air. She was fascinated with Derrick Rarian. Who was he? *What* was he? The artist Blake King had called him "the emissary of Mammon whose velvet words obscure vile thoughts while all the time he magnates to himself the treasures of the world."

And so she stayed. Discussed the art market, the up-coming auctions, recent acquisitions, reported forgeries. When she asked him what he had meant in saying that he "destroyed things" for a living, he changed the subject.

They ate dinner in the kitchen at a small teakwood table—a green-pea soup sprinkled with fresh dill, a creamy fettucini Alfredo, a salad of baby greens. Jackson served dessert in the living room, and poured each of them a snifter of cognac from a crystal decanter.

"Now do I get to see the collection?" Epiphany asked.

Derrick chuckled. "You've been extremely patient," he said. He got to his feet and held out his hand. "Right this way."

They made the rounds of the living room and she made appreciative exclamations over the melange of museum-worthy works—an eclectic mix from Byzantine icons to contemporary video works. But nowhere did she see the Blake. Nor did she see the other works that had appeared in her vision—the photos of clear-cut hillsides and sculptures of melting polar bears. "Is this all?" she asked as they finished the tour of the great room.

"Haven't had enough?" He stared a her for a moment, then said, "Come. I'll show you my favorites. The heart and soul of the collection."

They took an elevator down to a lower level, and entered a long white room, a true gallery. It felt at once familiar. She had visited it before in her vision. She scanned the walls. She remembered the Blake drawing being exactly ... there. Right next to that horribly beautiful photograph of a rusted pipe spewing froth into a pool of green slime.

Only it *wasn't* there. The space was noticibly empty, a gaping hole between the other works of art. "Looks like something's missing," she said.

"It's being re-framed." He met her questioning look with a hard stare.

She let him lead her around the gallery. It was a grotesque display of destruction and carnage—paintings of oil spills, photos of dead birds that looked to be made of black plastic, flames burning on the surface of a river. "Welcome to the Inferno," Derrick said with a tight smile.

"You said this is the 'heart and soul' of your collection. What did you mean exactly?"

Derrick looked around. "I love beautiful things. For a while, that's all I wanted to see. Beautiful things. Images that made me feel peaceful and hopeful and good. But then," he paused for a moment, "then I saw the hypocrisy of that position. I was not being true to myself, to my vision of what could be. What *should* be. I was finally able to look in the mirror and see my true face."

"And that face was?" Epiphany prompted.

"The face of Mammon. The face of greed." He was silent for a moment, then said, "Look, I work for a petroleum company. Since the mid-seventies we've known that the pollution from the petroleum industry was compromising the health of the planet, yet we kept that information from the public. Why? To make money of course. Coal, oil, petroleum extraction has raised the traditional mythology of a subterranean world of fire and brimstone and made it a reality on the planet's surface. The Underworld is eradicating the Upperworld. All for the sake of money. It's actually a very simple concept."

"But you said you love beauty. Why would you embrace destruction?" Epiphany asked.

"I had convinced myself that I only wanted the money for the beautiful things it would buy. But then I realized that I made the money by destroying beautiful things. There was a dichotomy in my thinking. A flaw. Why not just embrace the obvious? I was destroying the world in order to surround myself with beauty. Why not see the terrible beauty of destruction? Then there would be no inconsistency. And so," he gestured to the gallery, "I acknowledged my true passion. What is it they say? 'Better to reign in Hell than to serve in Heaven'?" He gave a mirthless laugh. "I have made my choice."

"May I ask a personal question?"

He raised an eyebrow. "All right."

"Do you ever consider yourself to be evil?" Epiphany asked.

"Evil?" Derrick looked thoughtful. "I'd like to believe that I've transcended such categories." He pointed to a lushly painted aerial view of the Gulf of Mexico with flames spiraling up from a black whirlpool. "Is this painting evil? I see it as beautiful. The deep green of the water. The swirls of red and orange leaping skyward from the depths. It's a thrilling image. Did the artist mean to condemn or to celebrate? Does it matter?" He turned to Epiphany. "What do you think, Rebecca?"

"I love the connection to *The Inferno.* Don't you have any art that is specifically tied to Dante's work? Perhaps an … illustration?"

"Actually," he said. "I *do* have such a work."

"But,' Epipahny glaced around, "where is it?"

"It's the piece that's missing. The one that's out being framed."

"Really?"

"Really." His smile was slick as ice.

Epiphany arched an eyebrow. "I know that you have it," she said.

"Have what?"

"The Blake."

"Oh," he said with a shrug. "And how would you prove it?"

"I have a buyer," Epiphany said evenly. "A gentleman from Dubai. He's willing to pay whatever you ask."

Derrick crossed his arms and gazed at her. "Is that a fact?"

"He's been collecting illustrations from *The Inferno,* a collection similar to yours of oil-related disasters. He's quite keen to have Blake's picture of the *Boiling Pitch Pool of Corrupt Officials.*"

"Is he?" Derrick appeared to be considering, and for a moment Epiphany thought he might take the bait. Then he gave her that sinister, velvety smile of his and said, "Even if I had the Blake, I wouldn't agree to sell it. You'll have to do better than that. Tell your handlers I'm disappointed in their lack of creativity. I think," he added smoothly, "that you'd best be going now."

Stunned and humiliated, Epiphany headed for the door. At the gallery entrance she stopped and looked back at him. "If you knew this was a set-up, why'd you play along?"

He gave a low laugh. "For my own amusement," he said. "Jackson will show you out. Good night, Ms. Mayall."

Chapter 27

"You WHAT?" Maro cried. "God, what a mistake! Now he knows we're on to him and he'll be sure to put the Blake someplace where we'll never find it."

"I'm so sorry. I thought I was doing the right thing. He seemed to be buying my act, but ..." Epiphany shook her head. "What did I do wrong?"

"You can't just ... I could have ... *Jeez,* you could have gotten yourself killed!"

Epiphany had telephoned Maro when she got back from Dayton. Miserable and humiliated, she first thought she wouldn't tell him about her failed plan, but she wanted him to continue the investigation. He had immediately driven out to the Mayall farm to get a full report on her ill-advised adventure.

"I'm just thankful you didn't get hurt," said Susan.

"Don't beat yourself up," said Hannah. "You did what you could, and I think it was very gutsy of you. I certainly wouldn't have been able to pull it off."

"Thanks, guys," Epiphany said, "but I still feel like shit."

"It was reckless," Maro said. "But I know you were trying to help." He turned away and muttered something under his breath about "bad judgment." Epiphany had a sudden strong impression of anger mixed with fear. And guilt. Something from his past. Something had gone terribly wrong, and he blamed himself. She had inadvertently sent him down the same path.

He glanced back at her and their eyes met for a moment before he looked away. "Well," he said, "The game's not over yet. We still have some options."

"Such as?"

"I want to zero in on Hugh Stillman and see if we can find out what he knows about the theft. Maybe we can also get him to give us some info on the role Chance played." He gave Epiphany a hard look. "Maybe you can have a chat with Hugh? He won't talk to me."

"Well," Epiphany said, "I can *try*." Maybe she could redeem herself?

"That's all I'm asking. Just be careful, okay?"

"Yes, sir."

Maro shook his head.

"And that security guy," Epiphany said. "What was his name?"

"Ray Lucas," said Maro. "Yeah, I'll check him out."

Maro gave Epiphany a stern look. "But please, would you talk with me before you decide to undertake any other … schemes?"

Epiphany felt like a scolded child. "Yes, Mr. Gaido," she muttered.

He let out his breath in a little hiss. "You can call me Maro," he said.

She looked up at him. "Okay. And you can call me Epiphany."

"Yes, ma'am," he said.

⁂

Epiphany and Hannah spent Sunday taking it easy—enjoying Susan's breakfast, taking a walk along the creek, gearing up, Epiphany thought, for the next act. The weather was bright and unusually cool for a July day in southeastern Ohio, almost a little foretaste of fall.

On Monday they got an early start and arrived at the OU campus just after nine. Epiphany had telephoned Maro and asked if he wanted to meet them at the museum, but he declined, saying he didn't want to spook Hugh Stillman. He wanted to be sure Epiphany could find out as much as possible about Hugh's part in the theft.

Hugh wasn't in yet, so the two women spent fifteen minutes chatting with Zoe, John Bernhardt's former secretary, who was still working at the museum office. When they asked how Hugh had been, she thought for a minute and then said, "Jumpy."

Hugh arrived a few minutes later looking a little discheveled, as though he hadn't taken time to think about his outfit—his shirt was wrinkled and his tie carelessly tied. He didn't seem very happy to find Epiphany and Hannah waiting for him, but he invited them into his office and offered coffee.

"So, ladies," he said, smiling tightly, "I haven't seen you for awhile. How's the investigation going? Any new leads? Or have you decided to take my advice and leave it to the professionals?"

Epiphany felt a little rush of irritation. Maybe Hugh had a point. She hadn't gotten very far with her undercover mission. But she smiled back and said, "Still trying to be helpful and do what we can to find out what happened."

"We have a few new leads," Hannah added.

"Really?" Hugh said. "Well, I'd love to hear about them."

"We have a pretty good idea how the Blake was taken from the gallery," Epiphany said.

Hugh's mouth twitched, but he said nothing.

"You know about the tunnel, of course," Epiphany continued.

"The tunnel?" Hugh's eyes widened.

"The one that runs from the museum basement to the dock on the river."

"Uh, how did you—"

"I have an informant," said Epiphany.

He was looking uneasy now. Somewhere between dazed and frazzled. Epiphany let him stew for a moment before she said, "My, uh, contact told me she saw Chance Hilliburn going into the tunnel with a package wrapped in a plaid blanket."

Hugh stood up, nearly spilling his coffee. "That's impossible! Who is this informant of yours? Clearly they don't know what they're talking about!"

Hannah said, "There's an easy way to clear this up, isn't there? Let's take a look at the security cam tapes."

"You don't have the authority to—" Hugh stammered.

"Actually I do," said Epiphany. She pulled a piece of paper from her purse and handed it to the bewildered curator. "I'm working with Maro Gaido," she explained. "You remember Maro? That nice young man from the insurance company? He asked me to take a look at the tapes to see if there were any, uh, discrepancies. Any indication that the tapes had been altered." She smiled. "I'm sure you'll want to cooperate, won't you Mister Stillman?"

Hugh sat back down. His face had turned ashen, his eyes brown pools of fear.

"Hugh?" Epiphany said. "The tapes?"

He swallowed and said, ""I don't have them."

"Then where are they?"

"Look," Hugh said, "you really don't know what you're getting into. This is way bigger than you think. Take my advice and back off. It's not worth it, believe me." His voice was thin and desperate.

"It's not worth it to find out who stole the Blake and why? And how the theft was connected to John Bernhardt's death?" Epiphany took a deep breath. "Oh no, Mister Still-man, I think it's very much worth it, and I think you'd better tell us what you know." She leaned toward him. "Now!"

He looked away, twisting his hands and shifting in his chair.

"Do you want me to go to the police? Maybe have a chat with the FBI? Bring up my concerns with your boss?

Hugh stared at her.

"Well?"

"All right, all right." After a minute he said, "You're right about Chance. He took the Blake."

"Did you help him?"

"It's complicated," he muttered. "There's a lot more to it than you think."

"Did you help him?" Epiphany repeated.

Hugh sucked in his breath. "I … allowed him to do what he did. Look," he continued, "they told me just to go along with it and not get in the way. I didn't actually *do* anything."

"They?" Epiphany said. "Who are they?"

"It wasn't just Chance. There were … other people involved."

"Such as?"

"Ray."

"Ray Lucas? The security guard?"

"Yeah. He helped. Facilitated. Cleared the way. And he also …" Hugh paused and gave Epiphany a stricken look.

"He made me edit the tapes. But after that PI reviewed them, I panicked and got rid of them. I told the police that the tapes had disappeared. I thought maybe … my fingerprints were on them or something. I don't know." He shook his head.

"Are you willing to testify that Chance took the Blake and that Ray Lucas helped him?" asked Hannah.

"No!" Hugh said. "I'm telling you, don't mess with these guys! You're looking at the tip of the iceberg here."

"I'm sure the FBI can help you," Epiphany said. "Get you into a witness protection program or something."

Hugh gave a shrill laugh. "You're not listening, are you? The police are in on the whole thing."

Epiphany's eyes widened. "Are you sure?"

"They're going to look the other way. They don't give a damn if a piece of art's gone missing."

"What about John's death?"

"They ruled it a heart attack and that's that. Don't you see," Hugh continued, "it's all a set-up."

"*What's* a set-up?" asked Hannah.

Hugh's hands made circles in the air. "The whole thing. It's all tied together."

Epiphany sat back. "That's what I thought. The theft, the fracking, John's death—they're all connected, aren't they?"

Hugh bent his head and covered his face with his hands. "Please, don't do this to me. You don't understand. They'll go after my family." He dropped his hands and stared at Epiphany. "They'll do whatever they need to get what they want."

"And what do they want?" Epiphany asked.

"Money," said Hugh.

Chapter 28

"So you have a witness who won't talk and no evidence to charge anyone with anything?" Susan said. "That doesn't sound good."

Epiphany groaned and buried her head in her arms. Then she straightened up and said, "Damn it! We've got to find *something* we can use to make our case."

"But to whom?" said Hannah. "Hugh said the local police are no help. They want to steer clear of this mess."

"There's still Maro," said Epiphany. "At least *he* wants to solve this case. And," she paused and took a breath, "I expect he'd also like to find out who murdered John Bernhardt."

"Which has already been written off as a non-murder," said Hannah. "Thanks to the local officials. But Maro was certainly concerned about that … heart attack gun."

"But since you can't prove that Mister Rarian stole the art work, you can't charge him with anything," Susan said. She looked from Epiphany to Hannah and back. "Girls," she said, "pardon my French but I think you're screwed." She got up and hobbled to the stove. "More tea?"

"Why not," Epiphany said. "Maybe it'll help me think."

"Okay," said Hannah, "Let's back up and follow the dots. We know Chance took the Blake, and that Ray Lucas helped him get it out of the building through the tunnel. Hugh's job was to look the other way, say nothing and get rid of the security tapes. But he won't testify even if he's charged, which he won't be because the local police don't want to be involved in what they think is a 'victimless crime' such as art theft."

"We also know the responsible party is Derrick Rarian," said Epiphany. "He wanted the Blake, and he had his boy Chance get it for him. But Rarian's apparently outsmarted us, and we don't have any evidence to charge him with anything."

"But what about John's murder?" Susan asked, putting a steaming cup of tea in front of her daughter and settling herself in a kitchen chair. "Maybe you should concentrate on that."

"Right," said Hannah. "We've sort of hit a dead-end on the theft, so why not focus on John's death, and how it fits in with the disappearance of the Blake?"

Epiphany's cell phone buzzed. She hoped it was Michael. She hadn't talked to him or her granddaughter Maddie for a couple of days, and was eager to hear their familiar voices, but the number on the screen was an Ohio number she didn't immediately recognize. She did, however, recognize the voice. It was John's widow, Francesca.

"How are you, dear?" Epiphany asked.

"Holding up pretty well, I guess," Francesca replied. "My daughter's here with me. She's been such a help these past few weeks. Listen, I've come across some documents I thought would be of interest to you. It's rather complicated, so I don't want to try to explain over the phone. Do you think you might be able to drop by in the next day or two?"

"Hannah and I were planning on coming into town tomorrow afternoon. How about after lunch. Around two?"

"That would be fine. See you then."

That night Epiphany had a puzzling dream. She is in a town that seems to be foreign and very old. The streets are narrow and paved with stones. She walks through meandering alleys and comes to a river spanned by several bridges, their arched footings reflected in the water. The sun is setting, revealing an undulating line of blue hills in the distance, and the sky is flooded with gossamer pink and coral clouds. She can make out several tall spires and the rounded dome of a church or cathedral.

Then she realizes that Maro Gaido is walking along beside her. "Do you see this man?" he asks and shows her a photograph of Derrick Rarian. "Do you know who he is?"

"Of course I do," Epiphany replies. "He is the Devil."

Maro winks at her and chuckles. "Good for you. Then you know why he's here."

"But what—" Epiphany starts to ask, but Maro disappears in a wisp of fog. Just like Margaret Schilling, the ghost from the lunetic asylum. Is Maro also a ghost?

When she glances around, all of the colors have faded, and everything is in black and white, like an old movie. There is a line of men on one side of the street. They are all dressed in black robes. On the opposite side of the street is a row of men dressed in white. They are lobbing paper airplanes at each other and shouting insults. "Pig! Hypocrite! Liar! Crook!"

Maro re-appears. "Look at them, the Blacks and the Whites. Who would have thought it would lead to this."

"Lead to what?" says Epiphany

"The war of the Guelphs."

"In Florence?"

"He's one of them," Maro replies.

"Who? One of what?" Epiphany asks.

"Of the three-hundred, of course."

"Three hundred what?"

He smiles in a patronizing way. "You'll find out. Just pay attention."

She woke up feeling frustrated and angry. The night sky was just beginning to lighten toward the east. She tried to go back to sleep, but couldn't stop thinking of all the obstacles that seemed to be multiplying even as she tried to get past them. "What would Albert do?" she asked herself, and then had to laugh. Albert, her dear funny friend back in Watoolahatchee living in his strange purple house with his lace curtains and Victorian antiques. She loved his round face and his strangely tiny hands—like a little mouse. But he always had the best advice. What would he advise? She got a very clear picture of Albert in her head. He looked at her over his glasses and said, "Read the script."

"I've been trying to sort through his papers," Francesca said, "but there's just so much to go through." She glanced around at the cardboard file boxes stacked along the walls of the library. Hannah and Epiphany were sitting in the brocade-covered wing chairs next to the fireplace. Pearly afternoon light filtered in through the white gauze curtains, casting weak shadows on the colorful Kilim carpet.

"It must be daunting," Hannah said. "All those years of research and writing. Don't you have anyone to help you?"

"His students have been wonderful," Francesca said. "I don't know what I'd have done without Gretchen. And Zoe has been a big help. But I just don't want to miss anything. Anything important." She took a breath and gave her guests a weary smile. "Sorry, it's been a bit overwhelming."

Francesca straightened up and sorted through the pile of papers on the desk before her. "This is what I wanted to show you. A whole box was devoted to the Inferno exhibit with all of John's notes and research. I came across—let's see. Ah, here it is. This folder has something quite disturbing. It's about a secret organization called the Committee of 300. I thought you should see it."

"Three hundred?" Epiphany said.

"Yes," said Francesca. "Do you know anything about them?"

The previous night's dream flooded through her mind—He's one of them, Maro had said in the dream. One of the 300. She held out her hand. "Could I see that, please?"

Francesca handed her the folder and Epiphany opened it. "Venetian Black Nobility," she read aloud. "Roots of Today's Ruling Oligarchy."

"The ruling families of Venice and Genoa in the twelth century," Hannah said. "They had a monopoly on trading rights and became fabulously wealthy."

"The Guelphs," Epiphany said. "That's what Maro was trying to tell me in my dream. The House of Guelph was one of the Venetian familes. The family later split into two factions: the Black Guelphs who supported the Pope, and the White Guelphs who supported secular rule. Dante was part of the White faction. That led to him being exiled from Florence, and was the basis of his poems." She looked down at the papers in the folder. "I wonder what this has to do with …" She looked at Hannah.

"What?"

"Oh my God, Hannah," Epiphany said. "He's one of them."

Chapter 29

Dinner was over, and Susan had gone to watch Lawrence Welk on PBS. Hannah and Epiphany sat at the kitchen table with the papers from John's folder spread out between them.

"The Committee of 300 is a product of the British East India Company's Council of 300," Hannah read aloud. "The East India Company was chartered by the British royal family in sixteen-hundred. It made vast fortunes in the opium drug trade with China and became the largest company on earth in its time."

Hannah flipped through the folder. "I don't know, Pip," she said. "It all sounds like a wacky conspiracy theory to me. I mean listen to this, 'There is a plan for a New World Order devised by an American/European financial elite of immense wealth and power with ancient historical roots, called by some the Illuminati. This oligarchy controls the politicians, the courts, the educational institutions, the food, the natural resources, the foreign policies, the economics, and the money of most nations. And they control the major media, which is why we know nothing about them.'" Glancing at Epiphany, she said, "Do you think John bought into all of this?"

"I doubt it," Epiphany said. "He was very much the conscientious scholar, not much given to wild theories or undocumented rumors. Still ..." She looked back down at the paper she held. "This set of notes is all about the petroleum industry and its role in shaping history. 'The power of the dollar and the power of the U.S. military has been uniquely intertwined with one commodity, the basis of the world economic growth engine since before the First World War. That commodity is petroleum,'" she read.

"It goes on to point out that all of the major conflicts since that time have been about the oil industry, including World Wars One and Two, the founding of Israel, the development of British and American oil companies, the growth of American financial institutions, and finally the war in Iraq and subsequent chaos in the Middle East. All part of the plan to dominate the world on the part of a small group of hugely powerful stakeholders."

She flipped through more pages. "Banks, weapons manufacturers, pharmaceutical companies, big agriculture, the so-called seven sisters oil cartel—this does make an interesting if not thoroughly convincing case for some kind of secret global organization responsible for everything from wars to assassinations to who gets to be president of the U.S. Listen to this. The section ends with these words: 'Let no man vainly imagine that he can take on the Committee of 300 and win ... '"

"Okay," said Hannah. "Let's suppose some extra-legal, international entity is controlling everything. How exactly is that connected with the theft of the Blake and John Bernhardt's murder?"

"Let's follow the clues," said Epiphany. "Suppose Derrick Rarian is a member of the Committee of 300. Wealthy, connected, flying both above the law and under the radar. He has a kind of mania about collecting artworks that deal with petroleum, and embraces all the negative consequences of the industry. The company he represents, Ace Energy, has come to southeastern Ohio to search for yet more ways to extract money, in the form of petroleum, from the earth. This extraction will cause problems for the local population of people, critters, and plants, but who gives a rat's pitooty when there's money to be made?" She got up and began pacing in front of the darkened window.

"That is when one John Bernhardt gets in their way," she continued. "He objects to the destruction of people and the environment and, worse yet, does something about it by putting up an art exhibit calling attention to the punishment of corrupt and greedy rich folks, and then writes anti-fracking articles to alert the locals that they will be in deep doo-doo if Ace has its way." She stopped pacing and looked at Hannah.

"And that," said Hannah, "is when Ace has to go to work and stop this menace to the American Way of Life. They intimidate Hugh Stillman, bribe Ray Lucas, and instruct Chance Hilliburn to snatch the Blake."

"Spoils of war," Epiphany said.

"Then they take out John Bernhardt and make sure the police say he died of 'natural causes' and that there is no investigation into what really took place."

"And you know what?" said Epiphany.

"What?"

"They've gotten away with it."

Hannah looked back at the stack of papers before her. "Apparently," she said, "they always do."

On Wednesday morning, Epiphany called Maro and asked if he was available to meet with her and Hannah. An hour later, they were sitting on the sofa in Maro's hotel room near the university, sipping coffee and watching the rain trace vertical silver ribbons on the window.

Epiphany related the efforts she and Hannah had taken to try to pin down at least a scrap of evidence they could use against the suspects, but except for possibly charging Hugh Stillman with obstruction of justice or being an accessory to burglary, there was nothing of substance.

"Were you able to find out any more about Ray Lucas?" Epiphany asked.

"Everyone wants to let Ray off the hook," Maro said. " I keep hearing what a great guy he is and that he's been with the university forever and that he's been going through a rough time with his wife being sick and having to go up to Columbus to get treatments. It's like he's martyr of the month or something. However," —he pulled his cell phone from his coat pocket—"I was able to get some info on his finances. It seems he had two rather tidy sums of money deposited to his checking account. One last month for five thousand dollars. And another last Friday for the same amount." He looked at the two women and shrugged. "In both cases, the deposit was in cash, so no way to trace its source, but where would he find ten grand in cash lying around?"

"I didn't know you could access account info," Hannah said. "Isn't that sort of ... illegal?"

"Depends," Maro said with a smile.

"If his wife's sick, he probably needs the money," said Epiphany.

"That's motive," said Hannah. "And he certainly had the opportunity to help with the theft. He's the one who locked up the gallery after the Blake was stolen."

"And probably told Hugh to get rid of the security tapes," Epiphany added.

"But who would have paid him?" said Hannah.

"Rarian?" Epiphany suggested.

"I'll keep digging," Maro said, "and see if I can't get some more dirt on our Mr. Lucas. Meanwhile, I have another bit of news that may interest you."

Epiphany gave him a questioning look.

"I got word from a former colleague of mine in the Antiterrorist office that two guys were arrested at Heathrow yesterday. They came in on a flight from Columbus, Ohio, and had fake passports."

"What happened to them?" Epiphany asked.

"They were detained briefly, but weren't on any watch lists, so the agents let them go after they promised to show up in court and pay the fine."

"Oh, I'm *sure* they'll be happy to do that," said Hannah.

"Right. They're likely long gone by now," said Maro, "but it might answer the question of who took out Bernhardt."

"Do you have photos of them?" asked Epiphany.

"Right here." Maro scrolled briefly, then held the phone out to Epiphany. She stared at the photos of two young men with dark hair and frightened eyes.

"Maybe we could have Zoe take a look at them," she suggested. "She remembered seeing two guys outside the entrance to Siegfred Hall just before John was murdered."

"If she could ID them, at least we'd have a better idea of what happened," said Maro.

Zoe was in John Bernhardt's old office in Siegfred Hall when Maro, Hannah, and Epiphany arrived. She greeted them warmly and Maro explained the reason for the visit. Zoe was eager to help, but when she looked at the photos of the two young men, she shook her head.

"I really don't know. I didn't pay much attention to them at the time. They were young and had dark hair and looked foreign, but that's all I recall. The photos could be of them" —she shrugged—"or not."

Maro put the phone back in his pocket. "I think I'll see if I can trace their path after London. We might at least be able to find out their destination and have a better idea who hired them. I'm very concerned about their use of new weapons technology. Hate to see it get into the wrong hands."

"I'm sorry I wasn't more help," said Zoe.

"It was a long shot," Maro said. "Even if you were able to identify them, they're likely safe at home by now."

Chapter 30

When Hannah and Epiphany arrived at the farm, they were amazed to find the front door locked. “Mom never locks her door,” Epiphany said, giving the brass knob another twist. “I’ve been meaning to talk to her about why she should be more careful.”

“That’s odd,” Hannah said, looking around at the soggy landscape. The rain had stopped, but the sky was still a dull grey and the tree branches sagged with moisture. Then she pointed toward the driveway. “Look, Pip. Tire tracks. Looks like someone left in a hurry.”

The tires had gouged a path in the wet mud and gravel of the drive.

“Who could have been here?” Hannah wondered aloud.

“Maybe Sam came by to deliver Mom’s groceries or something.” Epiphany turned around and gave the door knob another yank, then knocked. After pounding on the door two more times, she started toward the steps. “Let’s try the kitchen door.”

“God, I hope she’s okay,” Hannah said.

Then the front door opened and there was Susan, dressed in a plaid house dress, a gingham apron around her waist. "Fanny! I saw you through the window. Thank goodness you're here!" Susan hobbled across the porch to embrace her daughter.

"What happened, Mom? Who was here?"

"He said his name was Chance," Susan said as Epiphany helped her inside and eased her down on the sofa. "I wouldn't have let him in, but he said he was a friend of yours."

"Chance?" Epiphany said. "Chance Hilliburn?"

"That's it. Hilliburn. I remembered you mentioning him."

"I wouldn't call him a friend."

"I figured that out pretty quick." Susan shuddered. "He's very disagreeable."

"What did he want?"

Susan shook her head. "Fanny, could you get me a glass of water please?"

Epiphany hurried to the kitchen. When she returned, Hannah was holding Susan's hand.

"Thank you, dear," Susan said. She took a gulp of water, set the glass down on the sidetable, and looked at Epiphany. "He wants to buy the farm."

"What?!" Epiphany cried. "Why on earth—"

"He said the company he works for, Ace something, wants the land to expand their business in the area, and that they would pay above market value for the property."

"What did you tell him?' Epiphany said.

"I told him no, of course," Susan replied indignantly. "I told him my home is not for sale at any price."

Epiphany and Hannah exchanged looks. Epiphany turned back to her mother. "Then what did he do?"

"He laughed. Can you imagine, Fanny? He laughed and said I would change my mind. I told him to leave, and he stomped out and took off like a bull out of a barn. Spewed gravel all over the lawn."

"I saw the tire tracks," Epiphany said.

"Dreadful man. Just plain ugly."

"So that's why you locked the door," said Epiphany.

"I was afraid he'd come back," Susan said.

"You did the right thing, Mom. Be sure you keep that door locked, okay?"

"I just hate that," Susan said. "I've always welcomed guests into my home. It's the neighborly thing to do."

"Well," said Hannah, "Mr. Hilliburn isn't exactly neighborly."

"He certainly isn't," Susan agreed.

Hannah and Epiphany stayed up until after midnight, sitting at the kitchen table going through the stack of John's files that they had borrowed from Francesca. The night outside was sultry, the air filled with moisture. Epiphany could hear the drip-drip-drip of water from the branches of the buckeye trees. Two moths were battering themselves against the window in a hopeless battle to get inside.

"I wish we knew what we're looking for," Epiphany said with a yawn. She put down one file and picked up the next.

"Yeah," said Hannah. "*Anything relevant* is sort of a broad category."

"I appreciate John's thorough research on the finer points of Dante's descriptions and how they correspond to the illustrations created by the artists in the exhibit, but what we need is something that explains why he was targeted by Ace, aside from the fact that they didn't like his journalism."

"I've gone through a bunch of articles from various sources that he used as references for his articles," said Hannah, "but they're pretty general. Mostly descriptions of the fracking process and reports of environmental issues that might be related to it." She put down the manila folder she was holding and began twisting her neck in slow circles. "We need something specific."

"Wait a minute," Epiphany said. "I think I may have found something. Look at this."

Hannah got up and leaned over Epiphany's shoulder. "What is it?"

"A letter from the Department of the Interior and a bunch of statistics about earthquake hazards in southeastern Ohio. There's also a letter from a geologist at Ohio State in Columbus. And John's notes on the connection between fracking and how it would affect this area if all of the permits that have been issued moved forward and were operational."

The two women scanned the pages. "Good Lord," Hannah said. "This indicates that fracking operations could destabilize the bedrock that runs for about one-hundred-twenty miles through the whole central and southern section of Ohio. Listen to this. 'This map shows a possible fault that was only recently discovered after fracking activities along the northern section of the fault resulted in the brittle sedimentary rock collapsing, causing an earthquake that registered 5.0, larger than any other quakes ever recorded in the area. The sandstone along the fault is formed by the consolidation and cementation of layers of loose sand held together by silica or iron oxide that can destabilize under pressure.'"

"And then it goes on, 'Ground motion from seismic waves tends to be magnified by thick deposits of clay or sand and gravel of the type found in southeastern Ohio. These waves tend to travel for very long distances throughout thousands of square miles even in a moderate-sized earthquake. Damaging ground motion would occur in an area about ten times larger than for a California earthquake of comparable intensity.'"

Hannah and Epiphany looked at each other. "This is why John had to be eliminated. He was going to use this evidence to warn people about the horrendous consequences that Ace's fracking program could initiate."

"So they brought in a couple of hit men with no ties to the area and used a secret new weapon to murder John, knowing that none of the local officials would understand what happened," said Hannah.

Epiphany nodded. "John's death is only partially connected to the theft of the Blake. It's really about shutting him up so he wouldn't stir up anti-fracking sentiment and alert people to the risks involved."

"So the theft was a sort of red herring," said Hannah. "It was meant to distract everyone from the real crime, which was John's murder."

"Exactly."

"But what can we do? There's no evidence."

"We need to talk to Maro again," said Epiphany.

Chapter 31

"I'm going to have to leave town for a couple of weeks," Maro said. "I've been suboenaed to testify in a case I worked on last year and it may take some time."

"Can't I do something?" Epiphany's voice echoed her frustration. "Go to the FBI or some other agency?"

"You could try, I suppose. But I don't think you'd get very far."

"Why not?" Hannah said.

Maro sighed. "It's complicated. See, the Bureau is a very convoluted beast. It's a lot about turf and bureaucracy—like the military. The art crimes agents are like tiny fleas on the back of a huge dog. They can be a nuisance, but they can't throw their weight around because they don't have much to throw. Also, as far as the bosses are concerned, they aren't much interested in recovering stolen property such as art. They're more interested in getting arrests and convictions.

"Look," he continued when Epiphany and Hannah stared at him, "the FBI is very decentralized. There are fifty-six field offices spread around the country. The head of each office takes charge of his 'turf.' Investigations are run by the agents in the field office where the crime occurred. Since there's no office in Athens, an agent would have to work out of the Cincinnati office."

"And they're not particularly interested in art crimes?" Epiphany guessed.

"Nope. Bank robberies. Frauds and forgeries. Money-laundering. Drugs. Supervisors are rotated in and out of offices, and most of them don't give a damn about art crime. That's one reason I … retired."

"Then they're willing to just let Rarian get away with stealing the Blake?" Hannah asked.

"One of my contacts told me they've determined it will be increasingly difficult to gather enough evidence to prosecute him. Hell," he added, "the Blake could be hanging above the sofa in his St. Moritz condo by now, so even if we dug up enough evidence to get a search warrant, we'd likely come up empty." He looked from one dismayed face to the other. "I'm truly sorry, ladies, but at this point there's nothing more I can do."

Epiphany looked despondent. "This just gets worse and worse," she said. "I know Chance stole the art, and that Hugh and Ray Lucas helped him and that Rarian has the Blake. And I also know that they were involved in murdering John Bernhardt. Likely because he was speaking out against the company Chance and Rarian work for. And yet there's no way to make them pay for what they've done?"

"That's about the size of it," Maro said. "At least for now."

"Well, that … sucks!" Epiphany said.

Maro gave a thin smile and Hannah laughed aloud. "Nicely put, Pip," she said.

"Seriously," Epiphany said, giving Maro a stern look, "isn't there anything we can do to continue our own investigation of John's death?"

Maro shook his head. "You should at least wait until I can work with you."

"When will that be?"

"I really can't say." Noting Epiphany's scowl he continued, "Look, please don't do anything more just now. It could be dangerous. Don't underestimate these guys."

"I have to find out what happened," Epiphany replied. "I owe it to John."

For a long moment, Maro looked down at the grey-green hotel room carpet. Then he glanced up and said, "I have a friend in Columbus. She's in the state legislature, recently elected and full of optimism. She's been leading the charge against allowing more fracking in the region, so I'm sure she'd be sympathetic to your cause. I'll give her a call and see if she has time to get in touch. The legislature is in recess right now, so this would be a good time to talk to her."

"What's her name?" Hannah asked.

"Bea," said Maro. "Bea Falco."

Maro, true to his word, set up the meeting before leaving for Chicago. The next day, Epiphany was seated in a white wicker chair on Senator Falco's veranda.

"It's not that they don't understand what we're saying," the senator said. "They understand quite well and that's the problem. The very idea of climate change goes directly to the source of their funding, the fossil fuel industry." Bea Falco reached for her glass of iced tea and took a drink. Then she continued, "In terms of political leverage in the Republican Party, nothing comes close to the power of the fossil-fuel conglomerates and their demand for deregulation so they can drill, dig, and pollute at will. So they have to deny the concept of climate change. It's a deal-breaker."

"But if they understand the consequences, how can they go on doing what they're doing?" Epiphany asked. "If they don't care about themselves, you'd think they'd care about their children. And their grandchildren."

"You'd think," Bea agreed. "But faced with the choice of amassing ever larger amounts of material wealth or protecting the lives of their children and the health of the planet, they have chosen the former and the only way to live with that is to deny that there is a problem. The only other alternative is to deliberately embrace evil."

"Rarian," Epiphany said.

"Excuse me?" Bea's dark eyes flickered with interest.

"Derrick Rarian. Do you know him?"

"I know *of* him," she said. "VP at Ace. But how do you know him?"

"Long story," Epiphany replied. "But I just recalled something he said. I was talking to him about his art collection, and he said he made money by destroying beautiful things, but he had embraced the beauty of destruction. He had transcended evil and would neither condemn nor celebrate the consequences of his passion."

"Interesting," Bea said. She was silent for several minutes, thinking.

Epiphany studied her. She was a small woman with short-cropped gray hair and a round face, yet she had an aura of energy about her, something strong and determined. Sturdy, Epiphany's Dad would have called it. Perhaps it was the way she held her head—slightly tilted, chin thrust forward. Or maybe it was the way she moved—deliberately but with an economy of motion.

Bea's home was a rustic log house with ample porches running the length of both front and back. Bea told Epiphany the house had been in her family for two generations, and that after her husband, Damian, a geologist at Ohio State University, had passed away a year ago, Bea had moved back to take over the homestead.

Epiphany felt an immediate kinship. The house sat on the top of a gentle rise surrounded by twenty acres of pasture that stretched out to a line of oaks and hickory trees. The place was an easy drive—about sixty miles—from Susan's farm in Mt. Eden. Hannah, concerned that Chance might try to further intimidate Susan, had opted to stay with Epiphany's mother while Epiphany traveled to meet Bea Falco.

"I read your late husband's essay on Ohio earthquakes," Epiphany said.

Bea looked up. "Where'd you find that?" she said. "It was never published."

"I came across a draft of it in John Bernhardt's papers. I think he planned to use it as a source for the third antifracking article that he was writing for the Athens newspaper. But, of course, that article never got finished. Or published."

Bea nodded. "Figures. Too bad Dr. Bernhardt died before he had a chance to finish the good work he was doing. We can use help from the academic world trying to educate the public. Too often the academics keep a low profile. I expect they don't want to lose grant funds, or get the state legislature angry at them. They've lost enough funding as it is."

"How did your husband die?" Epiphany asked.

Bea gave her a sharp look.

"I'm sorry to be so personal," said Epiphany, "but if you don't mind telling me, I'd like to know the cause of death."

"He had a heart attack," said Bea. "It was rather sudden. We had no idea he had a heart problem."

An image flashed into Epiphany's mind—a dark-haired man in a white lab coat lying facedown on a grey vinyl tile floor. "He died at work?"

"Yes, he did. He was in his lab at the Ohio Seismic Network where he worked as a geologist monitoring seismic activity in the region. I found him there when he didn't come home after work. I called and called, but there was no answer, so I drove to the lab and …" She took a deep breath. "It was quite a shock."

"I'm sure it was."

"But how did you—"

"I … see things," Epiphany said. "I guess Maro didn't mention that I work as a psychic."

"No. He said you were a former student of Dr. Bernhardt's and that you were following up on his involvement with the antifracking campaign."

"That's true. But I'm also trying to find out how John Bernhardt died."

"I thought it was a heart attack," said Bea.

"So they say. Although he had no previous history of heart problems."

Bea's dark eyes stared into Epiphany's. "Just like my Damian." She frowned. "But surely there's no connection." Her eyes searched Epiphany's face. "Is there?"

"I don't know. But here's what I *do* know." She told Bea about the heart attack gun, the so-called HAG. And she said that Maro seemed concerned that the weapon had somehow fallen into the hands of criminals hired by Ace Energy to eliminate their opposition.

"Maro didn't say anything about that to me," Bea said.

"It's almost impossible to prove that a heart attack was caused by the HAG," said Epiphany. "I expect he didn't want to put you through a long, costly investigation that would likely come up empty-handed."

"The publicity probably wouldn't have helped my

campaign. As it was, I got the sympathy vote." She smiled. "Damian would have loved that."

"Really?"

"He had a quirky sense of humor."

"He wants you to know that he's proud of you," Epiphany said.

Bea gave Epiphany a quizzical look. She opened her mouth to speak, then closed it and turned away. After a minute, she turned back and said, "Let's talk about what we're up against, shall we? If Damian's death was somehow involved, it wouldn't surprise me. His most recent data on the connection between fracking and earthquakes is very convincing, and the oil and gas industries are determined to keep that kind of evidence out of the hands of the public."

Epiphany listened while Bea related a brief history of what had been going on since the late nineteen-seventies when ExxonMobil discovered through their own investigation that the climate was being disrupted, and that their product—petroleum—was responsible. Bea quoted an industry study that in 1982 determined that "Mitigation of the greenhouse effect would require major reductions in fossil fuel combustion. There is concern among scientific groups that once the effects are measurable, they might not be reversible … Some potentially catastrophic events must be considered."

"And yet they made no attempt to warn the public or change their operations?" Epiphany said.

"No. Instead they spent the next three decades and millions of dollars lying about what they knew in an effort to slow any action and protect their profits."

"Sounds a lot like the tobacco industry," Epiphany noted.

"Absolutely," said Bea. "In the case of the tobacco industry, the Department of Justice took action by prosecuting the tobacco companies under a piece of legislation called the

Racketeer Influenced and Corrupt Organizations Act. The law states that no company can knowingly mislead the public in an attempt to protect profits at the expense of our health, safety and national interest. The tobacco industry had to pay two hundred billion dollars in 1998 to settle a suit with the DOJ, and there's plenty of evidence that Exxon committed the same kind of crime."

"Then why haven't they been investigated?" Epiphany asked.

"There have been some local investigations in New York, and a few Congressional leaders have called for a study," Bea said, "but unfortunately too many politicians are indebted to the oil industry for their careers. They don't want to bite the hand that feeds them. So they scuttle the calls for investigation and attack the investigators with charges of being alarmists, if not outright liars. And the cartel is so big and so powerful—corrupt officials, chambers of commerce, organized crime, the international corporate oligarchs."

"You've been at this awhile, haven't you?"

Bea nodded. "I was an attorney for an environmental group called Earth Justice for a number of years before I decided to go into politics. This battle's nothing new for me. But" —she looked out at the green expanse of pasture and the dark line of the tree rim—"it hasn't gotten any easier."

"But you've stayed at it?"

Bea smiled. "A wise man once said, 'The greatest sin is to see something that's morally evil and do nothing.'"

Part IV

The eyes of the future are looking back at us and they are praying for us to see beyond our own time.

—Terry Tempest Williams, American author and conservationist

Chapter 32

The drive back to Mt. Eden was uneventful except for the fog that began to drift across the low hills and settle into the hollows. Epiphany drove east along the edge of Tar Hollow State Park, a wilderness area of deep ravines and dense woodlands. Shortleaf and pitch pines grew along the ridges of the Appalachian foothills, a source of pine tar for the early settlers in the region who used it to lubricate their wagons and other equipment—the forerunner of WD40.

She arrived at the farm just before dark. The welcoming glow of lights in the windows reminded her of her childhood, of the happiness she felt when she finished her chores and was anticipating the warmth of the kitchen and the smell of something good for dinner. The thought made her sad for what was lost and happy for what had been. The double edge of memory.

Hannah greeted her knock at the locked door. "Hi, Pip. How'd it go with the senator?"

"I'll tell you over dinner. Everything okay around here?"

"No problems."

Epiphany let out a sigh of relief.

"Hi, hon. Dinner's almost ready," Susan sang from the kitchen.

Epiphany and Hannah exchanged smiles. "Hard to starve around here," Hannah said.

Susan had cooked a large platter of fried smelts for dinner—little fish about the size of sardines that were crisply delicious. And best eaten with your fingers, Epiphany told Hannah, demonstrating the technique. Hannah praised the tangy coleslaw, and Epiphany reminded her mother that she was still waiting for Susan's special recipe. "Michael and Maddie will be so happy," she said. "Every time we have coleslaw, all they can talk about is how good Grandma Susan's is."

Over dinner, Epiphany told Hannah and Susan about her meeting with Bea Falco and the strange "coincidence" of her husband's death by heart attack.

"That's got to be connected," Hannah remarked.

After finishing up the dinner dishes, everyone decided to turn in early and take up the subject of Bea's information in the morning.

Epiphany realized when she got into bed that she was exhausted. It had been an intense week of meetings that led to revelations (Hugh's admitted involvement in the theft), disappointments (Maro leaving), scares (Chance's visit to Susan), and new allies (Bea Falco). Her head was swimming with facts and possibilities and half-formed plans. She fell immediately into a deep sleep.

She is running through the woods. The tree branches slap at her face, and she flails her arms at them. She can see a bright light in the distance, an orange glow that is moving, undulating, spurting upward like lava from a volcano. She is afraid the trees will catch fire. Ash is drifting around her like heavy snow, covering the ground with a gray slush. It is harder and harder to keep running. She can barely lift her feet.

"Pip! Wake up!" Hannah's voice sliced though the dream.

"What? What's happening?" Epiphany said with groggy alarm.

"The barn's on fire! Come on. Get up!"

Epiphany sat up. The window was aglow with orange light and she could smell the smoke.

"Where's Mom?" she asked.

"Downstairs. We called the fire department."

"Lord," Epiphany said, throwing off the covers. "It'll take the volunteers a while to get here." She got unsteadily to her feet and groped for her robe.

"What should we do?" Hannah cried.

"I'll call Sam Miller," Epiphany told Hannah. "I'm sure he'll come give us a hand until the firetruck gets here. You stay with Mom. Don't let her do anything foolish."

Hannah disappeared and Epiphany found Sam on her cell phone contact list. She told him what had happened and he said he'd be right over. Then she found her jeans and a sweater, pulled on her clothes and hurried downstairs.

Susan was standing by the window, hugging herself and weeping while Hannah tried to comfort her. "Thank God," Susan said, "we don't still have the horses. I couldn't bear that."

Epiphany heard a car coming up the drive and ran out to meet Sam. He gave her a quick hug. "You got a couple of hoses we can hook up?" he said. "We might as well try to slow it down 'til the truck gets here."

The next half-hour was a blur of activity. Sam and Epiphany did what they could with two garden hoses as Susan and Hannah watched helplessly from the front porch.

The fire truck finally arrived, careening up the driveway and parking in front of the barn. The four volunteers jumped out and began pulling out equipment and connecting hoses.

They went about their business calmly but with energy, and took control of the efforts to douse the flames.

Exhausted, Sam and Epiphany joined Hannah and Susan on the porch and watched the spectacle, huddling together like anxious sheep.

In the end, the barn was pretty much a total loss, but the damage was confined to the structure itself and didn't affect the pump house, garden shed or other nearby buildings.

The firemen stayed until they were certain the fire was out, then began loading up their equipment. One of the men came up to the porch and apologized for not being able to do more. "Any idea how it started?" he asked.

"None," Susan said. "Nobody's been out there for at least a week."

The fireman frowned. "Well, *somebody* was out there. We saw footprints in the mud on the far side of the building. And some tire tracks too."

"That's very strange," Hannah said. "I was here all day and I didn't see anyone. Except the mailman. He drove up to deliver a package, but it turned out to be the wrong address." She and Epiphany exchanged glances.

"Mom," Epiphany asked. "Did you see the mailman?"

"I was taking a nap," said Susan. "But Hannah took care of it."

The fireman looked back at what remained of the barn. Charred posts stood at strange angles beneath the partially caved-in roof, as if struggling to keep it from further collapse. "I'm going to recommend that somebody come take a look, if that's okay with you folks. The sheriff might want to investigate. Seems strange to me, just catchin' fire for no reason."

Sam stayed until the firetruck left. Epiphany walked him out to his car. He looked grave and was strangely quiet. As he slid in behind the wheel, he looked up at Epiphany and said, "You be careful, hear? Keep your eyes open."

Epiphany nodded. "I will."

"I'd be real surprised," Sam said, "if this was an accident."

A deputy arrived the next morning, even though it was Saturday, and made a show of poking through the rubble and collecting little samples of this and that. He interviewed Susan and Hannah and made some additional notes, then put away his clipboard and stood looking at the ruins. A few wisps of smoke still curled from the smoldering wood.

"I don't know," he said, pushing his cap back on his head. "I can't find any signs of arson."

"What about the footprints and tire tracks?" Hannah asked.

"Coulda been made by the vols," he said. "They mean well, but they just don't have much trainin'. Don't pay attention to details." He handed the three women a concerned smile. "I might could send along an arson forensics team. I'll see what the chief wants to do."

After he left, Epiphany said to Hannah, "I wouldn't bet on seeing any forensics team." She watched the patrol car leave the drive and turn onto the main road.

"Another cover-up?" Hannah said.

"And another warning."

Chapter 33

That afternoon, Hannah drove Susan into town to help her do some shopping. Epiphany opted to stay at the farm. She took the opportunity to conduct her own investigation of the fire scene.

The air was warm and muggy, and the sunlight seemed to be filtered through a murky haze. Some of the barn's larger beams were still oozing smoke. They lay strewn across what had been the barn floor like fallen warriors on a charred battlefield.

Epiphany shuffled through the ashes, kicking at clumps of shingles and stopping to examine bits of burned cloth and blistered metal. Susan had tried to remember what was still stored in the barn, but didn't think there was anything important. "Old tractor tires, maybe a few bags of horse feed. I haven't been out there for—goodness, likely a couple of years."

The remains of a canning cupboard revealed some broken jars filled with what could have been green beans, though they looked more like blackened pencil stubs—all that remained of a final harvest. Epiphany stood still for a moment, remembering harvests past. Putting by the summer's bounty of tomatoes, beans, peaches. Helping her mother wash the canning jars and boil the lids and line up the finished array of homegrown provisions that would last the family through the winter.

"Them was good days, wasn't they?"

Epiphany started at the voice, then saw the Old Man standing a few feet to her left in front of the charred remains of a manger. "Yes," she said, nodding. "Very good."

"They's still here, you know," he said. "Long as you remember them."

"I'll always remember," she murmured. Then, looking around at the carnage, she added, "Who could have done this?" The moment she said the words, Chance's face came into her mind.

"That's right," the Old Man said. "He's the one does the dirty work all right."

The two hounds suddenly appeared, one on each side of the Old Man. Bounder, the larger of the two, looked at Epiphany and whined. Then he trotted to what was left of the doorway and stopped to look back at her. He whined again.

"He can help you," the Old Man said.

Epiphany started toward the door. The hound waited for her, then began to sniff and paw at a clump of rubble.

"Found something, have you?" She looked at the blackened pile, but didn't see anything. Bounder began to dig furiously with both paws. Then he stopped and let out a yelp.

Epiphany dug at the clump with her foot, then tried to brush away the mass of wet ash. There was something beneath the muck. When she saw four stiff fingers sticking up through the mud, she gasped and stepped back. Then she realized she was looking at a glove. It had stiffened from the water and slush. Gingerly, she bent down and pulled it out. It was a work glove, the kind a gardener might use. The fabric was partially burned, but she could tell it had originally been thick grey leather with a red-plaid stripe around the cuff. And what was left of the leather looked surprisingly new.

"It's not mine, that's for sure," Susan said.

"Could it belong to Sam?" Hannah asked.

Susan shook her head. "I don't think so. Never saw him wearing any gloves like that. Guess we could ask him."

"I looked it up online," said Epiphany. "It's not just any old garden glove. It's a special safety glove that's meant to protect a person from strong chemicals or sparks from electrical equipment. They cost around a hundred dollars."

"Goodness!" exclaimed Susan. "A hundred dollars for a pair of gloves?"

"Maybe one of the firefighters?" said Hannah.

"Possibly," Epiphany said. "I'm going to check it out."

The next day was Sunday, so Epiphany decided she should wait until Monday to try to trace the owner of the glove. In the meantime, she and Hannah read over their notes and put together a list of what they needed to do.

"We should talk to Hugh Stillman again," Epiphany said. "I think he's still hiding something."

"That's one scared puppy," Hannah agreed. "They really got to him."

"He said they'd go after his family if he talked to us. But who is *they*? Chance? Rarian? I'm confused."

"If only we could find that high tech gun that killed John. At least then we could make a case for a larger investigation."

"I'm going to try a remote-viewing experiment," said Epiphany, "and see if I can get a fix on the gun's location."

She waited until dusk was just beginning to fall— that blissfully peaceful period just after sunset when the sky becomes transparent but stars are not yet visible. Following the path that led across the meadow toward the creek, she sat down halfway across the field, in the midst of an outcropping of wild flowers that looked like miniature daisies.

Using the relaxation techniques she learned early in her training, Epiphany quieted her mind's internal chatter and directed her attention to an image of the HAG, the secret heart-attack gun developed by the CIA to carry out assassinations that would be undetectable.

The image of the gun was very clear—a modified Colt Government 1911 pistol that looked like a standard semiautomatic revolver with a straight barrel and a simple, straight grip.

Once she established the target subject, Epiphany gathered her energy and projected her biophysical awareness toward the target, carefully sweeping across the general area of the OU campus, and zooming in on areas near Siegfred Hall where John had been shot.

Nothing.

She tried again, this time zooming out to cover a larger range. When the gun still failed to show up, she modified her approach by not limiting her search to a specific place, but just allowing herself to coast as though riding on a slow wave.

Water. Not running like a creek, but rippling quietly, lapping at a muddy shoreline. She is above a lake looking down at it, but not from a high altitude. Steps lead down to the water. A staircase or ladder. And a sort of platform made of wood.

Then she is right above the surface of the water, looking down to the murky bottom. There is something lying there, almost totally submerged in the mud. It's difficult to tell the size of the object since there is nothing to compare it with, but Epiphany is certaint it is the HAG.

But where is she? A lake. But what lake? Where? Epiphany glances around, but there is just the lake and the distant treeline and a bit of rolling pasture. She relaxes, floats, calms her mind. And catches sight of a little white sign that says *Dow*.

Chapter 34

"Dow Lake? It's in Strouds Run Park," Susan said. "You remember, don't you, Fanny? We used to take a picnic and go there with our friends the Gilmores. You and little Andrew had a great time playing hide-and-seek, and getting into all sorts of mischief."

Epiphany remembered a little. How old was she—four? Maybe five? A lake and lots of dandelions. And one time a strawberry cake. Okay. That was Strouds Run Park. And the lake was named Dow.

"What should I do?" she asked Hannah. "Go to the authorities and say 'I think there's a top secret CIA heart-attack gun in Dow Lake?'"

Hannah rolled her eyes and took another bite of blueberry muffin.

"What about that nice young man from the insurance company?" Susan said.

"Maro? I think he went back to Chicago. He said he had to testify in a trial and didn't know when he would be able to come back to work on this case."

"What about Sam?" Hannah said. "Maybe he'd have an idea."

"Worth a try, I guess," Epiphany said.

Sam came over about an hour later and sat on the porch

with Hannah and Epiphany. Epiphany told him the whole story about the two young foreigners John had seen outside Siegfred Hall. And about the little wound in John's neck. And Maro's concern about the secret gun.

"You mean it really leaves no trace?" Sam said, his eyes widening. "Not even in the blood?"

"The toxin dissolves quickly," said Epiphany. "Someone would have to do a blood test in the first half-hour after delivery, and they'd have to know to test for that particular poison."

"And since the toxin mimics heart attack symptoms, most first responders would be busy dealing with cardiac arrest, not testing for an exotic poison," Hannah added.

Sam considered. "A perfect murder weapon."

"Pretty much."

"And you think that's what happened to John Bernhardt? The two foreign guys shot him, and then disappeared and dumped the gun in Dow Lake?"

"I know it sounds bizarre," said Epiphany, "but I think that's what happened."

"And," Hannah added, "we think Chance Hilliburn set fire to the barn." She looked at Epiphany. "Tell him about the glove."

In doing her earlier online research on the mysterious glove, Epiphany found that the same type of glove was often used by oil-rig workers. She was certain the glove belonged to an Ace Energy employee, but how to prove it?

They went over the sequence of events. After half an hour, Sam sat back and nodded slowly. "This is all starting to add up. You've figured out who stole the art work and how, who has the stolen work, why John Bernhardt was murdered and who did it. And now you've located the murder weapon."

"But what do we do now?" Epiphany asked. "The local

police don't want to deal with it. Even the PI pulled out. Our witnesses are too scared to come forward."

"Ace Energy seems to be able to do whatever they like, and no one will stand up to them," said Hannah.

"No surprise there," Sam said, his mouth twisting with anger.

"Pip, maybe we could … Pip?"

But Epiphany was looking out at the pasture, fixated on something, her eyes following an arc across the cloudless sky. "Falcon," she said softly. Then she turned to Hannah. "We need to talk to Bea Falco."

It took a week to set up an appointment with Senator Falco. Hannah and Epiphany drove to Columbus. The Senate Office Building, part of the Capitol Square complex, was located about three blocks from the Scioto River that ran through downtown Columbus. Bea's office was on the second floor. She greeted them warmly and Epiphany introduced Hannah. They quickly brought Bea up to speed on their investigation and the latest discovery—the location of the murder weapon.

"So," Bea said, "you've been to the local authorities, but they have been dragging their feet?"

"They won't even send a forensic unit to check out the barn fire. Even after I found that strange glove in the debris."

"Stonewalling." Bea shook her head. "Ace must have really gotten to these people."

"They certainly got to Hugh Stillman," Epiphany said.

"And apparently to the police as well," added Hannah.

"Is there anything else we can do?" Epiphany asked.

"The state's attorney general can initiate an investigation," said Bea, "especially if there is an issue of potential environmental damage that would impact public health. But that's only part of the problem, right? We also have the theft of a work of art and a potential murder case. Plus arson and criminal intimidation. That's a bunch of bad stuff. The sorry thing is we lack evidence. Even the FBI seems willing to wait it out and hope the missing Blake will wind up on an auction list."

"But what about the HAG?" Epiphany said. "And the glove? Aren't those physical evidence?"

"Potentially." Bea was silent for a moment, thinking. "Let me do some digging. I want to run this past a few of my colleagues and see their reaction."

As Epiphany and Hannah prepared to leave, she shook their hands and said, "I'll get back to you at the end of the week. Let me know of any new developments."

Hannah and Epiphany got back from Columbus just before dark. The western sky had turned red-violet from the particles of dust and smoke that hung in the atmosphere.

"I wish it would rain," Hannah said. "Maybe it would clear out some of this smog."

They pulled into the driveway. Susan waved to them from the porch. Epiphany turned off the motor, but didn't move to get out.

"Pip? What's up?"

Epiphany turned to Hannah. "Maro," she said. "We need to contact Maro."

"Why?"

"Once he knows we found the HAG, he'll be back on the case."

The next morning, Epiphany was finally able to reach Maro's office after several tries. He was not available, but she left a request for him to call her.

Meanwhile, she decided to drive into Athens and see if she could convince Hugh Stillman to help them. "I need to let him know it might be safer to help us now than to wait for a subpoena if we do get anywhere with our investigation," she told Hannah.

Hannah decided to stay at the farm and do some research on the computer. Maybe there had been similar cases in the past that might provide a template for action.

The end of summer appeared to be dragging across the landscape. The leaves of the maple trees were not yet displaying any fall color, but they were yellow around the edges. Everything was drooping—tall grass bending wearily toward the ground, bushes partially devoured by clouds of grasshoppers. Epiphany took the back road through Wayne National Forest, but even the fir trees looked ragged and sad.

The OU campus was nearly deserted. Summer classes were over and the fall term had yet to begin. Epiphany parked the car in front of the Kennedy Museum and started up the walk, but she heard someone call her name and turned to see Chance Hilliburn coming toward her. She felt a shock of cold air, even though the sun was shining brightly. "Mr. Hilliburn," she said. "What brings you to the Kennedy?"

He made no attempt to disguise his anger, staring at her

with his small, mean eyes. "Ms. Mayall," he said, "I was just thinking about paying you a visit."

"Really? And why is that?"

He glared at her with such venom she had to stop herself from stepping back. *Don't let fear cloud your judgement.*

His mouth twisted in a lewd grin. "I'm on to you, missy."

"Oh?"

"Yessir, I checked you out. And I have a word of advice for you."

"Do you?"

"Yeah." He took a menacing step toward her, but she held her ground. "You oughta just go back to that wacko camp in Florida where you came from. And keep your mouth shut."

Epiphany bristled. "I don't believe that you—"

"Who put you up to this anyway?" Chance narrowed his eyes. "Was it that slimy little Jap from the insurance company?"

Now *that* made her angry. "You're nothing but a cheap bully," she said through clenched teeth.

"Get the fuck out of here!" he shouted, his face red with rage. "Or you'll wish you had!"

Epiphany appraised him with contempt. "No, Mr. Hilliburn. I intend to stay right here and keep putting the pieces of the puzzle together until I nail your mangy ass. Now get out of my way."

She started to brush past him, but he grabbed her arm. His bloated face was inches from hers. "You're making a big mistake. Don't say I didn't warn you."

With that, he let go of her arm and gave her a push. She stumbled, but caught herself and glared at him. "Go to hell," she said.

Chapter 35

Epiphany was still shaking with anger as she walked into the museum's reception area. Gretchen was not at the desk. In fact, the place seemed deserted. "Hello?" she called.

A security guard appeared in the gallery doorway. "I'm sorry, ma'am, but the museum is closed."

"Then maybe you should lock the door."

He gave her a sheepish grin. "I was just fixin' to do that."

"Is Mr. Stillman here by any chance?" she asked.

The guard shook his head. "Everbody's off this week for vacation. They'll be back the last week of August."

Great, Epiphany thought as she turned to leave. She felt the whole investigation evaporating, slipping through her fingers. Maybe it was time to get out of Dodge.

When she got to the car, she checked her cell phone to see if Maro had called. But the phone was dead. She realized she'd forgotten to charge it. One stupid mistake after another.

On the drive back to Mt. Eden she considered her options: stay and try to figure out a way to initiate a full investigation of John's murder. But it was still not listed as a murder. And how could she prove it was? Even if she managed to produce the alleged murder weapon, the HAG, there was no way to connect the discarded gun to John's "heart attack." The two young men were long gone—probably back in the Middle

East and unreachable. Even if Hugh Stillman was willing to testify, all he knew was that Chance and Ray Lucas had taken the Blake. She couldn't even prove that Derrick Rarian was in possession of the stolen artwork. I've got nothing, she told herself. This was so discouraging. And Chance's words came back to her: *You're making a big mistake. Don't say I didn't warn you.* He might not just harm her. He might go after Hannah. Or Susan. Or even her family in Florida.

Or, she could give up and go back to Florida. Her granddaughter Maddie would be starting the new school year in less than two weeks, and Epiphany felt she should be there. She shouldn't leave her son Michael all alone with too much work to take care of—running the house, helping Maddie, taking care of the cat, plus trying to get his own classes at Linden College underway. She knew he wouldn't complain, but she felt guilty.

So, what to do next?

A strong scent of clove. And then the fragrance of roses. Where did that come from?

She is suddenly aware of someone sitting next to her. She glances to her right and sees a lovely young woman sitting in the passenger seat. Her profile is exquisite, ethereal. Her skin a perfect creamy porcelain and her long blond hair is pulled back and arranged in a loose bun at the back of her head. A few golden tendrils curl down around her neck.

Epiphany pulls off the road and stops the car. As it comes to a halt, the woman turns to her and says, "I am Susan Travis, your great-great-grandmother. I have a message for you."

"Susan," Epiphany whispers. "Albert said you would come to me."

The woman smiles. "And here I am." Her clear blue eyes fix Epiphany with an intense gaze. "You must stay yet a while longer in this place," the woman says in her soft, calm voice.

"Your mother is strong, but she will need your help. Will you stay?"

"Of course," Epiphany says in a low voice. "Of course I will."

The woman nods. "Thank you," she says. And disappears.

"Maro called," Hannah announced as Epiphany walked into the living room.

"Thank goodness. What did he say?"

Hannah waved a post-it note at her. "He said to call this number."

He picked up on the second ring. "Gaido here."

"Maro? It's Epiphany."

"Thanks for calling back. Hannah told me you had some important news. She wanted you to talk to me directly."

"I know where the HAG is."

She heard him inhale. "Where is it?"

"In Dow Lake. That's a reservoir not far from the campus here in Athens. Someone must have ditched the gun in the lake on their way out of town."

"Then you've seen it?" he asked.

"Well," she paused, "I've *envisioned* it. But I'm sure it's there," she added quickly.

There was a moment's silence. "Okay … I need to make a phone call. I'll be right back in touch."

"Right back" ended up being two hours, but then Maro called to say he was heading for Ohio and would be staying at the Campus Inn in Athens. "I should be there by dinner time," he said.

"Shall we meet you tomorrow morning at the Inn?" said Epiphany.

"I'll be there."

There was a significant thunderstorm that night—grand bursts of lightning and rolling volleys of thunder. Epiphany hoped Maro's plane had gotten to Columbus before the fireworks started.

The next morning was bright and noticeably cooler, another harbinger of fall. Hannah and Epiphany parked across the street from the Inn and found Maro waiting for them in the lobby. He was dressed in jeans and a black tee shirt. His dark hair was cut short and he wore sunglasses, even though he was inside. Some kind of disguise? He tossed a copy of the *New York Times* aside and greeted them cordially, but with that restrained politeness she found uncommonly attractive.

"How was your flight?" Hannah asked. "The weather got a bit rough last night."

Maro shrugged. "I've seen worse." Then with a little smirk he picked up his backpack and said, "All right, ladies. Take me to your HAG."

It was a short drive from the OU campus to Strouds Run Park, a twenty-six-hundred-acre wilderness area crisscrossed with hiking trails and clusters of rustic cabins. The surrounding forest was just beginning to show the promise of fall colors—a few spots of yellow and orange emerging from the green canopy.

They picked up a parking permit and followed the road to the edge of Dow Lake, an artificial reservoir held in the cupped hands of the hills. There was a grassy picnic area and a dirt road that curved down to a boat launch.

"I think it may be somewhere near the launch area," Epiphany said. "I saw some steps and a sort of platform with a railing."

Hannah parked the car, and they walked down the path toward the launch. But Epiphany stopped and looked around. "This isn't right. The path was steeper. With steps. Like a staircase."

They walked a bit farther along the shoreline. Then Maro spotted a park ranger and asked about other launch facilities. "There are two more. One just up the road, and another on the other side of the lake." He showed them the locations on the map they'd picked up at the parking kiosk.

The second site was not as Epiphany envisioned the target area, but when they drove to a more secluded area on the lake's north edge, she at once said, "This is it. See that concrete retaining wall? The steps go down from there to the water."

There was a metal handrail beside the steps and a floating wooden dock at the base of the slope. "This is definitely it," said Epiphany.

Standing beside the floating dock, Maro looked down into the murky water. "Do you remember where it was?"

"The right side of the dock. It was almost totally buried in the mud."

Maro pulled a small metal disk from his backpack. The disk was about a half-inch thick and roughly the size of a biscuit cutter. It had a metal cable attached to the top.

"What on earth is that?" Hannah asked.

"Retrieval magnet. If there's a gun down there, this will catch it." He walked out onto the dock and dropped the magnet into the water, moving it slowly back and forth alongside the dock. After several passes, the cable went taut. "Got a strike," Maro said.

He pulled the cable up slowly, and there it was: a black, short-barreled pistol covered with slime and trailing hydrilla. "Bingo," said Maro. He glanced at Epiphany. "You're going to make me a believer yet."

"Just doing my job."

He was smiling as he pulled his cell phone from his pocket and photographed the gun. Then he took a plastic bag from the backpack. He bagged the gun, disconnected the magnet, and sealed the top of the bag. Then he hoisted it onto the dock.

"Now what happens?" Hannah asked.

"Now I send this to USERT, that's the FBI's evidence response team, and have them test it for latent fingerprints."

"But it's been in the water all this time," said Epiphany. "Can they still get prints from it?"

"Possibly," Maro said. "Print residue can last up to two months, depending on conditions. In this case, the gun was in cold freshwater, which means we have a better likelihood of finding usable prints. Salt and warm water destroy the prints more quickly." He shrugged. "Of course, the hit man could have been wearing gloves, but at least we should be able to trace the serial number and get some idea how they got hold of it."

On the ride back into town, Epiphany could "feel" Maro looking at her. She knew he had questions, so she wasn't surprised when they pulled up to the Campus Inn, and he said, "How the hell do you do that? I mean, do you just have some kind of vision or what?"

"It's called remote-viewing," she said. "I'm surprised you haven't heard of it. I understand the Russians have been using psychics for years to gather information. I thought the FBI was doing the same thing."

"I've heard about that from the guys in Special Ops," Maro admitted, "but I didn't pay much attention. Guess I figured it was not very ..."

"Scientific?"

"Right."

"Maybe you should take another look."

"Maybe I should." He got out of the car and lifted the plastic bag onto the sidewalk. For a moment, his dark eyes met Epiphany's through the car's open window. Then he nodded. "Thanks," he said, "You really have been a big help." Then he turned and walked away.

Epiphany watched him until he disappeared into the lobby. She let out a little sigh and turned to find Hannah looking at her. "What?"

"I think he likes you."

"Hannah! You can't be serious!"

"Hmmm."

"He's Michael's age, for goodness' sake."

"And your point is?"

"I certainly ... I just ... No! That's totally outrageous." Epiphany yanked the gearshift and the car lurched forward. "I won't listen to another word of your nonsense."

Hannah looked away, smiling. "Just sayin'"

Chapter 36

Back at the Mayall farm, Epiphany found another phone message waiting for her. "It was the senator, Bea Falco," Susan said. "She said she'd be at that number until around five."

Epiphany got Bea's voice mail and left a message. The weather was so nice that she and Hannah decided to take a walk. Epiphany took her cell phone along in case Bea called.

They strolled across the meadow and down the path toward the creek. Epiphany was telling Hannah about the fight to make Athens County a "Charter Government" in order to limit the development of toxic fracking wastewater wells in the area.

"Athens County has become the number-one destination for wastewater disposal in the state," Epiphany said. "There are eight active injection wells around here, and they could cause a lot of trouble."

"What's the worst problem?" Hannah asked.

"Well, there's the containment problem—trying to keep the toxic water from migrating into the aquifers and contaminating the drinking water," Epiphany said. "But I think the earthquake issue is even worse. No one's sure what might happen with activating new fault lines. But like everything else the energy corporations do, the biggest problem is trying to stop them. The legal maneuvering is unconscionable."

"I'm curious to see that polluted pond you told me about," said Hannah. "Could we take a look?"

"Sure. It's not far."

They made their way along the path beside the creek, and soon arrived at the bluff where the stream from the pond emptied into the creek. The smell of creosote was strong.

The two women scrambled up the sandy trail and got to the top of the ridge. Before them lay the field and not far away was the pond with its sad forest of dead trees.

Hannah shook her head. "Now that's just disgusting." She looked at Epiphany. "How did it get here?"

"Sam thinks that when Ace Energy had problems getting the wells permitted, the company just started dumping the wastewater in this lagoon."

"This is their land?" Hannah asked.

"No, it's state land. Which means that someone at the state level had to lease it to them or give them permission to use it. It's all just so ... political."

As they approached the pond, a swarm of flies burst up from the shoreline. A closer look revealed the bloated body of a dead raccoon lying in the mud beside the water. The irridescent water lapped slowly at the raccoon's rigid front paws.

"Okay," said Hannah, "I've seen enough."

"Hey, there," came a rough shout. "What are you doin'?"

Startled, Epiphany looked up to see a uniformed figure coming toward them.

"This here's private property," the man said as he approached. "I'm gonna have to ask you to leave."

"Sorry," Hannah called. "We didn't see any signs."

"Then you didn't look real good," said the man. He was medium-height and was wearing a blue uniform. Epiphany was sure she had seen him before, but it took her a minute to recognize the face. It was Ray Lucas, the museum security guard who had helped Chance take the Blake.

But this was not the time for accusations. He must now be working for Ace. She wanted to follow up on that piece of information. So she took hold of Hannah's hand and called out, "Oh, we're so sorry. We'll leave right away." With that she started briskly toward the bluff. Ray watched them go.

Then Epiphany's cell phone buzzed. "It's Bea," she told Hannah. As they walked back toward the bluff, Epiphany told Bea about the discovery of the HAG and Maro's plan to try to get some fingerprints from the weapon. "Of course," she admitted, "if the prints belong to one of those guys that got away, then it won't make much difference."

After a few more minutes of conversation, Epiphany sighed and said, "Yeah, I understand. It was a long shot anyway, but thanks for trying. Right. I will. Bye."

"Bad news?" asked Hannah.

"Bea wasn't able to get the state attorney general's office to call for an investigation. They told her there wasn't enough evidence to override the local authorities. Maybe finding the HAG will help motivate someone, but for now the investigation is closed. At least locally."

Hannah gave Epiphany a mocking grin. "Why don't you call your favorite private investigator? He could probably come up with some answers."

"Maro?" Epiphany felt a small glitch of excitement that she quickly doused. "I don't think … I mean, I wouldn't want to bother him."

"I'm sure he wouldn't mind."

"I really don't think that would be … wise."

Hannah smirked. "Okay, play hard to get."

"Hannah!" Epiphany protested. "Don't be ridiculous."

But after she went to bed that night, she indulged in a few

wishful thoughts about Maro Gaido. Sure, he was interesting. And attractive in a mysterious, exotic way. And smart. And funny.

But she had lived for years without a "man in her life," and had decided she was fine with it. No complications. No entanglements. No distractions.

Except he *was* a distraction. "That's enough," she said aloud. "Forget him. Go to sleep."

But he still floated there in her mind like one of the Spirits, there and not there. The ghost of memory.

"What if we could get Hugh Stillman to testify?" Hannah said.

"Worth a try I guess," Epiphany said. They were getting low on options. "Let's go talk to him."

They found Hugh in his office and talked through several possible scenarios.

"You could be subpoenaed, you know," Epiphany said.

"But there's no trial," said Hugh.

"What if we get a hearing? We're starting to find more evidence. It's only a matter of time until we have probable cause and can request a search warrant."

Hugh plucked nervously at a button on his grey sweater.

"I'm sure we can get a judge to grant anonymity orders," Hannah said. "Your statement can be taken by video with voice alteration."

"They'd still know who ratted them out. I'm the only one who knows what happened."

Hannah and Epiphany looked at each other.

"Look," Hugh said, "I want to help you. Really I do. But you've got to understand what you're up against."

"We *do* know," Epiphany said. "That's why we can't stop now. It's not just the stolen Blake, it's also John Bernhardt's death and the contamination of the local water supply. There is a whole lot at stake here!"

Hugh stared miserably out the window. Then he sighed. "All right then. Tell you what. If you'll meet with me and my attorney, maybe we can find some way to move forward."

"Thank you!" Epiphany said. At that moment, she would have gladly kissed Hugh Stillman.

Chapter 37

Diedre Carson had been a defense attorney for more than twelve years. Hugh Stillman, who was an old friend from their graduate years together at Ohio State, had never needed her professional services before. Now, however, he was meeting with her at his office to discuss his role as a "confidential informant" for the re-opened investigation that was now headed by Maro Gaido and a friend of his from the FBI.

Hugh made it clear he was willing to make a statement only if he could be assured complete anonymity based on his fears of retaliation. Legal precedents were very clear: authorities had the "privilege" to refuse to disclose a CI's identity to anyone, thus protecting "not only the informant's name, but also those portions of communication from and about the informant which would tend to reveal his or her identity" if it was deemed that the witness would be in danger if his identity was revealed.

Diedre advised Hugh that, given the circumtances, his best course of action was to tell the investigators what he knew in exchange for anonymity and to avoid any charges himself, which might have included obstruction of justice and perjury.

Hugh agreed to a video interview with voice-alteration that would give the judge enough information to establish "probable cause," and to issue a search warrant for Derrick Rarian's home. In the event that the stolen artwork was found, the judge could then issue a warrant for Rarian's arrest for receiving stolen property. Since the value of the property exceeded five hundred dollars, the case would be treated as a felony.

The next day, Hugh kept the appointment for the interview. He repeated the details of the crime he had divulged to Epiphany: he had cooperated with Chance Hillibrun and Ray Lucas to provide an opportunity to remove the Blake drawing from the museum and transport it via the basement tunnel to the river where a boat was waiting to receive it. He knew the identity of the recipient of the stolen art, Derrick Rarian, but had not revealed that information to anyone. He had also followed Ray Lucas's instructions to edit the security tapes to delete the frames that showed Chance removing the work from the wall and taking it out of the gallery. And, he had later disposed of the tapes when he became alarmed that they might contain evidence of his tampering.

"If you're okay with it, I could use your help." Maro's voice was unusually energetic and excited. Epiphany could almost see the surge of bright colors in his aura. Such enthusiasm!

"Of course," she said. "Where do I meet you?"

"My plane gets into Dayton at one this afternoon. If you meet me at the airport, we can hook up with the FBI team from Dayton and the Xenia police, and get to Rarian's before he has time to react. The Xenia police have the search warrant, so we're good to go."

"What can I do to help?" Epiphany asked.

"Help us locate the Blake. Rarian might have hidden it somewhere in the house or on the grounds."

"I'm on it," she said.

"Ten-four," he said with a chuckle. Then, "See you at one."

"Roger that, Mr. Gaido." She ended the call and smiled. "Hannah," she called, "guess what!"

Anxious about any possible retaliation from Ace Energy, Epiphany asked Hannah to stay at the farm and keep an eye on Susan while she was away. She made a reservation at a Xenia bed-and-breakfast, packed an overnight bag, and headed west on Route 56 toward Dayton.

The morning was bright and breezy with just a hint of gold beginning to gild the edges of the hickory and buckeye trees. Cows watched placidly from their pastures as she passed. She noticed a flock of geese flying high in their typical V-formation, early travelers getting a jump on the fall migration. Nature's cycles following their ancient patterns, unperturbed by the brief passage of the species called "human." Helped to keep things in perspective.

She reached Interstate 70 around eleven and joined the westbound flow of traffic past New Vienna, Springfield, and the Dayton suburbs. The terminal at Dayton International Airport was a futuristic-looking fantasy of glass and metal. She left the car in short-term parking and made her way to the main terminal with its rounded skylights and sleek corridors.

A huge mural dominated the wall above the sign that read "All Gates." Portraits of hometown heros Wilbur and

Orville Wright looked down at the crowd. An inscription on the mural informed travelers that "Two brothers from Dayton taught the world to fly."

With an hour to wait until Maro's flight was due, Epiphany stopped at a café and ordered a Greek salad and an iced tea. She was just finishing when she heard the announcement that United Flight 5751 from Chicago had arrived at gate 14. She paid the bill and made her way through the crowd, stopping briefly to help an Asian woman with two small children who was trying to find the baggage claim.

Passengers from the flight trickled out into the terminal. She knew before she saw him that Maro was near, then spotted him coming through the doorway. He wore jeans, a dark shirt and a lightweight black leather jacket. And sun glasses. He stopped for a moment to scan the crowd, then saw her and nodded a greeting. She felt a tingle of excitement as he came toward her. Damn, he was attractive. Wouldn't she just love to ... *Stop that! Behave yourself.* "Hi, Maro," she said.

He gave her a tentative smile. "Thanks for coming to meet me," he said.

"Of course. Do you have baggage to claim?"

"Nope. I'm good to go."

Chapter 38

Epiphany and Maro drove south on I-75 through the city, and pulled into the parking lot in front of the Dayton FBI office. Maro introduced Epiphany to two federal agents as "a consultant on the case," and they settled down in a private office to review their plan.

The Dayton agents had brought in the Xenia police to assist with serving the search warrant. Aware of Derrick Rarian's history and his connection with Ace Energy, the police chief recommended that a SWAT team be assigned to the operation as well. Epiphany would be allowed to accompany the agents to the scene, but for safety reasons would not be able to enter the Rarian residence.

It was late afternoon by the time the team arrived at Number Eight, Shadow Drive, Rarian's lavish "weekend place." Maro and Epiphany stayed in the car while the two federal agents conferred with the police. Part of the team deployed to the rear of the grounds to prevent an escape.

"Do you have any impressions about the location of the Blake?" Maro asked.

Epiphany had been concentrating on exactly that question for the past three hours and wished she had a different response. "I'm afraid I'm not getting anything," she said.

Maro chewed on his lip, frowning. "Nothing?"

She shook her head. "Give me a minute. Now that I'm close to the house, I might get a better reading."

She closed her eyes and concentrated, letting her mind retrace her experience of walking through the mansion when she visited Rarian originally. The grey marble foyer with its dramatic spiral saircase. The vaulted living room overlooking a Japanese garden. She toured the public areas—the living room, dining room, kitchen—then envisioned taking the elevator to the basement gallery where, she was sure, the Blake had been installed. She had noticed its absence, but was sure it was somewhere close by. Was there a storage room? She remembered seeing an elaborate storage facility with metal shelves, an archive that held the bulk of Rarian's extensive collection. Was that here, or somewhere else?

Her eyes flew open as she realized with a sudden shock that that although the upstairs rooms were exactly as she remembered them, the basement gallery was empty. Just a deserted, white-walled room where what Rarian had described as the "heart and soul" of his collection had been displayed.

"What?" Maro asked, seeing her expression.

"It's gone," she said.

"The Blake?" His voice was strained.

"All of it." She looked at him. "It's not here, Maro. And neither is he."

The team went through the exercise anyway—Knock and announce: (*FBI! Search warrant! Open the door!*). Forced entry: (It took a while. The bronze door was difficult to dislodge.) The sweep and clear: (There was no one in the house.) The public areas were totally intact. Even the bedrooms were undisturbed—clothes in the closets, polished shoes on their rack, bathroom supplies in place.

But when they cautiously moved to the lower level, they found it totally stripped—bare walls, empty closets, not so much as a paper clip or a roll of tape.

Once they'd secured the scene, Maro asked Epiphany to come with him to the basement to determine if she "saw" anything.

"There were four men working here," she told him. "They wore red jumpsuits with an" —she gestured to her shoulder—"Ace Energy logo. I see them taking the art from the walls and wrapping it in paper and then in bubble wrap and loading it into crates. One of them has a laptop, and he's entering data into the computer. Maybe a list or spreadsheet.

"Then I see them loading the crates onto the elevator and taking them out the door. There is a truck or a van waiting behind the house and they are loading the crates into the van. It's an unmarked van. White. Large. More like a delivery truck. Now it's driving away.

"It's dark now and I'm hearing something. A whirring sound. The tree branches are whipping back and forth and the sound is getting louder. There are lights in the sky, floating. Moving toward me. The sound is loud. Oh, I see it. A helicopter. It's landing on the lawn behind the house. Two people are running toward it. They are helped on board, but one of them stops and looks back.

"It's Rarian! I can barely see him, but I see his hair in the reflected light. It's definitely him. Then he ducks into the helicopter and it lifts off and disappears into the sky."

Epiphany and Maro stared at each other. Then Maro said softly, "He got away."

Epiphany nodded. "And he took his collection with him."

"He could be anywhere," Maro said. His voice sounded distant and scratchy over the cell phone. "The Ace folks told us he's officially 'on leave,' but that's all we could get from them. And guess who else is suddenly out of reach."

"Who?" Epiphany asked.

"Chance Hilliburn. He's been transferred to the Ace office in Qatar. So essentially, he's also out of our jurisdiction."

"Then even if we have evidence, it would be hard to get either of them back here?" Epiphany asked.

"Almost impossible."

"What about the HAG? Did you get any prints?"

"Negative. Either they wore gloves or they wiped it clean before they tossed it." She could hear the disappointment and frustration in his voice.

"Then we're back to square one," Epiphany said.

"That's right."

Dejected, Epiphany turned off her cell phone and set it aside. *Damn,* she thought. *That really sucks.*

"Look on the bright side," Hannah said, "At least that goon Chance is gone. Your mom doesn't need to worry about him showing up and harassing her about selling the farm."

"They can always send someone else," Epiphany said. "They're not going to give up. After all, why should they when everything's rigged in their favor?"

"That's just depressing."

They were both quiet for several minutes. "I have a thought," Epiphany said. "Maybe we should talk to Blake King. He gave us some good leads last time."

"Why not?" Hannah said.

Epiphany raised her hand to knock on Blake King's door, but at that moment the door swung open.

"I have a message for you," Blake said. He looked disheveled. His collar-length hair was matted, and he wore muddy jeans and a ragged, red-plaid shirt. He gestured for Epiphany and Hannah to enter and closed the door behind them.

"East and West have met and mingled," he said, his words coming quickly. "And they produced a shooting star." He raised his hand. "No, wait. Not a star, but rather a comet, for it will complete its necessary cycle and return. Sun-ships and chariots are revolving now, surrounded by walls. Their only tools are seeds of doubt and a raft of heavy metals, but they will come again in glory. You may be sure of that. The word that comes to mind is *mercy*."

Epiphany and Hannah looked at each other.

"I will bring water to quench your thirst," said Blake, and headed for the sink. He handed them each a glass and sat down on the cot, indicating for them to sit in the two chairs beside the window. He waited, watching as they sipped their water.

"We've come to ask for your help," Epiphany said. "Our investigation has come to a dead-end, and we don't know where to go next."

Blake nodded slowly. "The earth, the sun and moon are

three immense wheels turning upon one another. A cog indents its spirit effigy a hair's breadth off and misses. Confessional courage is a thing gone rare. You can tell when the jig is up."

"We know what happened," Hannah said, "but we can't prove any of it."

"Tell me your tale of woe," Blake said.

Epiphany and Hannah took turns filling him in on what they had discovered since their previous visit—Hugh Stillman's confession of knowledge of the theft and his unwillingness to testify, the ill-fated attempt to apprehend Derrick Rarian, the arson incident that burned down Susan's barn, and finally the finding of the heart-attack gun that turned out to be worthless as evidence.

"So as I told our friend, Maro Gaido, we're back to square one," Epiphany finished.

"Nē plūs ultra," Blake said solemnly.

"Go no more beyond this point?" Hannah translated. "You mean we should stop our investigation?"

Blake got to his feet. "Come," he said, motioning them to follow.

They left the cabin, crossed the lawn, and went through a gate. A dilapidated barn, its once-red exterior now a sooty grey, stood at the end of the pasture. Blake heaved open the heavy double doors and Epiphany and Hannah followed him inside.

"Behold what Malbranche hath wrought," he said as he flipped on a light switch.

Before them was a huge sculpture constructed of scrap metal and other found objects including rusty cables, plastic body parts, and pieces of painted cardboard. What appeared to be an iron cauldron sat on a base of twisted junk that looked like the residue of a violent explosion and fire. The interior of the cauldron included a set of mirrors and spirals of red LED lights that blinked on and off, creating the illusion of a pot of red-hot, boiling liquid. Suspended from the ceiling were two human forms: a naked pink plastic female mannequin that hung upside down above the glittering cauldron, and beside her, right-side-up, a plastic male figure dressed in a blue uniform.

"Wow," Hannah said, staring at the bizarre installation.

"So, this is Malebranche?" Epiphany said.

Blake stood looking at his creation. Then he raised his arms and said in a loud, singsong voice, "I Want! I Want! Wants brief prayer kisses its quick inheritance and settles on the moon. Oothoon's sacred body lies ravaged, dissected by the blades of a thousand anatomists eager to rip open the treasure house of Nature. Ask the Bacon! Ask the Glanvill! The Empire of Man will prevail over the Inferior Creatures. Conquest and enslavement are the legacy of the penetrating member. If you require a sign, look for Hunger! It is everywhere! It will not be satisfied until every tree is bare and every pasture empty. Consider the palatability of horses, and afterward we hung our heads and turned to roasting dry bones. Nature is finished, and we have barely begun!"

"Where does it lead?" asked Hannah.

Blake turned to face her. "Sunless light and wordless logic intertwined. Invite the creature into your home and it will devour you. Crosses and holy water are no match for silicon. Ahriman is laughing up his sleeve."

He looked back at the sculpture and said more softly, "They are gone to their rewards in the Dark Futurity of the Kingdom that will seek its own level within the Circle. Let them embrace the Abyss." Then he added, "But the Bald One will succumb to the pitch-pool. At least that justice will be done."

At that moment, the sculpture began to vibrate, its components dancing crazily. The wooden beams of the barn creaked ominously, and dust sifted down from the loft.

Blake half-pushed-half-led the two women out of the barn. The pasture was undulating in ripples like a lake. Epiphany felt a blast of energy and heard a crash as the barn collapsed behind them. She fell forward as the earth heaved like a writhing beast. Hannah was screaming something, but Epiphany couldn't hear her through the roar of the shifting landscape.

Then it was over. Dust rose from the earth like steam. It was unusually quiet—no birds, no insects, not a whisper. Epiphany looked around. Hannah was sitting on the ground about ten feet behind her. Blake was kneeling next to her. Then he got up and came to Epiphany. "All right?" he said.

She nodded. He put a reassuring hand on her shoulder, then helped her get to her feet.

"I hope your cabin's okay," Epiphany said.

Blake looked toward his house. "Without a thing's falling apart, there can be no falling. Fragments, when they come to rest, seed the place. We speak the words of eternity."

Hannah joined them, breathless and red in the face. "I think maybe I'll go back to New York," she said with a wavering laugh.

"Where it's nice and safe?" Epiphany asked.

They made their way across the field. The countryside looked deceptively normal and the cabin was still standing, although the chimney was slightly tilted. A few loosened bricks lay at the base.

"I'm so sorry about your sculpture," Epiphany said.

"Absurdity is the oldest of nativities," Blake said with a smile.

"Look," Hannah said, pointing. "Look at that cloud of smoke. I wonder what's on fire."

Epiphany looked toward the horizon and her hand flew to her mouth. "Mom!" she cried.

Chapter 39

The drive back to the farm was not easy. Trees and power lines were topsy-turvy. In places chunks of asphalt had sunk several feet beneath the roadbed. At the village of Orland the bridge had collapsed, so Epiphany took a meandering back road that was barely more than a path. It took almost an hour to cover the fifteen miles, but when they came in sight of the house, Epiphany let out a little cry of thanks: it was still standing. And the towering cloud of smoke was coming from somewhere to the north of the Mayall property.

She and Hannah jumped out of the car and ran to the house. The front porch was tilted and one of the windows was broken. Shattered glass littered the floor. And the front door was locked. Epiphany didn't know whether to laugh or cry as she fumbled for a key. "Mom?" she called.

No answer. Once inside, Epiphany saw that the bedroom door was open, but there was no sign of Susan. She raced up the stairs with Hannah close behind her. The three small bedrooms were intact although littered with fallen objects—books, photos, anything small and moveable. Another window was broken in the upstairs bathroom.

Epiphany grabbed her cell phone from the rug in front of the dresser. Why hadn't she remembered to take it with her? There was a voice mail message from her son, Michael.

"Mom. Just heard about the quake. Are you all right?"

She sent a quick text: "We're fine. Call u this pm."

They took a look at the basement, but Susan wasn't there. Then Hannah spotted a note on the kitchen table. "Took Susan to the hospital in Logan. Call me. 740-986-7172. Sam"

"Oh God," Epiphany breathed. Her hands shook as she tapped in the number. Hannah stared at her, biting her lip.

"Miller here."

"Sam? It's Epiphany. Is—"

"She's gonna be okay," Sam said. "Got a broken ankle and some bruises, but otherwise she's fine. Gave me a scare when I found her, though."

"Where was she?"

"Back porch. Reckon she tried to get outside, but the shelf over the door came loose and whacked her on the head. Don't worry. Rhoda and I are right here with her. You and Hannah okay?"

"We're both fine."

"I'll let her know. She's been fussin' about you."

"Thanks so much, Sam," Epiphany said, sinking down on a kitchen chair and letting her breath out in a long sigh. She nodded to Hannah and mouthed "okay." Hannah grinned and gave a thumbs-up. "Tell her we'll be there as soon as we can. The roads are kind of messed up."

"Will do. Be careful. Lotta wires down."

On the way to Logan, Epiphany and Hannah spotted several helicopters circling the column of smoke and heard sirens in the distance. "Hope they have it under control," Hannah said.

"Wind's from the south," said Epiphany, "so the farm should be okay."

"I wonder what caused it?"

"Who knows—power lines? Transformer explosion?"

They both forgot about the fire as they approached the town. An overpass had collapsed, blocking the main road. Epiphany had to circle through a maze of back streets to get to the hospital.

The town looked as though it had taken a direct hit from a tornado—walls collapsed into piles of rubble, trees sitting at odd angles, sunken depressions in the street. "It looks like a Kandinsky," Hannah noted, refering to the Expressionist artist known for his frenzied abstractions of people and places.

"Definitely a war zone." *Nature strikes back,* she thought.

The hospital was largely intact and swarming with people—ambulances lined up in front of the ER, gurneys clogging the halls. But they found a very calm and efficient nurse at one of the stations and got Susan's room number.

Sam was sitting in a chair next to the bed while Rhoda was perched on a stool. Susan wore an oxygen tube in her nose and was tethered to several machines that blinked and beeped, recording her body's processes. But when she saw Epiphany, she held out her arms. "Fanny," she croaked, "thank goodness you're all right!"

Epiphany hugged her awkwardly, trying to avoid the medical paraphernalia.

Sam stood up, and Epiphany gave him a hug. "Thanks so much."

"We'd best be gettin' back to our place," he said. "I still need to check on the horses and make sure they're all accounted for." He turned to Susan. "You take it easy, young lady."

She nodded, her eyes brimming with tears.

After Sam and Rhoda left, Epiphany pulled the chair close to the bed and took her mother's hand. "I don't want you living so far away," she said. "I'm serious, Mom. I think it's time you moved to Florida."

Susan met Epiphany's eyes for a moment, then she turned her face away. "We'll talk about that later." Then she looked back at Epiphany. "I'll tell you one thing, though," she said, her voice hard and flat. "I'm not selling the place to those no-good oil people. They've caused enough trouble around here. They need to go."

"I hear you," Epiphany said. "We'll make sure they keep their dirty paws off the Mayall family homestead."

She and Susan both laughed.

Epiphany was exhausted and feeling overwhelmed by the time she and Hannah left the hospital. They decided it would be foolish to try to go back to Mt. Eden given the condition of the roads and the damage that Susan's house had sustained. The power would be out, and there could be other dangers—broken gas lines, foundation cracks.

After trying several places, they were able to get a room at the Holiday Inn in Logan. The hotel was only slightly affected by the quake. The water and power were still functioning. The young woman at the reception desk informed them the pool was closed for repairs. But the restaurant was open.

After a turkey sandwich and a glass of wine, they headed for their room and found it clean and well equipped—the two double beds looked inviting after the traumas of the day.

Epiphany put in a quick call to Michael to assure him they were all okay. Then she climbed into bed and was soon asleep.

When she woke a few hours later, she wasn't terribly surprised to find John Bernhardt sitting in the desk chair next to the bed. "I'm sorry," she said softly. "I'm afraid I haven't been much help."

He shook his head, smiling at her over his glasses. "You did everything you could," he said. "I'm grateful to you."

"I wanted justice," she said. "Still do."

"'They sow the wind, and they shall reap the whirlwind,'" John replied. "But it will take some time. The best thing you can do now is to go home. Your family needs you. And you need them."

The next morning, the Logan Daily News had a big article about the fire. Epiphany took the paper with her to the hospital and read the story to Hannah and Susan. "'The fire apparently started when an Ace Energy tanker truck was pumping a load of contaminated water into the holding lagoon at a hazardous waste dump site just off Highway 374 north of Mt. Eden. The earthquake, which struck at 12:42 P.M., caused a short in the pump's electrical switch and the resulting fire soon spread to the pond. The water was so full of toxic chemicals that the pond itself caught fire. The driver of the truck escaped without injury, but the site security guard, Ray Lucas, 59, of Nelsonville, fell into the pond and drowned.'"

"Oh my God," Hannah said. "The corrupt official fell into the burning pitch-pool. Just like Blake said he would."

"Both Blakes," Epiphany observed, thinking of the lost

William Blake drawing of the corrupt magistrate being thrown into the burning cauldron.

"What are you talking about?" Susan said, looking from one face to the other.

"Long story, Mom," Epiphany said.

Hannah stayed for another week and helped Epiphany get Susan home from the hospital. They got the broken windows replaced and cleaned up the yard. Thankfully, there was no major structural damage, and the power had been restored.

Sam and Rhoda came by almost every day to check on Susan's progress. Her ankle was in a cast, but otherwise she was recovering quickly. "Takes more than a little earthquake to get this gal down and out," Susan said, giving Sam a jaunty wink.

Before leaving, Sam said to Susan, "I've got a little proposition for ya, Mrs. Mayall." He glanced at Epiphany. "If ever this daughter of yours talks you into goin' home with her, Rhoda and I would like to buy this place from you all. We want to expand a bit and maybe look at raisin' some sheep. We could rent out the house and make some improvements to the outbuildings. You keep that in mind now, hear?"

Epiphany caught her breath and looked at her mother. Susan was beaming. "Thank you kindly, Mr. Miller. If I decide to put the place up for sale, you'll be the first to know."

Hannah left the next morning, heading for Cleveland to start on her research project at the museum. Epiphany promised to "come visit soon," and to let Hannah know if she heard from Maro or Bea about any action on the investigations into the stolen drawing or John Bernhardt's death.

"Just try it for a few months," Epiphany said to Susan over dinner that evening. "Just for the winter. Sam will keep an eye on the place. And we will keep an eye on you."

"Well, it would be nice to get away from the cold weather. Last winter was a little … difficult. Hard to get around when it's icy."

"Easy to fall," Epiphany said.

Susan gave her daughter a disapproving look. "I didn't fall."

"But you could have."

"Hmm …" Susan looked at her plate, then glanced up and met Epiphany's eyes. "All right. I'll try it for the winter. But, mind you, I might decide to come back here in the spring."

"Fair enough."

Chapter 40

The car was packed—suitcases in the trunk, Susan's walker in the back seat, cell phone plugged into the outlet. Epiphany had made all her last-minute calls to Francesca, Zoe, and Bea, and one to Maro Gaido to tell him she was going back to Florida. He assured her that he was still working on the case, informally. "It will take some time," he said, "but we hope to locate Rarian and a few of the other guys we think were involved. We'll get them eventually."

"Like the Mounties," Epiphany teased. "You always get your man?"

She thought she could hear him smile. "We try."

"Right," she said. "Well, then I'll say—"

"Epiphany? Wait. Um, this is kind of out of left field, but can I give you a call if, uh, if I ever need your … services?"

"My psychic services?"

"Yeah, I mean …"

"Of course. You've got my number."

"Right. Okay then. Maybe I'll … see you sometime."

"I'd like that." *What the hell am I doing?* But she felt a strange little pinch in her stomach. *I will see him again,* she thought. *I'm sure of it.*

Susan was having a farewell lunch with Sam and Rhoda. They had asked Epiphany to join them, but she said she wanted to take a walk before starting the long drive back to Florida. She had made reservations in southern Virginia for the first night, and in Savannah, her favorite ghost town, for the second. From there it was an easy drive to Watoolahatchee. Susan got uncomfortable if she spent more than four or five hours in the car, so they would take it easy on the drive to Florida.

Epiphany took the path across the pasture and down into the gorge. The trees were really getting into fall—leaves beginning to turn gold and maroon, beautyberry and butterfly weed in full array. The air smelled damp and sweet, like decaying leaves and wet earth. She hiked along the creek, following its twists and turns. When she reached the base of the bluff, she decided she had to take one more look at the polluted lagoon.

A newspaper article said that because of the potential fire hazard, the state had revoked Ace Energy's lease on the property. There would be no more dumping of toxic chemicals at that site. Shutting down one site out of dozens was a small victory, but Epiphany savored it anyway. It made her feel that maybe John Bernhardt's death hadn't been in vain.

She made it to the top of the bluff and followed the small stream toward the pond. The landscape looked like the crater of a volcano—blistered stumps and piles of sludge. The "water" was almost non-existent, just a gooey mess of inky syrup that looked as though it might bubble over and flood the meadow with the sticky tar of greed. She shuddered and turned away.

The Old Man was standing on the edge of the bluff. She waved to him and he waved back. As she walked toward him, the two hounds manifested, one on either side. "Will I see you once I'm back in Florida?" she asked.

"Wouldn't be surprised. Good place to spend the winter."

She laughed. "Do ghosts feel the cold?"

"I'll ask around," he said. "Safe travelin', hear?" With that, the Old Man and the hounds faded into mist.

Epiphany turned for one last look at the lagoon. Did Ray Lucas, she wondered, feel the burning pitch that had consumed his corrupt actions? Would he continue to feel it forever? Was Hell a place? A state of mind? A metaphor? Perhaps it was a virtual reality designed to bring the sinner into a more enlightened state by demonstrating the harm he/she had done. If spiritual growth was the ultimate goal of every soul, the lessons would not always be easy.

As she walked back to the house, she made a conscious effort to notice every detail—every bush and tree and leaf and petal. The melody of the rushing stream, the whispering of the wind. The scent of dried leaves.

She paused for a moment at the pasture gate, her eyes sweeping over the familiar landscape. In her mind she could picture the animals—the cow with the black and white spots, the old bay gelding her father liked to ride, little Sparkles, her beloved pony. And Bridgette, the collie who had been her childhood pal.

Were they all still there in some past time, like images caught on film that the mind of memory could play back again and again? In front of her was the charred ruin of the barn, and beyond that the white siding of the house with its wide porch and black shutters. Would she ever see this scene again? Perhaps not, but it would be there forever in her heart.

She caught sight of her mother waving to her from the front door. Epiphany hoped she was making the right decision to take Susan away from this beautiful and familiar place. Maybe the warm embrace of the family would keep her from being too homesick.

It was time to go. With a little sigh, Epiphany left Dante's Eighth Circle behind her and headed for home.

Epilogue

Derrick Rarian tilted the white leather recliner back a bit and gazed out the oval window of the Global 6000 ACE Energy corporate jet at the French countryside twenty-thousand feet below. In less than three hours the plane was due to arrive at the Aerodome Tivat, one of two international airports in the country of Montenegro, Rarian's new base of operations.

He had left Cleveland shortly after midnight, and slept soundly during the overnight flight across the Atlantic. The aft stateroom of the aircraft was like a lavish cocoon—luxurious seating, a comfortable sofa-bed, a sumptuous en-suite bath fitted with a shower, and a spacious wardrobe/dressing room. The stateroom seats were ergonomically crafted with adjustable headrests and recliner-style leg rests. And independent temperature and entertainment systems. The cabin was blessedly quiet, too. He could barely hear the purr of the two Rolls-Royce turbofan engines that powered the G-6000.

Rarian consulted the gold Heuer Carrera watch on his wrist, and noted that it was now eight-fifteen A.M. in Cleveland. 2:15 P.M. in France. That would put him in Montenegro around 4:30, plenty of time to drive to Kotor and settle in before dinner. While his villa was being renovated, he would be staying with his old friend Hayden Camden, who he had known since they were at Yale together. Hayden's vacation "cottage" wasn't far from Rarian's villa.

He'd never thought about moving to Montenegro, even after learning he had inherited property there, but the idea was growing on him. The country had good connections worldwide for the array of business interests that occupied him. The available technology was first rate, unlike some places he'd visited—those disadvantaged wastelands suitable only for *commoners,* as Her Majesty put it. Rarian had the advantage of claiming his position on The Committee at birth—he was descended through his mother's side from the Black Nobility of Venice said to trace their lineage to the Emperor Justinian and also through his several business connections. And via the network he had carefully built through his "brothers" at Yale and the London School of Economics.

Leaning back against the soft, cool leather, Rarian took a few minute to savor his deft escape from the dreary incidents in Ohio—the old man's death, the Senator's snooping, the bumbling investigator and his laughable psychic sidekick. Such people were simply a nuisance. But they had been easily dealt with. Fortunately, he could put them behind him and look ahead to a future bright with escalating profits and amusing distractions.

Rarian twined his long slender fingers together, and placed them behind his head. Closing his eyes, he conjured up an image to soothe him, something to remind him of his destiny: a skull floating on a sea of oil, flames erupting from the empty eye sockets and bursting from the top of the head. In the lowest circle of Hell, a demon waited, counting the moments until he was released to assume command. The Underworld would rise and consume the Upperworld. The vast culling would commence. Plague, war, flood, and famine—the ghostly herd of the Apocalypse—would ravage the earth, and the *useless eaters* would be eradicated.

Then the true Golden Age could begin.

Note:

The diatribes and prophetic messages of the character Blake King found in this book are taken in part from "News from Golgonooza," Vol 1-16. Published by The Church of the Blake Recital and authored by Aethelred Eldridge, Millfield, Ohio, 1973.

Author Interview - Mallory M. O Connor

This interview is based on a conversation with *Literary Titan*'s editor.

***L.T.** Epiphany's Gift follows one young girl through her life as she struggles to cope with an extraordinary gift. What was the inspiration for her gift and the struggles she faced?*

M.OC As a child, I had several powerful "visions" and/or paranormal experiences. Because the experiences were so exciting and so unusual, I was surprised to find that when I talked about these experiences, adults didn't want to hear about it. They told me it was my imagination. Or worse. So, I stopped talking to anyone and kept my experiences to myself. Later, I began to read about other people who had unusual "visions." I began to study the writings of religious mystics and found many similarities to my own encounters with "another level of existence." In 1979, I met a psychic medium and we became friends. Although my "mystical" experiences were not the same as her "impressions," we found we had a lot in common and have remained friends ever since.

***L.T.** I really enjoyed the well developed character in the book. Was there anything taken from your own life and put into the story?*

M.OC Along with my childhood experiences, I included a number of "autobiographical" elements in the story. One is my work as an art historian and my fascination with artists such as William Blake and his visionary illustrations, especially the works he did of Dante's *Inferno.* I also incorporated my interest in Asian art and culture in the character of Maro Gaido, an art crimes investigator who is half Japanese. I wanted to explore his views about art from a non-Western perspective. And, I set *Epiphany's Gift* in southern Ohio where I lived for four years while attending Ohio University. I was fascinated with Appalachian culture and wanted to immerse myself in the area and its special landscape.

***L.T.** This book blends several genres exceptionally well. Was this your intention or did this happen organically while writing?*

M.OC When I first started writing *Epiphany's Gift,* I intended to create a series of stories that combined paranormal events with art crimes. I wanted my readers to understand the problem of art theft and the significance of taking cultural treasures out of the public arena and into private collections where they are only seen by a few individuals. I believe that art has a lot to teach us about how our civilization developed and why we are who we are. So, I think that art belongs in a larger world that is open to the public.

But I also wanted to explore the issue of climate change and environmental degradation. I was encouraged by Dan Bloom, a climate activist and editor of the *Cli-Fi Report,* to explore various aspects of global warming and its consequences in my writing. In *Epiphany's Gift* I take on the issue of fracking and its consequences. In subsequent books, I plan to focus on a number of climate-related issues including the spread of tropical diseases, effects on water resources, and catastrophic weather events.

So, my stories will be about paranormal events, art crimes and global climate change. Something for everyone!

Reading Group Guide

1. What is Epiphany's "gift" and how does it effect her life? Why does she initially reject her gift and later deide to embrace it?
2. What kinds of psychic experiences does Epiphany have? Have you ever had an unusual "paranormal" experience?
3. Have you ever consulted a psychic? Was it what you expected?
4. Do you think there is any "scientific" evidence for psychic phenomema? Can you see any practical applications for psychic talents?
5. Epiphany is very close to her family. How would you descibe her relationship with her mother? With her son? With her granddaughter? With her ex-husband? How do they relate to her?
6. Do you think that Epiphany was justified in leaving her husband and moving to Florida to follow her dream of being a psychic medium? Who helped her make this decision?
7. What's your impression of Epiphany's friend Hannah? How is Hannah different from Epiphany? Why are they such good friends?
8. What do you make of Maro Gaido? What is his reaction to Epiphany and her "gift?" Why do you think he

is such a skeptic? How does his opinion change over the course of the story?

9. What do you make of Blake King? Is he insane or merely eccentric? Why do you think he acts and talks the way he does? Why does Epiphany consult him and listen to him?
10. Is Derrick Rarian the villain of the story? What do you make of his "aesthetics of destruction?"
11. As the story ends, Epiphany is heading back to Florida with her mother. Do you think she made the right decision? Do you think that Susan will decide to move to Florida permenently? How do people decide when it's time to leave the past behind and give up something/someplace that's been their home for many years?
12. Did you learn anything from reading this book about psychic pehnomena? About global climate change? About art?

Printed in the United States
By Bookmasters